Faith

4CLOVER SERIES BOOK THREE
SHAUNA McDONNELL

Shauna McDonnell

❀ Created with Vellum

TO MY INNER CHILD, I LOVE YOU.
THANK YOU FOR YOUR CREATIVITY, WISDOM, AND JOY.
YOU TAUGHT ME THAT TO CONQUER FEAR, I HAVE TO HAVE
FAITH.
FAITH IN MY WORTH.
FAITH IN MY POTENTIAL.
AND MOST OF ALL, FAITH IN YOU.

🍀

TO MY GORGEOUS AMERICAN FRIEND, DANI.
YOU CLAIMED CIARAN FROM THE VERY, VERY START, THIS IS
ME GIFTING HIM TO YOU. TAKE CARE OF HIM, HE'S ONCE IN
A LIFETIME!

SHAUNA X

This book is book 3 of the 4Clover series. Although the storylines intertwine, they can be read in **any** order.

Before you embark on Ciaran and Lily's story, I want you to know this is a book about growth. At times our heroine will seem selfish in her pursuit of self worth and love; but I promise you, if you stick with her you will see she is no longer a victim held down by her childhood chains. She's a woman, a warrior, a boss-fucking-bitch! After all, healing is a process, it takes time, strength, and dedication! I hope you enjoy this story as much as I enjoyed writing it.

Much love, Shauna

SHAUNA'S GUIDE TO IRISH SLANG

GOBSHITE/EEJIT - IDIOT
BELLEND - DICKHEAD
PISSED - DRUNK OR ANGRY
(DEPENDS ON THE SETTING, LOL)
LILT - TWANG OR SOUND
BITTA CRAIC - GOOD FUN
JAYSUSIN' - FUCKING
SNAKES AND LADDERS - CHUTES AND LADDERS
WILL I FUCK - I WON'T

AUTHOR'S NOTE

This book is written in British English, spellings may differ from American English. A lot of my characters have Irish names. So, I've made a pronunciation chart.

Cian (Keane)
Cillian (Killian)
Ciaran (Kieron)
Conor (Connor)
Croí (Kree)
Sean (Shawn)
Bronagh (Brona)

🍀

My goal was to make this book as interactive as possible; each chapter has a song for a sub-title. If there is anything, I love more than reading, it's music.

�֎

The playlist is available on Spotify: Faith, Boys of 4Clover. Happy listening.

All my love disappeared

And I'm laying right here

While the silence is piercing

And it hurts to breathe

I don't have much but at least I still have me (I still have me)

And that's all I need

So take my faith but at least I still believe (I still believe)

And that's all I need

I don't have much but at least I still have me

— DEMI LOVATO

PROLOGUE

BROKEN BY ISAK DANIELSON

OCTOBER 2012

LILY

"Who the fuck is he, Mary?"

His filthy hand tightens around my mother's neck, squeezing with so much force the air drains from her lungs. Gasping, her face turns an unnatural shade of bluish-grey.

"Stop, Dad. Please, let go, you'll kill her." I pull at his shoulder, conjuring every ounce of strength I have, desperate to tear his unwavering grip from my mother's body, but it's useless.

He is too strong.

Too drunk.

Too out of control.

With one swipe of his free hand, he knocks me off my feet, leaving me a defeated heap on the whiskey-stained floor.

My mother's eyes close as tears flow down her swollen cheeks. When they reopen, her amber irises find mine. I see it, her silent plea.

Run, Lily. Get out of here, baby girl. Run.

The monster slams her exhausted body against the door frame and the wooden panel splits with the impact.

"Do you think I'm a moron, Mary?" His dark hazel eyes narrow as he spits in her face. "You are my wife, the only person you spread your legs for is me. Do you understand?"

His grip loosens, and an audible gasp rushes from my mother's lips. "Yes, Damien. I understand."

I've learned never to talk back, and always tell him what he wants to hear. Questioning him and his psychotic theories will get you nowhere — other than on the receiving end of his fists.

My mam would never cheat on him, but somehow, he's got it into his drunk mind that she has. There is no way to prove him wrong, he'll believe what he wants to.

After crawling across the room on all fours, I hide behind the couch and grab my phone off the coffee table.

My mother's cries fill my ears as I dial Cillian's number, over and over, with no success.

Come on, Cillian. Answer the fucking phone. I need you. We need you.

"Hi, you've reached Cillian, leave a message."

Keeping my voice as low as possible, I beg my brother to come home. "Cill, I need you. He's lost his mind. He's going to kill her. Come home, we need you."

I try a few more times, but it's pointless. Wherever my brother is, it's obvious he can't hear his phone.

Think, Lily! Fucking think.

Frantic, I scroll up through the contact list until I land on his name: Baby Hanson.

The dial tone rings once, twice, until finally, his deep, velvet voice seeps through the line, instantly bringing me comfort. "Hey LB..."

Background noise drowns him out, but after a few seconds of shuffling, I can hear him clear as day. "Lily, is everything okay?"

I can't stop the influx of tears from streaming down my face.

"Ciaran," I whisper.

My mother screams, and my body shakes with fear, cutting off my ability to speak. "Stop, Damien. You're hurtin' me."

"Good, maybe next time you won't be so fuckin' eager to share your pussy with every useless bastard in the area."

The bang that follows sends shivers through my core, and suddenly everything goes silent.

I almost forget about the phone clutched tight against the side of my face. It isn't until Ciaran's panic-stricken tone echoes through that I remember he's there.

"Lily, hide. Hide now. We're coming. We'll be right there. Can you be strong and hide somewhere for me?"

I nod my head even though I know he can't see me.

Suddenly, the phone gets pulled from my grasp, my da flings it across the room and it hits the wall with an unmerciful crash. His six-two intimidating frame towers over me — radiating anger.

His hazel eyes are nowhere to be found, instead, they are dense black and burning with rage.

"Who the fuck was on the phone, Firecracker?"

My eyes close as my teeth grind. I hate that name; he is the only one who calls me that.

When I don't answer, he grabs hold of my hair and pulls me to my feet.

"I SAID... WHO THE FUCK WAS ON THE PHONE?"

Tears burn my eyes as pain shoots through my scalp. My vision blurs as he tightens the stranglehold grip.

"Answer me, you little cunt."

The overpowering scent of whiskey fills my senses as he brings his face closer. "Was it Cillian? The waste of sperm you call your brother. He won't save you, Firecracker. He's about as useful as a wet paper bag."

"Da, please. Let go, you're hurtin' me." My voice sounds foreign, broken, and defeated.

"What about that punk that's always hanging around? The Maguire kid? Was it him?"

I swallow the fear barrelling up my throat and force words to leave my mouth. "No."

His jaw clenches, and his eyes narrow. "You're lying! Are you fuckin' him, Lilyanna?"

"No."

"Stop lying, you're just like your whore of a mother!" He spits, and something unnatural flashes in his eyes. Fear comes back tenfold, shooting up my spine, and forcing my body to go rigid.

"I think it's time I show you what a real man feels like, Firecracker."

Bile rises, churning in my gut and bubbling up my oesophagus. "Don't, please." I shake my head. "I'm begging you."

Silenced with his hard-hitting fist, my head swings to the left as blood streams from my mouth. "Shut the fuck up. I'm sick of the women in this house always telling me what to do."

His greedy hands force my trembling body to the ground, tearing at my shirt, ripping it open and exposing my black lace-covered chest.

Finally, my body fights back, squirming beneath his piggish hands.

"Get off! Get. Off. Me. Mam? Mam, where are you?"

"She can't hear you, Firecracker. She's out cold. Nobody can save you now!"

The underlying pleasure in his words makes me sick, but I don't give up. My nails dig into his forearms and I apply as much pressure as I can.

"Fuccckk! You little bitch."

His hand reaches for my throat as he fights to keep me beneath him. Grinding his hips, his protruding bulge rubs against my centre. "Stop moving, you little cunt."

He gropes my breast with his free hand as I kick my legs in a piss-poor attempt at bucking him off.

Moving his hand lower, he grips my centre above my leggings. "Next time you even think about sharing this with anyone, I will personally see to it you're ruined beyond repair."

"I didn't... I haven't." The plea leaves my mouth, but it's unless.

He's unhinged, drunk off his ass and feeding fuel to the monster beneath his skin.

The front door flies off the hinges and Cillian, Cian, and Ciaran barge into the room.

Suddenly, Cillian tears my da's heavy body off me. The sound of bone-cracking-bone pierces through the living room as I struggle to steady my shaken breath.

Within seconds, brawny arms engulf me, and Ciaran's deep-velvet voice soothes my bleeding soul.

"I have you." His warm breath whispers against my skin.

Brushing the hair from my face, his sea-green eyes bore into mine. "You're safe. It's okay, Lily Bug. He can't hurt you. I won't let anyone hurt you, never again. Count with me, LB. Count with me."

Part One

The Opening Act

CHAPTER ONE

JUST THE GIRL BY THE CLICK FIVE
November 2013

LILY

"Are you sure?" The gentle whisper of Rosie's voice quips from behind me. "This screams, *bad idea!*" She's extra careful, trying her best to not make too much noise.

We've both been successful in our mission so far, which, may I add, is virtually unheard of for me. *Nobody puts Lily in the corner.*

The only other sound this gloomy autumn evening has to offer comes from my favourite yellow Doc Martens boots as they crunch against the falling leaves with every step I take.

Shit! Why did I wear these shoes? They're not exactly my most stealthy pair.

Maybe I should have gone with something more subtle, like Rosie's black converse. *Silent, but still styling.*

Looking over my shoulder at my Snow-White look-alike friend, I tease her with a cheeky, up to no good, smirk. "You know, maybe you're right, we should turn back."

"And listen to you bitch and moan for the next two weeks. No, thank you."

This is why we are best friends. Rosie knows I would never back down from a well-deserved act of retaliation, and that's what this mission is. Ciaran thought he would win this time.

Colossal mistake, Maguire.

Okay, so I'll admit it, I'm a sore loser. I don't enjoy being challenged by the opposite sex. Women can do anything men can. Well, except pee standing up, that shit is impossible, anyway, back to the point. I've been one-upped, and me being, *well me,* cannot stand for that shit. So, I plan to rectify the situation. *Payback is a bitch, Ciaran Maguire, and that bitch's name is LILYANNA O'SHEA.*

Adrenaline pumps through my veins. All that stands between me and my current victory is a seven-foot garden wall and a locked door. The latter is not a problem, especially when you have a key.

Cillian needs to learn he shouldn't leave things lying

around his bedroom. God forbid, somebody with a nefarious plan might come along and take them. (Insert evil laughter here.)

"Lily? I don't think this is a good idea." Uncertainty lingers in her voice as she eyes up the small wall that stands in our way.

"Rosie, soothe your boobs. Nobody is home. Mr Maguire is at your house and the lads are out doing God knows what. We won't get caught. I promise."

At least I hope not. That would suck harder than a porn star.

"Anyway, why are you so worried? You're staying on this side of the wall. Your only job is to catch what I toss over. Simple."

Placing my hand on her shoulder, I squeeze, reassuring her she has nothing to worry about. "Now, lift me over this thing."

With a weighty sigh, she links her hands, holding them down low to help boost me over.

A grumbled observation escapes her rosy red lips, "It's your funeral."

I climb over the wall with the grace of a ninja turtle — *in my head at least* — and step onto the chair I purposely left there earlier today. Slowly, I tiptoe down the cobbled stones leading to the large shed at the bottom of the garden.

Victory will be mine.

After removing the key from my jeans pocket, I stick it in the lock and twist. The door opens with a loud creak.

Mr Maguire should grease this thing.

My eyes scan the makeshift recording studio, taking in all the instruments and general boy clutter until finally, they land on my target.

"BINGO!"

❧

Clink, clank, clank!

"Could you get any louder?" I scold Rosie as we attempt to sneak through my house without my Ma noticing. I swear she's trying to get us caught and with the amount of noise she's making, it's inevitable.

"They're heavy," she growls low, keeping her voice a pitch above a whisper.

"What in God's name are you girls doing? What the hell is that?" My mother's booming voice travels through the doorway. The sternness of her tone causes me to freeze in place.

Maybe if I stand really, really still, she won't see me. Oh, that's right, she already has.

Why is it that I never know what to do in these situations, play dumb or play dead?

"Hello Mary," Rosie greets her with a genuine smile.

Does she not realise that we've been caught red-handed? Ugh, amateur!

"Hi, Rosie," Ma acknowledges before turning her curious gaze in my direction.

I sized her up, scanning her petite frame with laser-sharp focus. I've always been a tiny replica of my mother. We share the same auburn locks, almond-shaped whiskey coloured eyes, and doll-like frame. The only difference between us is, she is a blank canvas, whereas I'm sporting many tattoos and piercings.

Desperate to keep my facial expression as blank as hers, I bite the inside of my mouth. "It's a drum kit." She doesn't need to know where they came from, although I'm sure she has an idea.

We live in Oldtown. With its highly impressive population of 412 people, let's just say, the chances of there being more than one drummer in this one-horse town is staggeringly low.

"Lilyanna O'Shea do not get smart with me, young lady. I am fully aware it's a drum kit. What I would like to know is, why the hell it's being dragged through my sitting room?"

Oops, I'm in serious trouble. She full named me and let me tell you something for the price of nothing, it is never good when Mary O'Shea pulls out the full name card. I repeat, it's never good.

Mustering up my cutest babyface, I bat my eyelashes a

few times. *Innocent Lily. Act innocent.* "Well, my beautiful mammy, the local drummer boy let all the air out of my tyres, so ergo, drum kit."

Okay, the beautiful mammy may have been a tad overboard, but desperate times and all that jazz.

All joking aside, her eyebrows rise so high they nearly get tangled in her hairline. The look on her face is one only a mother can pull off. Oh, you know the one they do when they are waiting on an explanation.

Well, you can keep waiting, Mary, I'm not giving you shit!

A full minute passes by, her daring me to answer with just a beady look in her eyes.

Is that something they teach in parenting 101? Because that move is highly impressive.

When she's certain my resolve won't break, she asks, "What do you mean by '*ergo*' drum-kit."

Placing my hands on my hips, I roll my eyes to the high heavens. You would think she would be used to this by now. Ciaran and I have been playing these games for years. Silly pranks, always trying to out-do one another. I'm not sure when exactly this tug of war started, but I know life would be a lot less colourful without our petty games.

"Mother, did you not hear a word I just said? Ciaran released all the air from my car tyres. So, in return, I stole his drums. An eye for an eye. Two wrongs make a right and all that."

Rosie stands silently beside me, I can tell from the redness on her face, she is trying to contain her laughter, and judging by my mother's expression, she's also finding this rather funny.

Although she will never admit it because you know, mom mode or whatever.

"Lily, that saying is two wrongs *don't* make a right. You will bring those drums back, right this minute."

Fuck you, mom mode.

I look towards Rosie, silently begging her for help. I can't let him win, and like the faithful best friend she is, she comes to the rescue.

"I think Lily had every right to take his drums. Not only did he release the air from her tyres, but he also smeared ketchup on her windshield, then filled her window wash with washing up liquid. When she tried to clear her window, it was nothing but foam and bubbles.

The look of horror on my mother's face probably mirrors my own — wide-eyed and lips pursed. "He did not?"

Nodding my head, I assure her, "Oh, but he did."

That's when the magic happens. Mary O'Shea gets a glint in her eye. The one that only comes out when an O'Shea woman is severely pissed.

Well, hello, Mama bear, glad you could join us.

"Right girls, where are we hiding these drums? I think it's time we teach Ciaran Maguire a little lesson. Nobody messes with my baby girl and gets away with it." She smiles sweetly, nearly causing me to go into cardiac arrest.

Guess I know where the saying, *I got it from my momma,* came from.

*

CIARAN

I burst through the front door of Cillian and Lily's house like a man on a mission.

What the hell is wrong with her?

I can't believe she stole my drum kit. How did she even lift them? She's five-foot-nothing and a half. It shouldn't be physically possible. I can almost hear her disputing that thought. *Semantics, Ciaran — Don't get caught up on things you can never explain.*

Storming into the kitchen, I make a beeline for the little redhead with a nasty attitude. I swear, one of these days, Lily O'Shea will be the death of me. There isn't another person on this planet that affects me the way she does. If she isn't pissing me off, she has me sporting some serious hardwood. Just the sight of her, sitting on top of the kitchen counter has me forgetting why I'm so mad.

Her flame-red hair is pulled into a messy knot on the top of her head, secured — *like always* — by two pens. She's wearing an oversized Nirvana t-shirt dress paired with black fishnet tights and her signature yellow boots. *Damn, she looks hot! Focus Ciaran.*

"Where are they?" I ask, probably a little too aggressively.

Waving her spoon in my direction, she shoots me an evil smile. "Well, hello to you too."

Digging said spoon into the tub of Nutella, she scoops out a staggering amount of chocolate spread then stuffs it into her mouth. With her mouth full to the hilt, she continues, "Where is what, exactly?"

Pulling the jar from her hands, I set it on the counter behind me, far out of her reach. "Don't give me that shit, Lil. Where are my drums?"

"I've no idea what you're talking about."

She turns to face Rosie, who is straddling Cillian's lap on the opposite side of the breakfast bar. *Jesus Christ. Get a fucking room.*

"Rosie, can you please tell this bag of dicks I've no idea where his drums are?"

I butt in before Rosie can reply. "Lily, I know you have them. Just tell me where they are! I need them for our show tomorrow."

"I already told you, I. Don't. Know. Did you check up

your ass, because it seems to me, something's definitely stuck up there."

Is she serious?

"Do you want to know how I know it was you?" I pull the piece of paper I found in my shed from my back pocket and unfold it. Clearing my throat with a fake cough, I attempt my best Lily voice — high-pitched and dripping with venom — to read the words she left behind. "Dearest Asshole, whatever will you do with these sticks when you have no drums to bang on? Oh, I know, you can shove them up your ass!" I wave the page in her face. "You even signed it."

Cillian and Rosie snicker in the background.

What the hell is so funny?

She tears the note from my hands and reads over her own words as if it's the first time she's seeing them. Lily throws the page back at me in protest. "Someone has set me up. I didn't write that."

Does she think I'm stupid? Honest to fuck, she must.

"Really?" I question.

"Yep, wasn't me." She hops off her perch and stalks towards me, where I'm leaning against the sink. She squares up to me, her tiny frame more intimidating than it should be for someone of her miniature size. Bouncing up onto her tippy toes, she tries to reach my eyes but barely comes to my mouth. Her eyes squint, and her nose scrunches in this cute little way as she looks up at me over her long lashes. "Ciaran, I didn't touch your drums. Now, could you please move? You're standing in the way of me and my chocolate, and we both know that won't end well for you."

She reaches behind me, trying to take back her chocolate spread.

Not so fast, Lily Bug!

Gripping her elbow with my hand, I force her gaze back to mine. I lift her chin with my free hand, and my eyes land on the dark, purple lipstick painted onto her pouty mouth. Her tongue runs across her lower lip, and I fight against the groan crawling up the back of my throat. *Fuck me.* "If you didn't write this note, please explain why the kiss mark left at the bottom is the same shade as your lipstick?"

CHAPTER TWO

THIS IS WHAT IT TAKES BY SHAWN MENDES

LILY

I LIFT MY HAND TO COVER MY MOUTH — LIKE THAT will help, I've been caught red-handed, or in this case, Burgundy lip'd.

Why did I leave that note?

Rookie mistake, but hindsight can be a real bitch.

Ciaran's stare is intoxicating.

Those sea-green eyes of his do funny things to my chest. The thumping of my heart echoes in my eardrums. Why does he affect me so much? My body is full of hatred, yet also bustling with desire.

I'm not blind. Anyone with two eyes would appreciate the wonder that is the Maguire twins.

Honestly, they're both beautiful. I'm talking about Leonardo Di Caprio back in his younger years, beautiful — plus tattoos.

But Ciaran, there's something about him that makes my hormones race like a formula one car.

His natural, ashy blonde hair is dyed jet black, making it easier for people to distinguish between him and Conor. However, I could always tell them apart, even when they were younger.

Probably because Conor never affects you the way Ciaran does.

Standing at precisely six-foot, Ciaran's lean, toned athletic frame towers over my small doll-like one. His handsome yet boyish face is beautifully tanned, and with the three freckles that kiss his left cheek — only adding to his cheeky charm — he's a stunning fucking asshole.

With a firm grip on my elbow, his face hovers just inches from mine. If either of us leans in, our lips would be touching. That thought alone makes my solar plexus tighten with nervous energy.

I drag in a deep yet audible breath, desperately trying to gain some composure.

Oh, for fuck's sake, why was that so loud? He will think

I'm trying to preserve his scent. Which, for your information, I'm not.

But, in case you're wondering, it's warm citrus with a hint of spice. Now, pair that with his minty breath and the lingering cigarette smoke and you've got a purely sinful scent.

I look over my shoulder, and silently pray Rosie receives the SOS I'm sending her with my eyes, but the little traitor has her tongue buried in my brother's mouth. *Gross!*

Some friend you are. A little help over here.

When I flick my eyes back to the asshat that makes me feel things I'd rather deny, I'm greeted with a sexy smirk that lights up his handsome face. How come I can never decide whether I want to slap him or kiss him? Lord knows that smirk has caused many a wet knicker, but not mine, not tonight.

Oh, hello, denial. How nice of you to show up!

I suppose I should own up to taking his drums. Just because he knows I have them, doesn't mean I'm giving them back. *Right?*

Placing my hand on my hip, I try to convince myself my plan didn't backfire like a Honda 50. "Okay, I admit it! I took your drum kit. But —" I poke him in the chest, "— in my defence; it's justified. Until I receive a formal letter of apology, I'm holding them hostage."

I side-step, attempting to manoeuvre around him, but he

stands firm, blocking my way. Heat flares between us, filling my body from head to toe. I need to move, and I need to do it now. "Excuse me? I have plans that don't involve —" Before I finish that sentence, Ciaran attaches his mouth to mine, silencing me with shock. Suddenly, I am consumed by a rush of dizziness, followed swiftly by a slap of reality.

WHAT THE FUCK!

I slam my hands against his chest, forcing him to remove himself from my personal space. "What the hell, Ciaran? You can't just go around sticking your lips on people. What is wrong with you?" The panicked roar of my voice, laced with so much venom, shocks the shit out of him.

What is wrong with people? I don't like it when people touch me without permission. My body, my choice. Why can't the men in my life respect that?

"Shit, Lil, I'm sorry... you were shouting and... Sorry, I was just trying to shut you up."

He runs his hand through his overlong hair and takes a step back, giving me some much-needed breathing room.

"Yeah, well, splendid job. It worked." Turning on my heels, I walk away as I fight back the tears threatening to fall. Faintly, I hear Rosie tell them she will follow me as I rush up the stairs away from the boy who just stole my first adult kiss.

The funny thing is, if he asked, I probably would have let him. Probably.

✤

I SLAM MY BEDROOM DOOR WITH SO MUCH FORCE IT would impress Master Yoda. A whirlpool of emotion engulfs my senses, and now I'm on edge, caught somewhere between upset and just plain angry. Taking several deep breaths, I hopelessly try to calm my breathing.

What the hell was he thinking kissing me like that?

I slump onto my bed, and stare at the glow in the dark stars stuck to my bedroom ceiling. I don't know why, but somehow, they always bring me comfort.

Ciaran knows I hate it when people insert themselves into my bubble. I like to be the one in control at all times. When people force themselves on me, I freeze up and shut down. Handshakes, hugs, kisses, as long as I instigate them, I can deal. Over the years, I've gotten better with minor acts of intimacy, and as long as I am the one in the driver's seat, I can breathe easily.

The tears I previously fought off, come back with a vengeance.

I won't let them fall.

I will not let them fall.

I've cried too many tears over the past few years. Each teardrop is a reminder of the girl who grew up too fast. It's been nearly a year since I've allowed myself to cry. It's been almost a year since I made that promise to myself, one I have no intention of breaking.

I, Lilyanna O'Shea, will never shed a tear over a man, never again.

People presume I'm heartless, void of all emotion. My appearance is always perfecting a resting bitch face, but the truth is quite the opposite — I feel. I feel too-fucking-much.

Behind my badass persona lies a broken girl — a fractured child whose life got destroyed. She put all her faith in a man meant to love, protect, and shelter her from the big sinful world, only to find that *faith* is such a fickle thing. The man who's supposed to guard her with his life — the one person every little girl should be able to count on — stole the light from behind her hazel eyes.

That girl, she's gone now, in her place is a teenager afraid to fall in love, in fear that it might damage her even more. She's just a shell, one who is not worthy of the drummer boy who makes her heart skip a beat. Ciaran deserves someone better, someone whole, who's capable of loving him fully. Someone who's not broken beyond repair. That's the prime reason I fight him. I push his buttons so he will push back. People say there is a fine line between love and hate. So, if loving Ciaran Maguire is out of the question, I'll hate him instead.

"Lily, can I come in?" Ciaran's deep voice echoes through the wooden door, surprising me. He was the last person I expected to follow me. The last time he was in my room was the night my da attacked me. He wrapped his arms around my trembling body and held me tight until eventually, I cried myself to sleep.

I push myself up into a sitting position, lift my legs to my chest and wrap my arms around my shins. "Yeah."

Silently, I watch as he crosses my bedroom and takes a seat on the edge of my bed.

"Where's Rosie?" I question, trying to ease some of the tension floating through the air.

"I asked her to wait with Cillian," he offers, staring at the floor. Finally, he lifts his gaze to my face, and something I can't quite place, lingers in his eyes. *Sorrow, maybe?*

He scoots a little closer, leaving just a fraction of space between us. Holding out his hand, he motions with a nod of his head for me to take it.

I blow out a deep breath, and finally give in to his silent command. Once my palm touches his, the familiar spark I always get when he is around flickers with hope.

His fingers interlock with mine, causing my heart to race with anxiety. He always does this — stirs up feelings I don't want to feel.

"I'm sorry Lily Bug, I didn't mean to upset you. I wasn't thinking. Can you forgive my stupidity and forget that kiss ever happened? Please."

Plastering on a fake smile, I nod my head. "What kiss?" I

rest my head against his shoulder and pretend I'm not disappointed.

Does he want to forget that he kissed me?

Why am I like this? I'm a walking contradiction.

He rests his head on top of mine. "Love to love you, Lily Bug."

"Love to hate you, Baby Hanson."

His cheeks redden as he tries to hide his smirk. The familiar sentiment we've been using for as long as I can remember, floats like stardust in the surrounding air. His body shifts away from mine, and I know I don't want him to leave. Not yet.

"Stay! We can watch a movie. I'm sure Cillian is busy with Rosie anyway." Far too much uncertainty lingers in my voice, but he doesn't comment on it.

He stands up, his back to me, destroying any hope of a movie night with him, or so I thought. Instead, he kicks off his black combat boots and drops his wallet and keys on my nightstand. Turning those bright green eyes on me, he flashes me the biggest smile, showing off the cheeky dimple on the left side of his mouth.

"Move over, Lily Bug. You hardly expect me to sit on the floor."

🍀

CIARAN

Lily is fast asleep, her head resting on my chest.

Pushing back the strands of her vibrant hair, I give myself a better view of her face.

Fuck me. She is so beautiful.

Her arched brows relaxed above her closed almond-shaped eyes, allowing her long black lashes to kiss her lightly freckled cheeks. Her small dainty nostrils gently flare with every deep inhale, and her succulent lips softly quiver as she releases each breath.

Lily O'Shea turned me into a soppy lovesick fool.

All I know is, one day, in the very distant past, I vowed to guard her with my life. She became the most precious thing in my orbit, and I made it my mission always to make her smile. Because fuck me, when she smiles, I hear the angels sing out with joy.

The movie we were watching ended a while ago, but I can't bring myself to leave. My arm has gone dead, but I don't care. This is the most peaceful I've seen Lily in months, and I won't disturb her. Lily and I have always been close, but over the last year, after everything with her dad, things between us shifted. I'm all too aware of every single move she makes, and this ever-fucking-present need I have to protect her is crushing.

Lily is an octagon. She has so many sides to her, she's

smart, fearless, sarcastic, loyal, caring, vengeful, playful, and finally, broken. It depends on who you are, as to which side you'll see. Then there are the select few who see them all, and luckily for me, I'm one of them.

The creak of her bedroom door opening makes my eyes shoot in that direction.

"Hey, sorry for interrupting. I just wanted to make sure she was okay." Rosie steps into the room quietly, careful not to wake Lily.

My eyes dart between her and the girl asleep in my arms. "She's good. She fell asleep a little while ago, I didn't want to move her."

Rosie's lips lift in a slight smile. "You're good for her, Ciaran. Don't let her tell you otherwise. She's a tough cookie, but she has a heart of gold. If you are prepared to climb her walls, what you'll find on the other side will be worth it. Promise."

"I know."

And I do, but I don't want to climb her walls, I want to break them down. No matter how long it takes — five years, ten, fucking fifteen years. It doesn't matter. I'll wait until she is ready.

"Okay, well if you're staying here, I'll sleep in with Cillian. I just didn't want her to be on her own," Rosie replies with a sad smile.

"Go, I have her. I'm not going anywhere."

Leaning forward, I brush my lips over the mass of red curls that flow across my chest. "Oh, before you go, could you grab me that blanket?" I point to the throw hanging over the chair in the corner.

Rosie grabs the black throw, handing it to me before she leaves. Once the door closes behind her, I cover us both, finally falling asleep holding on to my forever — even if she is not ready to admit that yet.

CHAPTER THREE

MMMBOP (LIVE ACOUSTIC) BY HANSON

CIARAN

THE MORNING SUN POURS THROUGH LILY'S BEDROOM window. The light emanating from its rays catches the clear crystal quartz pendulum swinging above her bed, reflecting a kaleidoscope of colours across the ceiling.

This isn't the first or even the second time I've woken up with Lily fast asleep on my chest. Ever since that night with her da, she's had recurring nightmares. Sometimes she can calm herself down, but other times, she gets so bad that Mary calls me. I'm not sure why I help, maybe it's because I was the one who comforted her that night, but whatever the reason, I'm here more often than not.

Our relationship is strange. We've never been more than friends, playing silly pranks on each other and making dares that neither one of us ever backs out of. It's how we communicate with the outside world. There's nothing better than the spark in Lily's eyes when I've pissed her off. But when we're alone together, I get to hold her vulnerabilities in the palm of my hands.

I can tell you the precise moment when Lily O'Shea became a constant in my life. I was six-years-old. My ma had died six months before, and her death flipped our lives upside down. Then suddenly, we were living in an unfamiliar house in a new town. Conor adjusted a lot quicker than I did. I never really felt like I belonged, then a little ball of fire rolled into my life on my first day of school, and finally, I felt happy again.

"Give them to me now, New Boy," the bully shouted in my face. I didn't want to give them to him. They are mine. My mammy bought them for me before she went to live with Holy God in heaven. Gripping the two drumsticks tighter, I hold on to them like a lifeline. If he wants them, he will have to pry them from my fingers because I'll never hand them over.

"No, they're mine. You can't have them." Where is Conor? Why isn't he helping me?

The smelly boy grabs my arm, struggling to tear the sticks

45

from my grasp. Using as much strength as I can, I yank back, making him fall on his butt.

Rage builds behind his eyes when everyone points and laughs in his direction. Leaning back on his palms, he lifts himself off the ground.

"That's it, New Boy. You're dead." He comes barrelling towards me, and I squeeze my eyes shut, waiting for the blow that's sure to come. Only it doesn't.

"SEAN!" A girl shouts. "Back away from Baby Hanson."

I open my eyes to see who had just called me a Hanson brother. So not cool. I'm a much better drummer than Zac Hanson will ever be.

Standing there in denim dungarees, a black and red ladybug t-shirt with matching red, scuffed, high-top converse, is a girl around my age. Her hair is roaring red, braided into two plaits, and she is scowling at the boy who tried to steal my sticks. I stand still, just watching her as she intimidates the boy with her hand resting on her hip.

"Sorry, Lily. I... I. Bye." The boy rushes off, petrified.

Lily, her name is Lily.

Spinning to face me, her lips curl into a smile. Oh, she is pretty.

"You okay, Drummer Boy? Don't mind Sean; he's mean, and nobody likes him. Plus, don't tell him I said this, but he stinks like old man farts and smelly cheese."

The smile on her cute face makes my insides feel weird. I

like her. *Maybe she can be my girlfriend? Dad said when he first saw my mammy's smile; there was no way he was letting her be anyone else's girlfriend.*

"I'm okay." *Rubbing the dirt off my jeans with my free hand.* "Thanks for scaring him away."

"No trouble, Baby Hanson."

Squinting my nose, I ask out of curiosity, "Why are you calling me that?"

"You play the drums." *With a roll of her eyes, she adds,* "Duh! And if I move my head to the side and squint my eyes a little, you look just like him with your long blonde hair. Minus the rollerblades," *Her carrot coloured eyebrows rise.* "Obviously."

"Obviously."

"Catch you later, Baby Hanson," *she announces, rushing back to her friend.*

"Later, Lily Bug."

Looking back over her shoulder with a wide smile, she waves.

The ping of an incoming message drags me from my memory. Taking extra care, I slowly remove my arm from under Lily and reach over to the bedside locker for my phone. Unlocking the screen, I pull up the new message from my twin brother Conor.

Conor: Dickface? Rehearsal started

half an hour ago. Pull your ass out of the friend zone and get over here.

Good morning to you, too.

Ciaran: My "delectably plump" ass is on the way. See you in ten.

❧

TONIGHT, WE HAVE A SHOW AT THE GOLDEN BARREL, and somehow, I've convinced Lily to come. Even though she usually avoids anything sociable like the plague. Now I just have to convince the others to help me out. Shouldn't be too hard — I hope.

"No fucking way Ciaran, I am not singing that," Cian protests when I present him with my idea to win Lily over once and for all.

"Why not? Admit it, you love that song," I tease.

"You're joking, right? Nobody loves that song."

"Everyone loves that song, Cian, you're just too macho to admit it," Conor says, smacking Cian on the back of the head. Turning back to me, he adds, "count me in brother. It will be a bitta craic."

Sliding my gaze toward Cillian, I wait on his thoughts.

"I'm in too. I know my sister might not show it, but deep down, she'll love it."

"For fuck's sake! Fine, I'll do it, but you're singing those higher notes. My balls dropped too long ago. There is no way I'm reaching those." Cian points at me.

"Deal."

We spent the next few hours practising, nailing down the forty-five-minute set in no time. Once Cian and Cillian leave to get ready for tonight, I pull out a beer from the mini-fridge and plonk down next to my brother on the worn, brown leather couch.

"So, what's going on with you and Lily?" Conor asks.

Running my fingers through my longish hair, I let out a heavy sigh. "Honestly, I've no idea. We have been playing these games for years, and just when I think she is finally letting me in, she pulls back. It's driving me insane. I feel like the only time we agree is when we are pulling silly pranks on one another. I just wish she would let me in."

Sounding like a vagina, he asks, "Have you tried talking to her about how you feel?"

I raise my eyebrow in response.

No, I haven't talked to her about my feelings. Are you smoking crack? This is the ice-queen we are talking about.

"Okay, point taken," he replies to my silent answer.

Don't ask. It's a twin thing.

"So, what's the plan tonight then, get up on the stage,

sing her a song and hope she finally wants to like you back? Seems risky, if I'm honest."

Cheers Bro, you're doing a stellar job calming my nerves.

"I don't know, but after everything with her dad, we have been walking this tightrope, one gust away from blowing off. The tension between us is almost unbearable. It's getting to the stage where I can't be around her. I constantly want to touch her or hold her. Take last night, for instance, when she was being her usually sassy self. What did I do? I fucking kissed her. It was just a peck, but she freaked out. Instead of coming home and letting her calm down. I went to her room, apologised, and then held her all night. When I woke up this morning, I had to run out of there like the building was on fire. I had a boner the size of the Eiffel Tower. Just the sight of her and my dick was harder than a higher-level math paper. I don't know how much longer I can take it. I need to do something. I need to know either way. Does she want me to wait? Or am I wasting my time?"

"I hear you, just be careful. I know you're crazy about her. I don't want to see you get hurt."

Me neither.

🍀

Fuck me; my palms are sweating. How does Cian do this all the time? I'd much rather stay behind my kit, oblivious to the crowd.

The show goes by — far too quickly for my liking — and now it's the moment I've been dreading since I arrived. I didn't think this through. What if she hates it? Fucking hell, what was I thinking?

Scanning the growing crowd, I spot Lily standing with Rosie and Bronagh in the front row. I texted Rosie earlier, asking her to make sure Lily didn't leave before I had time to show her how I feel. I don't know whether I'm relieved she's still here or terrified that she will panic and bolt like she usually does.

"You ready, Casanova?" Cillian questions when he spies me rubbing my palms against my grey track bottoms.

Genuinely feeling nauseous, I respond, "I think I'm gonna throw up."

Cian, being his usual asshole self, steps towards me. "You better not be backing out now. I spent half my afternoon learning how to play the fucking tambourine on your big number. There's no going back now."

God, I can't wait until some chick comes along and knocks him on his face.

"Right ladies, the crowd is getting restless. So, if you're finished discussing whether your menstrual cycles are NSYNC — let's do this," Conor jokes.

Dragging my Cajon over to the microphone placed in the centre of the stage, I take Cian's usual place then adjust his microphone so I can play and sing.

"Hey everyone, you are probably wondering why the drummer is sitting in front of the microphone. Well, there's this girl, and for as long as I can remember, she has monopolised my every thought."

A chorus of ahh's fills the hall.

"She drives me fucking crazy, but I'm also crazy about her. Anyway, I wanted to do something that would show her how much she means to me. I need her to know that no matter how high she builds her walls, I'm not afraid of heights, and if she lets me, I'm willing to climb them."

"We love you, Ciaran." A voice from the back of the room shouts.

Ignoring the crowd, I continue. "This girl is fierce but frightened. She is unbreakable but fragile. She is bold and beautiful. Wild and untameable. She is everything I want and all I'll ever need. This crazy girl marches to the beat of her own drum, and that is one of the many reasons I adore her. I'm hoping that after this song, she will give me a chance at winning her heart because I want to be the one who makes her smile again. Because, God, when she smiles — it's so blinding, the entire room lights up."

"If things don't work out between you two, call me." This time, coming from somewhere on the right.

A laugh escapes me. "Okay, enough of me rambling, here it goes."

Take a deep breath and count to four.

"One, two, three, four," I pound against the Cajon, counting Conor in with the opening bass note of our acoustic rendition of MMMBop by Hanson. Cillian hits the first acoustic chord perfectly, just in time for me to begin. Cian gets the crowd going with a steady clap before picking up his new instrument. I can almost see his eyes rolling in protest. When I reach the chorus, the boys all join in singing back up.

My eyes land on Lily; she is standing right in front of me, just below the stage. Her hands are covering her mouth, her eyes wide in shock. Pleading with only my eyes, I sing the next line directly to her.

The boys all sing back up while I try my best to hit those high notes. I'm no Cian Mulligan, but somehow, I nail each one. The crowd all join in, while Lily just stands there, staring. The last note rings out, and the audience erupts into hoots and hollers, but my eyes stay locked on the one girl in the room who has the power to break my heart. When she turns on her heel and runs out the door, I swear I hear it shatter against the bar's floor.

Shit!

CHAPTER FOUR

NAKED BY JAMES ARTHUR

LILY

"Lily! Lily, wait."

I come to a halt outside of The Golden Barrel, knowing full well that if I don't, my best friends will continue their pursuit. One thing Bronagh and Rosie have in common — other than they're both too sweet for their own good — is that they are very persistent.

Rosie catches up first, stooping over, struggling to catch her breath. "God, I'm so out of shape."

Bronagh studies me with sorrowful eyes. "Are you okay?"

Truthfully, I've no idea how to respond to that question.

Right this second, I've no concept of how I feel. All I know is, I need to get out of here.

I feel like I'm drowning as every emotion — brought on by Ciaran's performance — slowly floods my lungs.

Why? Why did he have to say something? I was happy existing in ignorance. I was content being two friends who secretly have feelings for each other. Why couldn't he just leave it at that?

"I don't know, but I need to get out of here. I can't deal with him right now. I need to process this. Can you guys take me home, please?"

"Whatever you need."

I remain silent the whole ride home, a prisoner to my thoughts. As much as I would love to start something with Ciaran, I just can't.

How can a girl like me have a boyfriend? Whenever he touches me, I flinch or worse, go into a full panic attack. How could I ask him to deal with my brand of crazy? The truth is, I can't.

That's why I can't show him how I feel; because then he'd stick around until I was ready, and that's not happening anytime soon. Maybe never. I can't guarantee him a future together. It would be better for both of us if he moved on.

Heading into my house with the girls on my tail, I stomp towards the kitchen where we find my ma drinking a cup of tea. "How was the show, girls?"

Opening the refrigerator, I mutter back a response. "Fan-fucking-tastic." I take out an ice pack, wrap it up in a nearby hand towel and place it on my chest right over my heart.

Ma eyes me with a question while the girls both snicker at my dramatic display.

"Lily, what in the name of the Lord are you doing with that ice pack?"

"I slipped and fell on some feelings. I need to ice my heart before it's too late."

Dramatic? I think not!

Laughter erupts around me.

What is so funny? Can't they see I'm in distress here?

Through her fits of giggles, Bronagh fills Mammy O'Shea in, telling her all the details of the evening. Apparently, Ciaran's display was 'adorably cute'.

More like highly embarrassing, but whatever.

"I always thought he had a thing for you. Nobody spends that much time struggling to get someone's attention without a hidden agenda."

Not helpful, Mary.

"Ma, I love you, but I'm not ready for Ciaran's advances. I know I've made some progress since seeing Dr J. But a relationship? I'm not there yet, and I might never be."

"Lilyanna O'Shea, don't think like that. I know you have your reservations about intimacy, but remember, Ciaran is not your dad. He's respectful. Maybe you should give him a chance."

"You're right, but unfortunately my brain doesn't agree. Arg, I'm just so mad right now. Why does he have to look so good? This would be so much easier if he became a non-sexual entity, like a sibling or —" I look around the kitchen, waving towards the counter. "— that kettle."

"Sweetheart, stop exaggerating. If you're not ready, just tell him. I'm sure he will understand. He's known you a long time, and if your attitude hasn't made him run for the hills, neither will your denial. He sees you, Lily. Scars and all. I'm sure if it's time you need, he'll give it to you."

"That's just it though; I don't want him to wait. I would never ask him to do that. He is twenty. He has the entire world at his feet. I'm sure he has better things to do than wait for poor little damaged Lily to get over her issues."

My emotions are surfacing — time to shut them down.

"I'm done with this conversation. I'm going to bed. Thanks for the lift, ladies. I'll call you tomorrow."

After walking the girls out, I drag my heavy head up the stairs. I'm emotionally exhausted and in dire need of a twelve-hour nap.

Settling beneath the covers, I focus on putting everything Ciaran related to the back of my mind, which is virtually impossible because my pillow smells just like him and all his Ciaranness.

Rolling over, I pick my phone up off the locker. Maybe that new tragic romance I'm reading will help me escape reality for a little while. Before I can pull up my Kindle app, I spot the new notifications blinking across my home screen.

3 new messages: Ciaran.

Blowing out a defeated sigh, I close my eyes and draw in a much-needed breath. *Fuck it!*

Against my better judgment, I tap the notification, allowing his words to fill my screen.

Ciaran: I know I'm probably the last person you want to talk to, but I just wanted to apologise. I realise now how fucking stupid that move was. Forgive me? *prayer hands emoji*

Ciaran: Please?

Ciaran: LB! Just let me know you're okay.

I stare at the messages for far longer than I'd like to admit, before finally deciding to reply.

Lily: Did you mean it?

Ciaran: Every word!

Lily: I can't. Not right now.

Ciaran: I know, Lily Bug. I know. :(x

🍀

CIARAN

Lily and I fell into an awkward friendship over the last two-and-a-half months. I don't think either of us wants to admit things have changed between us. This tension wasn't present before my stupid grand gesture.

Honestly, I'm probably not helping the situation; I don't know how to behave around her. Every longing glance or accidental touch only makes me crave her more.

Now, I'm leaving for six months, and I hate how things are between us. On one hand, I'm all for living the dream, getting to tour the world with our band has always been the goal. But on the other, I'm hesitant to leave because I know deep down, Lily is the dream.

There's this large *what if* looming between us and I hate it.

Two out of four of the 4Clover band members are in steady relationships. Cillian is madly in love with Rosie, and Conor and Bronagh are better than ever. I am man enough to admit I'm jealous. They have what I want.

Tomorrow, we set out for our first-ever tour, but before I can go, I need to know where I stand with Lily. She needs to tell me if there is no future between us because if that's the case, I need to move on. I can't stay stuck in this limbo forever. It's been months.

As I stand at Lily's front door, my nerves kick in.

What should I say? I know this is it, my last attempt. I can't keep putting myself in her line of fire. I can't keep offering her a happy ever after, not when she keeps her heart so far out of my reach. This is it, all or nothing.

I raise my hand to knock, forcing down the unnerving feeling in the pit of my stomach. *It's now or never, Maguire.*

Rubbing my sweaty hands across the rough denim of my ripped jeans, I blow out a heavy breath and wait for the door to open.

What feels like hours later, Lily opens the door looking just as beautiful — if not more so — as ever. I take her all in like it is the last time I will see her.

Well, I suppose it is—for the next six months, anyway.

She has her hair tied up in two space buns. Her face, free from make-up except for the heavy eyeliner around her amber eyes. A black choker adorns her neck, and she's wearing a black cropped slogan T-shirt with the words 'not enough coffee or middle fingers to deal with today' written across the front in bold yellow writing. She paired it with black ripped skinny jeans, tucked into her yellow Doc Marten boots.

Classic Lily.

"Hey Ciaran, what are you doing here? Don't you have to pack for your tour?"

"Um, yeah. I came to see you, um... before I go. Is there any chance you would like to take a walk with me?"

She hesitates for a second before finally grabbing her leather jacket from behind the door.

We stroll across the fields, neither of us making any move to break through the awkward silence. I honestly don't even know where to start. Hesitantly, I watch as Lily fidgets with the silver zip on the sleeve of her jacket.

Shoving my hands deep into the pockets of my jeans, I try to form the words I need to say. "So, I'm leaving tomorrow," I announce like she's unaware of the fact.

Her arms wrap around her chest, shielding herself from the cold February night air.

Stepping in front of her, I block her path. "Lily, I'm leaving."

Lifting her head, her whiskey eyes lock on my sea-green ones. Her nostrils flare as she bites down on her bottom lip.

"Say something," I beg.

"What Ciaran?" She shouts, her dainty arms spread wide. "What do you want me to say?"

Closing the space between us, I leave just enough room that she won't feel threatened. "I don't know. Tell me we have a chance. Or that I'm wasting my time. Just say something. I'm waiting, LB. I've been waiting."

"I know." Her eyes lower to the ground beneath her feet.

"I get that you might not be ready, but I can't keep waiting for somebody who has no intention of ever being with me."

She is quiet for a moment, taking in my words. Finally, she steps forward, closing the last sliver of distance between us.

Placing her hand on my chest, she looks up with tear-stained cheeks. "Ciaran, I don't know. I want to tell you I'll be ready, but that's a promise I can't make. Maybe this is what we need, six months apart, to figure out who we are. You need to live your life, experience things you have yet to experience. I don't want to be the one who holds you back. I can't ask you to wait for me because I don't know how long you will have to wait. And even at that, I can't guarantee I'll ever be ready. You need to go, follow your dreams, be young, foolish, and carefree. Date girls, and maybe even fall in love."

Covering her hand with mine, I blink back the hurt. "If that's what you want, then I guess that's all there is to say."

I lift her chin by placing my fingers beneath it. "Chasing you is like I'm running on a treadmill, never reaching the destination in front of me. I'm just running and running and running, getting nowhere. You want me to go out and fuck dozens of women on this tour, fine. I might just do that. Goodbye, Lily."

I drop my hand and walk away, leaving her standing in the middle of the empty wheat field. I've done all I can to reach her. The next move is hers.

CHAPTER FIVE

SHE'S SO MEAN BY MATCHBOX TWENTY

5 Months Later — Las Vegas

CIARAN

Night after night.

Show after show.

City after city, and crowd after crowd.

I'm turning twenty-one today, and I'm living my best-fucking-life.

Ironically, I should be on top of the world, standing at the front of a boat with my arms stretched wide like Jack from that chick flick, Titanic. Yet, here I am, fighting back the gnawing feeling that something is missing. Deep down, I know what, or should I say who, but I won't touch that with a ten-foot barge pole.

She's not ready, and if I'm being one hundred per cent honest with myself, neither am I.

So, for now, I'll remain in this awkward grey area, somewhere between her best friend and arch nemesis.

I'll fight the pull, the temptation, and most of all, her because it's easier this way.

It's better for all parties involved if I just stay on my damn side of the lines we've drawn.

That's why, when Conor tells me the girls are coming to Vegas to celebrate our joint birthday, I don't get excited by the fact she'll be here. I don't allow her face to fill my mind and take over my thoughts, and I don't believe that the best present I could get for this once in a lifetime milestone, arrives in less than two hours in the form of the fiery little she-devil known as Lilyanna O'Shea.

❧

"HEY MAN, WHAT TIME ARE THE GIRLS FLYING IN?" I question, taking a seat across from my twin brother Conor at the dining table in our shared hotel suite. We've been on the road living between tour buses and hotels, and as much as I miss home, a boy could get used to this.

Popping the hot croissant I stole from Conor's plate into my mouth, I blow out as the warm dough hits my tongue.

This is the life, five months ago we were just four Irish boys with big-ass dreams of becoming Rockstar's, then in the blink of an eye, we caught our break when our manager — who is also Cian's da — scored us a sweet ass gig with America's biggest band, Sinners.

The last few months we have travelled the globe, one gigantic city after another, and it's been epic.

"They're arriving in a few hours. Cillian and I are meeting them at the airport. Are you coming with us?" He lifts his cup of coffee to his lips, the steam rises, fogging up his reading glasses.

Do I want to go to the airport?

Hell yes, I do. I haven't seen Lily since May — when the tour stopped in Dublin for two days — almost two months without laying eyes on my biggest temptation. If anyone were stupid enough to ask me, I'd deny it like hell, but I miss her sassy ass tormenting me.

"Nah, I'll probably just hang with Cian."

That's it, Ciaran, play it so cool, he'll think you need a jacket.

"How's Bronagh? Was she nervous about flying?" I know my brother is dying to see his fiancée. She is six months pregnant with their first child, and they only found out two weeks before we left Ireland. It's been hard on them both. He didn't want to leave her, especially in her condition. But somehow, they're making it work.

"She's good, a little nervous, but she's glad to be getting here. We FaceTime every day, but it's not the same. Without sounding like a total pussy, I can't wait to hold her."

The smile on my brother's face is blinding, it's been a long road for them, but Bronagh is staying with us for the rest of the tour, and once we finish up, they'll head to L.A. — to the apartment Conor and I bought last month.

His lips twisting into a smug smile. "What about you? Are you looking forward to seeing Lily?"

The croissant I was chewing on catches in my throat. Making a fist, I bang against my chest bone, coughing and spluttering like an idiot. "Lily?" I question when I finally get control of my lung capacity. "Why would I be looking forward to seeing Lily?"

Deny. Deny. Deny!

"Do you think I'm an idiot?" Conor raises his eyebrow. "I know how you feel about her."

"Like I want to tie her up and throw her off a bridge?"

Conor's deep laughter echoes around the hotel suite. "Nope, like you want to tie her to your bedpost and have your wicked way with her."

"Calm down, Conor Grey, nobody will tie anyone to anything. Well, unless you and Bronagh are into that."

He wiggles his blonde brows. "How do you think she got pregnant? So, back to you and Lily, what's going on there?"

Slumping back into the chair, I huff out a breath, knowing all too well he will not let this go.

"Honestly, I don't know." *Truth, right there.* "We didn't exactly part on the best of terms."

Conor rubs his hand across the light stubble on his jaw. His brows pull together, forming a deep v above his eyes.

I wink at him then stand, pushing my chair back. I'm in desperate need of a piss and this conversation is heading into territory I don't want to discuss. "I'm off. Later, man. Let me know when the girls get here."

"Will do, pussy."

I raise my hand, flipping him off over my shoulder. "Dickhead."

❧

BANG, BANG, BANG.

"Cian. Open the goddamn door."

It's two o'clock in the afternoon, and this fucker is still fast asleep.

Finally, the door swings open and standing on the other side is Cian in all his half-naked manly glory. What? I can appreciate a good-looking dude. The guy's ripped. *No word of a lie; his muscles have muscles.*

He blinks a few times, rubbing his eyes with his left hand while adjusting his cock with his right. "What do you want, Thing 1? I'm trying to sleep."

"It's the afternoon, get dressed. The girls will arrive in T-Minus forty-five-minutes." Raising my hands, I show him all the plastic bags I'm holding. "I need your help with these." I flash him a wicked smile, the one reserved for when I'm up to something I shouldn't be.

"What's in the bag, Ciaran?"

Leaning forward, he tries to glimpse at my supplies, but I pull them out of his reach.

"A-ah-ha-ah, no peeking. Put some pants on, and let's get this show on the road."

Time to show Lilyanna O'Shea, just how much I missed her.

❧

LILY

Stepping outside McCarran International Airport, I spread my arms wide. "Hello, Las Vegas!" Dragging in a deep breath, I take in the heavy, dead air. "Aww, pollution."

Beside me, Bronagh sits on her pink suitcase while her baby bump makes for a fantastic tabletop for her bottled water.

"My God, it must be like a million degrees." She pulls out her mini handheld fan and turns it up to full speed. "It's already up at turbo and I'm still fit to pass out. What setting do I need to put this thing on? Trans-fucking-former."

"Are the boys here?" Rosie asks, scanning the waiting cars. Using her hand, she shields her eyes from the blinding sun as she takes a seat on her case like Bronagh. "Goddamn, it's hot."

"You two are unbelievable, we finally get away from all the rain and you're both complaining," I state, basking in the scorching heat.

"Yeah, well, try being six-months pregnant. I've so much fluid in my body that when the sun hits me, I turn into a freaking jacuzzi. I'm boiling from the inside out." Her phone rings in her hand, she looks down and a smile lights up her pretty face.

"Hey, babe." She is silent for a moment, letting him speak. Suddenly, she turns to face the opposite direction. Conor and Cillian come into view, strolling towards us without a care in the world. The two girls take off to get their men, while I stand, waiting with our luggage like some kind of fifth wheel. Great!

🍀

HE DIDN'T COME. NOT THAT I WAS EXPECTING HIM TO be here. Okay, maybe I was, but still, I thought he would want to see me, and the fact that he didn't bother to show hurts more than I care to admit. We have had minimal communication in the past few months. We've exchanged the odd text message here and there. The odd, *how are you? And any craic?* But other than that, silence.

I miss him, not that I'd ever tell him that, that's a secret I'll take to my grave.

Dragging my suitcase up the hotel hallway, I groan with frustration. Bronagh is sharing a suite with Conor, so Rosie, Cillian, and I are sharing a suite. Yay, me!

They took the master, leaving me with the smaller room by myself — which suits me just fine.

When I finally reach my room, I wheel my case through the door and take in the fancy decor. Coffee coloured carpet covers the floor and the walls are papered with a contrasting beige design that's trimmed with a black border around the edges. Elegant and expensive.

A large four-poster California King is set in the middle against a painted red wall. I walk over to it and allow myself to face plant onto the soft-cushioned mattress. *Ummm... so, soft.*

Reaching up towards the pillow, something coarse and hairy tickles my palm.

What the fuck is that?

I jump from the bed like it's on fire, and reach forward, hesitantly. There is something in my bed.

Gently, I tug on the duvet, pulling it back to expose the mattress.

"OH, MY FUCKIN' GOD!"

I scream so loud it bounces off the hotel room walls. They are everywhere. How did I not see them? They're on the walls, the curtains, all over the bed.

Cillian and Rosie rush in from their room in a panic. "What's wrong, Lily?" Rosie scans the area and her eyes land on crisp white sheets covered with large, black, hairy tarantulas.

I'm frozen to the floor.

I can't move.

I'm sure I am the mirror image of a deer trapped in headlights — eyes wide and frozen in place.

There is not much that scares me in this world, but spiders... I can't deal. I despise spiders.

Especially the big, hairy, eight-legged — did I already say hairy? — spiders.

"Cillian, please tell me those are fake spiders." I back away from the bed, following Rosie towards the door.

Cillian inches towards the bed, his movements slow and precise. He leans forward.

Oh, God. I can't look.

I stand in the doorway, a tremendous distance from my

contaminated bed. My hands cover my face, while I slyly peek through the cracks in between my fingers.

"Rosie, darling, would you hand me that pole?" He points towards the stick thing for opening the skylight. Rosie obliges, handing it to him at arm's length.

Carefully, he moves towards the bed as he reaches forward using the long wooden stick. He pokes at one of the hairy creatures, and I release a breath I didn't know I was holding. Suddenly, the enormous furry ball splats to the floor, unmoving.

"They're fake," Cillian announces. He picks up one of the other million fake spiders off my bed, dangling it in front of his face by the leg. "Jesus, these things look so fucking real, it even feels real."

"I will kill him!" I declare between my clenched teeth.

There is only one person in this hotel dumb enough to piss me off. Colossal mistake, mister.

Ciaran Maguire: You just started a war.

Buckle up sweet cheeks. I'm bringing out the big guns.

It's on like Donkey Kong.

CHAPTER SIX

RAISE HELL BY DOROTHY

LILY

THE HEAVY BEAT OF DOROTHY'S RAISE HELL BLEEDS
through my headphones as my stride matches the booming,
heavy bass line. I'm a woman on a mission. Pushing the cart
with determination, I clench my shopping list tightly in my
left hand and scan the shelves for all the items I need.

Four bottles of blue food colouring.

Check.

Three large packets of itching powder.

Check.

And one pair of scissors.

Check.

After I retrieve all I came here for, I head to the checkout and remove my earphones so I can greet the elderly lady behind the register.

"Hey."

"Hello, dear." She scans the items one at a time, each beeping as she slides the barcodes across the machine.

"That's an interesting combination of products," she states as I place them into my reusable, planet-friendly, shopping bag.

Reading the printed nameplate attached to her red uniform, I greet her with a smile. "Sheila." My lips curl into a side smirk. "May I call you Sheila?"

"That's my name, sweetheart."

Ah, Sheila. I'm far from a sweetheart.

"How do you feel about spiders?"

"Oh, I don't have any love for those things. Especially those big ones. They make my skin crawl," she replies with a shudder.

"Me too, I hate them. So, when a boy — well, more of a man-boy — filled my hotel room with a bunch of Misses Muffet's pets, I couldn't let that go. He must pay," I state, gesturing to my bag of goods.

"Aww, I see." Her hearty laugh brings joy to my black soul. "Well, if I was twenty years younger, I'd do the same." The crow's feet surrounding her eyes become more prominent as her mischievous grin reaches her eyes.

"I knew I liked you," I wink. "Have a lovely day."

"You too, darling."

I pop my earphones back in place and head for the door. *Time to raise a little hell.*

✤

On my walk back to the hotel, I realised I will need a little help for my plan to work. Standing in front of Cian's room, I raise my hand and bang aggressively on his door. "Open up."

I continue my assault until the door swings open and Cian stands before me in all his 6'4 glory. Pushing my way past him, I knock my shopping bag off his thigh for good measure.

"Well, if it isn't my favourite little redhead, please, do come in," he grunts before closing the door behind me.

I drop the bags on the nearby coffee table and twist to face him. "Good to see you, too, Cian."

My eyes scan the bedroom. Bottles of beer line the nightstand and dirty clothes litter the floor.

These boys are such slobs.

"I see you're still a domestic goddess."

"What do you want, Lily?" He questions, pulling an old hoodie over his bare tattooed chest.

"Okay, I'm gonna get straight to the point. I know you

helped Assface do some 'Welcome to Las Vegas' decorating in my room."

I don't, but I'm fairly certain he had a hand to play in it. Although, I can't prove it. Here's hoping he puts his foot in his mouth.

"I've no idea what you're talking about." He tries to play it cool, too bad the twitch in his left eyebrow gives him away.

"Nice try, Cian, but I know when you're lying. So, if you don't want me to go full sweet-but-psycho on your ass, I suggest you sit down and listen up."

Pursing my lips together in a try-me expression, I wait him out, and like the good Samaritan he is, he takes a seat

Pulling a bottle of cheap dollar store perfume from my carry bag, I wiggle it in Cian's direction. "First things first, I'm gonna need you to douse yourself in this."

☘

CIARAN

I'm scared, and so I fucking should be. It's been two hours since Lily landed in Las Vegas. Two long-ass hours since she stepped foot inside her hotel room, and nothing.

Not a single thing.

No retaliation.

No verbal tongue lashing.

Zilch, zip, nada.

It's been quiet, too quiet if you ask me. I'm looking over my shoulder, waiting, expecting her attack. So far, I've escaped, unscratched.

So far — being the operative words in that sentence.

I know I go on like an idiot, but even I'm aware there will be consequences for leaving those spiders in her room. I was asking for trouble with a capital T. I may as well have walked into a forest and poked a bear with a stick. If I know Lily and I think I do, she is scheming, planning her attack like the hell-in-heels she-devil she is. She'll wait until I least expect it. Then boom, she'll strike when I feel safest.

That's probably why I've been hiding out in my hotel suite. At least she can't get me in here.

Cian saunters into the living area, stinking of perfume. "What's up? Are you still hiding from Lil?" His deep laughter taunts me.

"Yup." I'm not ashamed of the fact I'm terrified of a five-foot-nothing Satan doll. Everyone knows her bite is bigger than her bark.

"When are you going to man up and grow a pair of balls?" He plonks himself down on the chair next to mine.

Jesus. H. Christ, he smells like a goddamn brothel. I wave my hand under my nostrils, getting rid of the stench that's burning my nose hair.

Ignoring his comment about my lack of balls, I — not so

subtly — change the subject. "Why do you smell like an orgy? Fucking hell man, have you ever heard of a shower?"

"That's why I'm here, I need to borrow your shower gel. I'm all out and I can't be arsed to go out and get some."

"Grand, it's in the bedroom, help yourself. Just put it back when you're done, I need to shower before dinner."

"Will do."

When he comes out of my bedroom with my shower gel in hand, he asks, "Hey, do you fancy grabbing a drink before dinner?"

"Yeah, sure. If I've to face the wrath of Lily, I'll need some Dutch courage. Meet you in the bar in fifteen?"

"Sure." He lifts the shower gel. "I'll pop this back before I head down."

WE'VE BEEN AT THE BAR FOR TWENTY MINUTES, AND Cian is acting strange as fuck. The sly grin permanently etched onto his smug mouth is making me squeamish, and I swear if he checks his phone one more time, I'll whack him in the head with it. Something is up, I can feel it, and I'd bet my life it has something to do with Lily O'Shea.

"What the hell has gotten into you?" I ask, raising a bottle of Bud to my lips.

"Nothing." His eyes flick between me and the door leading to the lobby.

"That's it, spill it!"

"Rosie just text, she's on her way down... with Lily."

"Shit!" Standing up, I down the rest of my beer getting ready to make my grand escape. "That's my cue to go. See you at dinner?"

"You know you can't avoid her forever," he offers as if his statement helps.

"Yeah, I know. But I reckon I can make it another hour at least. See ya later."

"Later." He tips his beer in my direction and I head out.

✤

STANDING UNDER THE STEAM OF THE SHOWER, I LET the water cascade down my back. *Fuck me, that feels great.*

You know you're in desperate need of a good fuck when the water spraying from a hot shower turns you on. I blame Lily, whenever she's near me, this happens. I get so tightly wound.

A bass line pumps in my ears, the melody taking over. Lyrics form in my mind. I hear it like fucking magic — 4Clovers next big hit. There's nothing like a bit of shower singing to get you ready for a night out. As I scrub myself clean, I belt out the song as it forms in my mind.

The ground shakes with the rattle of an
*   earthquake, she's the girl I can touch, but*
*   I can't taste.*
A raging fire that will burn me with her
*   flames.*
She's the match and the gasoline.
She's gonna be the death of me.
She's explosive, but what she doesn't know,
*   in her palms my heart she holds.*

I grab my shower gel from the floor and squirt it into the palm of my hand. Lathering it up and spreading it over my chest as the song takes over.

Have mercy for the fallen ones.
Please forgive me for the wrongs I've done.
Have compassion, oh, I beg, please.
I'm in love, I'm in love, I'm in love with hell
*   in heels.*

My hand moves to my dick. I stroke it once, twice, cleaning every one of my eight inches. *Yes, eight!*

Oh, darling, what I wouldn't try.
I'd walk through hell and back to make you
*   mine.*

How does it feel to sit on Satan's throne?
I bet it seems like you're right at home.

Bopping along to the beat playing in my mind, I cover every bit of my skin with suds.

Have mercy for the fallen ones.
Please forgive me for the wrongs I've done.
Have compassion, oh, I beg, please.
I'm in love, I'm in love, I'm in love with hell
         in heels.

Then, and only then, do I realise the residue flowing down the drain is fucking blue.

Blue!

Motherfucking Lily O'Shea!

Jumping from the shower, I head straight for the floor-length bathroom mirror. *Jesus, Mary, and Joseph!* Not only is my entire body supporting a blue-ish hue; all that dick palming has made my penis look like an extra in the movie Avatar.

Rushing into the bedroom, I search for my clothes. I'm gonna KILL HER!

I can practically hear her laughter from here. Throwing on my black Rolling Stones shirt and black ripped jeans, I take a seat on the edge of the bed and reach down to pull on my socks.

What the actual fuck!

That crazy bitch has cut the toes out of my socks. Checking every pair, I realise they're all the same. She is certifiably insane. Who the hell cuts the toes out of someone's socks?

I run my short nails over my chest and under my armpits, tearing my skin to shreds. *Wait, why am I itchy? Make it stop.*

My balls! Oh, my fucking God! My poor, itchy, blue balls.

Marching from the room like a man possessed, I go on the hunt for the girl who drives me insane.

This round goes to Lily, but you can bet your sweet ass, I will win this game.

CHAPTER SEVEN

HEART WITH YOUR NAME ON IT BY NEW MEDICINE

LILY

"Hey, Lil, are you ready to go?" Rosie strolls into my bedroom. *Which is now spider-free, thank you, Cillian!*

Rosie's glossy black hair frames her porcelain face to perfection, and her short black dress clings to her body like a second skin.

"Looking hot, Chica." I compliment her. "I'm just about done, take a seat," I wink.

Rosie plonks herself on the edge of the bed. "Take your time, the boys can wait."

Turning back to the mirror, I apply another coat of my

favourite burgundy lipstick — Media by MAC — and pop the lid back on, storing it safely in my studded black clutch bag.

Carefully, I remove the styling clamps holding my hair in place, allowing my fire-engine-red locks to fall into the Hollywood waves I've spent the better half of an hour trying to achieve.

Standing up, I give myself a once over. My normal frizzy hair is sleek, tamed to within an inch of its life and I applied my makeup heavier than usual. The bold winged eyeliner, flawless foundation, and my signature I'm-a-badass lipstick make me feel and look older than my twenty-year-old self.

Since we're heading out on the town, I retired my usual band t-shirts and Doc Marten boots for something a little classier. A stark white, sleeveless, tailored jumpsuit with a deep v cut out of the sweetheart neckline, paired with my favourite blood red Louboutin's Cillian bought me for my nineteenth birthday. My half sleeve of tattoos is on full display, decorating the fair skin from my wrist to the elbow of my right arm.

I hold my hands out wide, giving Rosie a little spin. "How do I look?"

"Like Ciaran's worst nightmare." A laugh escapes her painted red lips. "You will drive him crazy in that outfit," she adds, her eyes scanning me with appreciation.

"Mission accomplished," I waggle my eyebrows at her.

"Stop looking at me like that or I'll tell Cillian his sweet little Rosie wants to bone his sister."

"Sorry, babe... I don't swing that way," she winks. "But, if I did, your sexy ass would be on top of my list. Well, after Demi Lovato, that girl is fire."

I nod in agreement and grab my leather jacket, ushering her out the door. Time to face Ciaran for the first time in months.

☘

"It's been fucking mental, city after city, the crowds get bigger and louder at every stopover. People know our names now. It's a bizarre feeling." Conor explains how the tour has been going, telling us all about the shenanigans they've been getting up to since they left Ireland in the spring. We've all been friends our entire lives, so not having them around has taken some getting used to but I'm glad they are finally getting their big break.

"Cian met a girl," Cillian announces, which shocks the shit right out of me. And, if my reaction wasn't bad enough, Rosie is still picking her mouth up off the floor.

"Fuck off, asshole." Cian picks up a bread roll from the large round dining table and flings it at Cillian's head.

"Poor Cian got shafted. She snuck out of his hotel room without leaving her number," Conor sneers. "It's been months, and he's still moping about like someone kicked his puppy." Wrapping his arm around his fiancée Bronagh's shoulder, he pulls her tighter to his chest. He places a gentle kiss on her forehead, then gazes down at her with nothing but love and affection.

I've always secretly envied them. Their relationship is unbreakable. There are times I wish I could have what they do, then reality smacks me in the face and I remember, I'm damaged goods, unlovable.

"Oh, the player becomes the played. It's about time. His head was getting way too big anyway," Bronagh teases Cian.

"Where the hell is Ciaran?" Cillian checks his watch. We've been waiting half an hour for Tweedle Dee to grace us with his presence, but as per usual, he's late. Cian's eyes meet mine, the laughter lines around his eyes become more prominent when I snort. All eyes land on us, and we erupt.

"Lily?" Conor stares down at me.

"What did you do?" This one comes from Cillian.

Rosie and Bronagh look highly amused. And so they should. It was hilarious.

"Me?" I hold my hand to my chest. "Why do you assume I did anything?" My eyes roll back into their sockets.

Just then, the door of our private dining area swings open, and in walks... Papa Smurf. Oh *my God, he's so... blue.*

"Lily. A word!" Ciaran punctuates his statement with a hardened stare.

Ignoring the laughter and taunts from everyone at the table, I push my chair back, stand to my full height — which isn't very tall — and weave my way past Rosie and Cillian. I hold my head high. Time to face the music. *Thankfully, Ciaran is a melody I could listen to on repeat.*

❧

CIARAN

"Do you think this is funny?" I ask once we're alone in the hallway. Lily tries her damnedest to contain her amusement, but her burgundy stained lips press together, making her attempt futile.

"I'm fucking blue." I stretch my arms out wide, giving her a better look at the damage she caused.

Her hand flies towards her mouth, covering the smirk I know is there. Her nostrils flare and her eyes crinkle.

"Say something." I rub my eyes, pinching the skin between my brow with my index finger and thumb. Only Lily could give someone a stress headache.

Her silence is deafening as I pace up and down in front of her, probably wearing a hole in the expensive-as-shit carpet beneath my army boots.

Finally, thank the Lord, she answers. "I'm not even

sorry. You started this. It's not my fault you can't handle the backlash."

Tears gather in her eyes — not from crying, no, these are laughter tears. She whips her phone from the pocket of her white, painted-on jumpsuit and starts snapping pictures.

"Give me that damn phone." I hold out my palm, wiggling my fingers. "Hand it over."

"Not happening, Baby Hanson. These pictures are Insta gold."

"Lily," I warn. "Give. Me. The. Phone."

Never one to back down, Lily steps forward, closing the space between us. The six-inch heels she's wearing give her the extra height she needs. Tilting her chin slightly, her gaze latches on mine.

"Didn't your da ever tell you it's dangerous to play with fire?" she quips.

Her golden eyes narrow — the colour of whiskey, autumn leaves, or the sweetest of honey. She is so close, close enough that I can almost taste her on my lips, our breaths dancing together in the tiny space between us.

"Yeah, sure he did, but we both know you're not fire, Lily Bug. You are ice. Cold to touch, but in the right hands you melt."

Her tongue darts out, tracing her bottom lip, taunting me, teasing me. She's mistaken if she thinks I'll kiss her first.

If she wants me, she needs to make the first move. She leans closer — if that is even possible — our lips touching, barely.

"I suppose you think your hands can do just that?" Her daring tone forces a groan from my dry throat.

I swallow the bowling ball-sized lump and close my eyes briefly. Shit, I'm milliseconds away from saying fuck it, capturing her lips and kissing the ever-loving shit out of her.

I reach up, brushing her stray hairs behind her ear. "I don't think, I'm certain. We're explosive. I know it, you know it, everybody knows it, Lily Bug. The question is," I whisper against her lips, "what are you going to do about it?"

She hesitates for a second, probably fighting the internal battle I know she's having with herself. There was never any doubt that our feelings for each other were mutual. I've always known she felt the same way, but she wasn't ready.

Then it happens. The air rushes from my lungs as her lips press against mine. She buries her fingers in my slightly long, thick, dyed black hair. Her mouth tentatively explores mine. Behind my closed eyelids, fireworks explode, popping loudly in my eardrums, sparking a fire within my veins as her tongue dances, softly, slowly, seductively, against mine.

The scent of her signature perfume fills my nose — cherry blossoms with a dash of lavender. I wrap my arms around her dainty frame, pulling her closer against my chest. The only sound is our rapidly beating hearts and sped up breaths.

Everything else fades from existence. I could stand on a track in front of an oncoming train and I wouldn't give two shits; because kissing Lily is like time. Fleeting but needs savouring.

A slow clap pulls us apart, followed by some extreme hoots and hollers.

"Bout time."

"Get a room."

I peer over Lily's shoulder to find the entire gang watching our exchange. Lily buries her head against my chest. Her voice, muffled by my black shirt. "Please tell me they didn't see that."

"No can do, Lily Bug. I'd never lie to you. Not now, nor ever."

She groans against my chest, the sound travelling straight to my cock.

It's gonna be a long night, Mr Boneman. A very long — keep it in your pants — night.

🍀

AFTER DINNER, WE END UP IN THE HOTEL BAR FOR THE Legends of Rock night, which the hotel is hosting. Later we're planning on meeting up with the band members of Sinners, but it's still early, so here we are.

The house emcee — a drag queen named Fanny Lennox

— is entertaining the crowd with an off-key rendition of *I Put A Spell on You.*

The drinks are flowing and even though the girls can legally drink in Ireland, in America, not so much. Thankfully, all the lads are already twenty-one, so we keep the table stocked. Everyone is well past tipsy-town and heading straight for hammered-city, well, everyone except Bronagh.

"Ladies and Gents." Fanny Lennox grabs everyone's attention. "For tonight's entertainment, we are hosting this year's Queen of Rock 'n' Roll contest." The entire room erupts into cheers and catcalls.

"My fellow queen, Gaylor Momsen, will go around each table with the sign-up sheet. So, ladies, if you want your face housed in the Queen of Rock 'n' Roll hall of fame, along with a signed Guns' N' Roses band t-shirt from their 1988 world tour... sign up."

Lily stands — or more accurately wobbles — on her feet. "I've got this in the bag," she shouts. *Okay, no more tequila for her.*

"The contest is three rounds long. Round one will be general rock knowledge. Round two will be a talent-based round," she points behind her to every instrument you can think of. "Where the three best Roll 'n' Roll performances will advance to the next round. Finally, we have round three, which is a couple-based round. The famous best Rock 'n' Roll dance battle. Contestants, you will need partners for this, so choose wisely, their reaction could cost you the title!"

Lily announces to our table, "I'm winning that t-shirt." She points to Rosie, "and you're doing it too, it's always good to have a Plan B." She spins to face Bronagh. "You're lucky you are pregnant because you'd be up there too if I had my way."

She cranks her neck, searching for something. "Where is Gaylor Momsen? This queen needs her crown."

I sit back against the booth, laughing my ass off at her drunken display.

She turns to face me, mischief burning in her amber eyes. "Don't know what you're laughing at, Baby Hanson, when I make it to round three... which I will, you're my dance partner."

My laughter dies in the back of my throat. Here's hoping she's too drunk to make it past round one.

CHAPTER EIGHT

POUR SOME SUGAR ON ME BY DEF LEPPARD

LILY

THERE ARE VERY FEW THINGS IN THIS LIFE I'M CERTAIN of but me winning this competition is one of them. As I stand on the stage sizing up my competition, I know deep down to my black soul, I've got this in the bag. Does it matter that I've drunk way more than my three-drink maximum limit? No, it does not; because if it involves Rock 'n Roll, I, Lilyanna O'Shea, know my shit!

"Okay ladies, are you ready?" Tranny Lennox — or was it Fanny? Oh, who cares, they're both hilarious — screeches into her diamond-encrusted microphone. I wonder if they're genuine diamonds.

Focus, Lily.

I stand behind my buzzer with Rosie on my left, and some chick in a Nine-Inch Nails band tee to my right. There are eight girls in total. Two of which look like they belong on the Disney channel, not the Queen of Rock stage, but whatever. And the other four, minus Rosie, I'm not sure about. Doesn't matter anyway, because I'm about to go full Lily and fuck shit up!

"Hands above your buzzers."

Holding my hand above the button, I purse my lips and squint my eyes.

Game face, baby!

"Question one. Which well-known rock band released Back in Black in 1980?"

I reach for the buzzer, but Malibu Barbie beats me to it. The crowd waits in anticipation for her answer.

Bouncing on the balls of my feet, I repeat the answer over and over in my head.

AC/DC. AC/DC. AC/DC.

"Emm, it's that band..."

Oh, sweet baby Jesus. This will be easier than I thought.

"ABCD," she claps her hands together, bouncing up and down. So much so that her fake tits are seconds away from knocking her out.

Laughter fills the room, a laugh I know too well, Cian Mulligan. His deep brogue travels towards the stage.

"Nice try, sugar, but Barney the Dinosaur is not a rock musician."

I don't even try to hide my snickers. This will be easier than I thought.

Like taking candy from a baby.

✤

I WAS WRONG.

Well, there's a sentence I never thought I'd think, but fuck me pink and fluffy, these girls are kicking ass.

Not mine, never mine. But Rosie, the little puff pastry, got eliminated in round one. Right alongside the two airheads. Round freaking one.

Disappointment is too nice of a word to describe how I feel towards my best friend. I cannot believe that she doesn't know the name of Led Zeppelin's drummer. Not only has Ciaran been calling his penis Mr Boneman after the legend John Bonham for YEARS, but her boyfriend has a giant ass poster of him above his bed. Such an amateur!

We're more than halfway through round two, and I'm physically sweating in places I didn't know could sweat. Nine Inch Nail girl — whose name I learnt is Daria — is rocking out on the bass. She is showing off some serious moves. Not going to lie, the girl has talent. She's the one to beat.

Once she finishes up, it's my turn. I have two options here, the guitar, which I know how to play pretty well — thanks to years of lessons from my genius brother — or the drums, which I've been practising secretly for years.

Not because I have a crush on a certain someone, but because I enjoy hitting things with sticks. Was that believable?

Yeah, didn't think so.

My eyes dart between the two instruments.

Eenie. Meenie. Minie. Mo.

"Now for our final contestant in this round. All the way from Ireland... Give it up for Miss Lily O'Shea."

Fuck it! My final thought before making most decisions.

I slowly make my way over to the Yamaha 7-piece drum kit. Taking extra care so my drunk ass doesn't fall off the stage, I lower myself onto the stool.

Okay, Lil. You can do this.

Gaylor Momsen walks my way, stopping to ask which backing track I need before heading for the turntable.

After wiping the sweat beads off my palms, I pick up the two hickory sticks. I loosen, then tighten my grip a few times, becoming one with the wooden texture. I always do this before playing, the same thing I learned from Ciaran... I take a deep breath and count to four.

The backing track floods through the speakers, and the whaling of the electric guitar forces me to count my beats.

Fifteenth measure and go.

CIARAN

I have never been so turned on in my entire life. My dick is bigger than Texas and I'm sure my mouth is hanging wide open. I never knew Lily could play the drums. I can't comprehend what is happening, but she is killing it. Epically!

"What am I seeing?" Cian questions.

"Did you know about this?" Cillian interrogates Rosie.

"Erm, yeah. She started a few years back. Mr Maguire sneaks her into the shed so she can practise on Ciaran's kit. Her therapist said it's an excellent way for her to release stress." Rosie shrugs her shoulders, guiding her straw to her lips so she can sip on the fruity cocktail — As if watching her best friend not miss a single beat of Sweet Child O'Mine, isn't a big deal.

It is A HUGE DEAL!

Everyone at the table is chatting about Lily, but me, I can't take my eyes off her. Her arms move effortlessly at the speed of light as the long guitar solo kicks in. She keeps up, never once faltering, and fuck me, it's the sexiest thing I've ever witnessed. Her eyes close like she is allowing the music to make her, not the other way around. She looks perfect.

Perfect for me.

"Give it up for Lily." The ground beneath my feet quakes as the cheers from the crowd echo off the walls. People stand and clap, but I can't move. Nothing Lily does ever surprises me, but this... I'm shocked.

"What the hell just happened?" I don't know who I'm directing that question at. But someone needs to clarify because I'm genuinely confused.

"Why are you so surprised?" Conor's hand lands on my shoulder. "You two have this strange — anything you can do I can do better — foreplay going on for years." He barks out a laugh. "The only thing you could do that she couldn't was work that kit like a pro," he laughs. "Looks like she decided she would outdo you on that too."

"True that," Cillian agrees. "And with minimal effort too. She was lit."

There is a part of me that wants to disagree with them, but I can't. She was epic and judging by the clapping and whistling, everyone in the audience thinks so too. My eyes land on hers and a shit-eating grin dances across her face; one I want to kiss right off. I make a mental note to take out some life insurance because if there's one thing I know for sure... it's that Lilyanna O'Shea will be the death of me.

✤

THERE ARE THREE CHAIRS LINED UP ACROSS THE CLUB'S stage. Each one, occupied by a poor unfortunate sucker. How do I know this? I'm sitting centre stage because Lily summoned me to be her dance partner.

There have been plenty of times in my twenty-one-years of existence, where Lilyanna O'Shea roped me into doing something I wasn't comfortable with. But this, this takes the biscuit. I do not dance... ever.

After Lily's surprise drum skills, she sailed into the last round. There are three contestants left, the girl who shredded the bass, an older lady with lungs of steel, and Lily.

"Give it up for our men," the emcee announces, and the crowd goes wild, hooting and hollering at our discomfort. "Before we move on with our third and final round, I'm just going to go over the rules." Fanny Lennox informs. "This is a dance round... but there is a twist. Men," she motions towards us. "Your job is to remain seated at all times, while our ladies," she points towards the three females standing to the side, "dance for you, to one of the raunchiest rock songs of all time."

Fuck me dead.

"At the end of this round, we will have the crowd choose

the winner. The couple with the loudest response wins... easy."

Easy? Fanny has lost her damn mind. What's the opposite of easy? Is it difficult or hard? I'm going with hard — because that's exactly what I will be the entire way through this fucking performance.

"Ladies, take your positions."

I watch with wide eyes as Lily throws back another shot of tequila before sauntering my way.

"Thank Jesus, I'm drunk," she shouts. "Because there isn't a sober day in hell I'd be doing this otherwise." The giggle that escapes her mouth is almost foreign. Lily never giggles. She's a contagious cackle kind of girl.

"You ready for this, Baby Hanson?" The amused look on her face tells me how much she's enjoying making me squirm. Leaning closer, her breath tingles my ear. "Stop grinding your teeth, it's not a pleasant look on you."

"Stop trying to send me to an early grave then," I grit out.

"Nope, my fundamental goal in life is to make you miserable," she replies. The glint in her eyes shines like endless stars on a clear night.

"Horny and miserable," I mutter.

I can see it now, written on my tombstone... Here lies Ciaran Maguire, death by blue balls and the opposite of an easy boner.

Lily sits on my lap, her perky breast at my eye level. I swallow down the bowling-ball-sized urge to bury my face in them. Her hand's loop around my neck as the heavy beat of Def Leppard's Pour Some Sugar on Me blasts through the speakers.

The overhead fluorescent lights reflect against her skin, making the white of her skin-tight jumpsuit transparent. It takes everything in me to hold back the groan when the sight of her barbell nipple rings shows through the see-through material. *Christ on stike.*

Lily flicks her head backwards, exposing the skin of her elongated neck. Her roaring red hair swishes from side to side as she rotates her hips to the heavy guitar intro. The next four minutes and fifty-one seconds will either be my own personal hell or a glimpse at fucking heaven.

She swings her left leg off me, and in one quick motion, she's now facing the crowd. She bends at the waist, gliding both hands from her red high heels up and over her calves and thighs; finally, settling them on her hips.

Every move she makes is equally hypnotic and torturous. The desire to grab hold of her and drag her out of here, over my shoulder, is almost too much to bear.

Joe Elliott's voice continues to sing about a crazy little woman in a one-man show while Lily grinds on my now excruciatingly throbbing dick. I can guarantee you, anytime

I hear this song from now on, all I'll see is Lily's peachy ass waving in my face.

Finally, my resolve breaks and my hand reaches out to roam over her waist. I pull her in until she lands back on my lap. This time, her back is against my chest. She reaches behind her, wrapping her arm behind my head. Her sensual movements cause my heart to beat so fast, it's seconds away from jumping out of my chest.

When she swings her hips from left to right, I pray to every God, in every religion out there, I don't come in my jeans like a horny twelve-year-old boy.

Pushing off my lap, she drops low between my legs, and I gaze down at her gorgeous face, just inches from my cock. Punished, I am being punished.

I'm sorry, Jesus. I promise I'll go to mass twice a week, but for the love of God, please get her off her knees.

Her palms glide over my thighs, and my penis salutes her.

Get back in your box, mister.

The song eventually ends while Lily is still straddling my waist. She stands up, ready to back away, but I grip her waist tighter, not letting her go.

"Do not move," I growl. "My dick is throbbing and if I stand up, someone will lose a fucking eye."

She barks out a laugh which does nothing to tame my trouser snake.

The crowd breaks out into a full-blown chant. "Lily, Lily, Lily…"

The emcee walks onto the stage and raises her microphone to her overdrawn lips. "Looks like we have a clear winner. I present you with the newest Queen of Rock." She gestures to the girl in my lap. "Give it up for Miss Lily O'Shea."

"Congratulations, LB," I whisper against her neck.

"Couldn't have done it without you, Baby Hanson."

CHAPTER NINE

BLAME IT ON THE STARS BY ANDY GRAMMER

CIARAN

Bright, fluorescent neon lights flash across the dance floor like beacons, moving in perfect sync to the heavy beat the booming baseline brings. I'm not a fan of the club scene, but nowhere does it the way Vegas does. This place is insane. Leaning over the balcony rail of the VIP area, I scan the crowd below, seeking the one person who unknowingly demands all of my attention. Sweaty bodies sway as the music rattles the ground beneath their feet.

Then I see her flaming red locks, more vibrant than ever under the glow of the overhead spotlights. Hypnotised by her every move, I watch intently, her body calling to mine like a siren. With her arms stretched above her head, eyes closed and hips moving in time to the music, she is a vision dressed in white. In all the years I've known Lily, this is the freest I've seen her. A large smile spreads across her porcelain face, and when the song changes to some remix of *Single Ladies by Beyoncé,* she and Rosie go crazy. Both bouncing around like two lunatics who don't have a care in the world, mouthing the words and making up some rather questionable dance moves. It's refreshing, seeing her have fun, she's always been so closed off and cautious. It appears a lot has changed in the few months I've been away.

A hand appears in front of my face, shoving a beer bottle towards me. "Here, you look like you need this more than I do."

My eyes leave the girls briefly as I take the bottle from Cillian. "Cheers."

Resting his arms along the rail, he follows my gaze. "So, you and my sister, huh?"

Okay, so I see we're doing this now.

I've been waiting all night for him to comment on the kiss he witnessed earlier. Honestly, I'm shocked it took him this long. This could go one of two ways. He could knock me out and tell me to keep my hands off his little sister or give me his blessing. With how unpredictable Cillian O'Shea is, your guess is as good as mine. Surely, he'll understand, he was hot for his best friend's sister for years and now they're dating.

Lifting the beer to my lips, I take a generous swig, washing down the ball of anxiety brewing in the pit of my stomach under the weight of his intense-as-fuck stare. Unsure of how to proceed, I go with the truth. "I have no fucking idea."

A gruff laugh leaves his mouth before he pats me on the back with a manly slap. "Good luck."

My head whips around so fast, it nearly disconnects from my shoulders. "Is that it? All you have to say is good luck?"

"Yeah. Ciaran... I'm not Cian. He hated it when I started dating Rosie. I know you would do nothing to upset Lily, fuck you've been her rock for years. If you're what she wants, and you make her happy, I'm all for it. So, as I said... Good luck, knowing my sister, you're gonna need it."

Shouts and hollers erupt from behind us, forcing our conversation to end. This is a private lounge which only means one thing, the Sinners have arrived. Turning to face the doorway, Jax St. Claire — also known as Saint — stands proud as a peacock, with his arms stretched wide while the other band members wait impatiently behind him. Next to enter is their lead bassist, Saints younger sister Remi, followed closely by their drummer Dash and their lead guitarist Maverick. We've got to know these guys pretty well the past few months. They're good peeps, well except Saint. He's a cocksure bastard who likes to piss me off.

"Hello, you bunch of pussies!" Saint saunters into the room like he owns the place. As the lead singer of the world's biggest indie rock band, he possesses a confident swagger that comes with years of fame. "Do you call this a party? This is the most pathetic thing I've ever seen." Leaning forward, he grabs the bottle of tequila from the glass table and lifts it to his lips, taking a more than generous gulp. "Didn't I read somewhere that nobody parties like the Irish? You boys need to step up your game, I've seen bingo parlours with more excitement. Where are the girls?" His blue-green eyes lock on mine and a smug smirk curls on his lips. "I'm looking forward to seeing my favourite Irish lass."

Grinding my teeth, I hold back the urge to punch him in his smarmy face. Saint met Lily when we played their show in Dublin, back in May. They hit it off and for some unknown reason, they've become friends. Now he finds every opportunity he can to rub their friendship in my face.

Cillian's hand lands firmly on my elbow, forcing me to direct my glare his way. Muttering under his breath, he warns me, "Cool it, you know as well as I do, he's trying to get under your skin. Don't give him any ammo."

I nod my head, steading my breaths just in time for Lily to waltz into the VIP lounge. Saint eyes her up and down, his stare full of want and appreciation. *Two seconds, that's how close I am from flinging him off this balcony.*

Saint opens his arms as he steps towards Lily. "Well, well. There's my favourite little redhead."

Trying to seem unfazed by his over-eager display, I tip my beer to my lips and swallow back the bitterness while watching their every move. When Lily cautiously steps forward into his awaiting arms, the beer I just swallowed lodges in my throat, making me choke and sputter like a goddamn idiot. I'm no expert, but I'm pretty sure this is what jealousy feels like.

✤

LILY

"I need a drink," I yell at Rosie over the loud music.

Nodding her head in reply, she takes hold of my hand and together we manoeuvre through the crowd. Once we reach the stairs that lead to the VIP lounge, we flash the bouncer our VIP access wristbands, then begin our ascent up the spiral staircase. *Whose dumb idea was it to put stairs in a nightclub? I'm way too drunk to climb these and these fucking heels are a death trap.*

Miraculously, after a few sways and fumbles, Rosie and I make it to the top without breaking our necks. Pulling back the dark, purple velvet curtain, we step inside and see that the band Sinners have arrived.

"Well, well. There's my favourite little redhead." Jax St. Claire stands right in my line of sight. His aquamarine eyes focused solely on me. With a face carved by angels and a body that roars sin, Saint is exactly the guy your momma would warn you about. He's an enigma, the full bad-boy package. His tossed, chocolate brown hair, and a lean, toned, tall frame — with just the perfect amount of muscle — has every girl he meets falling at his feet.

Opening his arms, he waits for me to make a move. When I first met this arrogant bastard, something about him screamed familiar. He never once forced himself upon me. It was almost as if he could read me like an open book, and in an instant, I felt safe in his presence.

People say that like recognises like... and with Saint, his demons — the ones he buried under his Rockstar persona — they recognised mine. We developed a strange friendship, exchanging texts and phone calls, getting to know each other.

We're friends, nothing more, nothing less.

"Well, hello to you, too." Stepping into his awaiting arms, he wraps me up in a hug filled with warmth. He brings his mouth down to my ear, and whispers for only me to hear. "Maguire is seconds away from cutting my balls off.

What do you say, Pretty Lady? Wanna piss him off some more?"

A low chuckle escapes me. "Definitely." One night, over one of our lengthy calls, I told Saint all about Ciaran and our 'dysfunctional' not-a-relationship. Funny enough, it was Saint who told me to make my move, sooner rather than later.

Lily, he's a man, he ain't gonna wait forever. Make your move, Pretty Lady. Before someone else does.

It was that conversation that prompted me to join Rosie and Bronagh on this Vegas trip. I had a plan: come here, talk to Ciaran, and see where we stand. Then that kiss happened and I've no idea what is going on, but tonight, I'm far too drunk to be making any kind of decision. Without effort, my eyes seek Ciaran out. He's standing in the corner with Cian, beer bottle in hand, chatting to the other members of Sinners. Remi throws her head back at something Ciaran says, before running her fingers along his bicep, causing my gut to tighten. My body goes rigid under Saint's touch and molten rage floods my veins. Saint notices my sudden shift and his gaze flicks over his shoulder.

"Ahh, yes, that. Looks like my sister has made her move."

Looking up at him with wide eyes, I raise my brow and wait for him to elaborate.

"I told you. You need to make your move before someone else does. Remi," he discreetly nods in his sisters' direction. "She is someone else." Gently, he places his hands on my forearms and spins us in place, leaving me with my back to the group. Locking his aquamarine irises on mine, he tilts my chin with his calloused fingertips and lowers his voice, so it is barely audible over the pumping bass of the club's music. "How badly do you want your drummer boys' attention?"

When I refuse to answer with words, my eyes travel over my shoulder and give away all my secrets.

"That bad, huh? Okay, let's get it then. Dance with me. And I guarantee he'll be putty in your hands before the night turns to morning."

Just as he finishes the sentence, the song changes to a remix of Jealous by Nick Jonas. A mischievous smirk curls on my lips. "Let's do this."

With a wink, Saint leads me over to the small dance floor in the corner of the VIP area. "I hope you're ready for this. Shit's about to get sexual."

🍀

SAINT'S HANDS ARE ALL OVER ME. ALL. OVER. ME. IF I didn't know better, I'd say he's enjoying our — make-Ciaran-jealous — show a little too much. Song after song, he grinds against me in a way that would make my mother blush. Hell, who am I kidding, my face is probably redder than my hair.

With my back pressed up against his chest, we sway in sync as Jason Derulo pumps through the speakers singing about talking dirty. When the song shifts to the baritone sax, Saint's hands land on my stomach. He pulls me closer while he moves our hips in a slow, sensual, side-to-side motion. His breath is hot and heavy, hovering beside my ear. "Don't look now, but your boy is seconds away from throwing you over his shoulder and dragging you out of here. Caveman style."

I don't know about you, but when someone tells me not to look, that is exactly what I do. Sitting around the large table are Cillian, Rosie, and Cian. Maverick and Dash stand over to the right of the table, knee-deep in conversation. Finally, I spy Ciaran, sitting back against the booth-like seats.

As if I called his name, Ciaran's eyes flick up and seek me out. The intensity behind them burns into my skin, blazing with a fire that could burn down an entire forest. He has a beer bottle clutched tightly in his palm and if I had to wager, I'd say it's seconds away from exploding into tiny green shards. It's hard to see from the distance between us, but I'm almost certain his teeth are grinding as he watches my display. I almost feel bad but then my gaze hits Remi, the gorgeous, tattooed brunette that's moulded to his side and any remorse I had, flies out the window. Ugh, I need a drink.

I slide out of Saint's hold, and motion with my eyes for him to follow me to the small bar in the corner.

"Shots. Let's do shots."

"What can I get you?" The barman greets us.

Saint's eyes focus over my shoulder as he replies with a teasing smirk. "I'll have a deep throat and a blowjob. What about you, Pretty Lady, wet pussy and a screwdriver?"

A throat clearing behind me grabs my attention. Turning, I come face to chest with Ciaran's impressive pecs. His arms circle my waist, catching me before I fall on my ass. Looking down at me, his eyes bore into mine. "Hey."

Licking my lips, I add moisture to my dry mouth. "Erm, hi."

Uncertainty lingers in Ciaran's brow, seconds pass without either of us saying a word as the tension brews between us, sparking like a match to a flame.

"Can, eh... Can I talk to you for a second?" Ciaran's voice cracks. He narrows his gaze on Saint. "Alone?"

Saint picks up the tray of shots and shoots me a wink before heading over to the table where the others are pretending not to watch the exchange between me and Ciaran.

I focus my attention back on the drummer boy who makes my heart skip a beat and purse my lips. "What's up, Baby Hanson?"

"Are you trying to piss me off? First, you kissed me earlier. Then you grind all over my dick at the contest and now... now you've got your hands and body all over Saint?

Is this just a game to you? Cause it's one I don't want to play.

"What about you?" I sass. "Did you think I didn't see Remi crawling on you like a koala on her favourite tree? Besides, why are you getting so mad? It's not like we're together. In the words of Queen Bey, if you like it, then you should have put a ring on it."

Dropping his face lower, his lips are now a breath away from mine, our noses touching from the lack of space between us. "You want me to put a ring on it? Fine, let's go. We are in Vegas. I could make you mine before the night is through."

I push off his chest, creating the distance I need. "Shut up, you idiot! I was joking."

Turning on my heel, I walk away. Suddenly, Ciaran grips my elbow and spins me back into his chest in a move that's so possessive, I'm not sure if I should smack him or kiss him.

"Well, I wasn't. You are so hell-bent on proving to yourself that I'm not serious about you. So, this is me proving to you, I'm all in."

His left-hand caresses my cheek as his eyes scan every inch of my face. "Marry me, Lily Bug. I. Dare. You!" The dimple on his left cheek deepens with his wide smile. "What do you say, Lil, wanna take a leap of faith with me? All you gotta do is jump, and I promise... I'll catch you."

CHAPTER TEN

MARRIED IN VEGAS BY THE VAMPS

LILY

IF THERE WAS EVER ANY DOUBT, IT'S NOW GONE. IT'S official, I'm certifiably insane.

Somewhere between the whiskey and the shots of tequila, I, Lily O'Shea, lost her goddamn mind. It's the only explanation I have as to why I'm standing in the overly tacky waiting room of The Little White Chapel, with my newly acquired marriage licence clutched tightly in my left hand. Sure, if I was to plan my dream wedding, this would probably be the last place on earth I'd pick, but sometimes life throws us a curveball and we just gotta go with it. Besides, If I squint — hard — the fire engine red carpet, stark white walls, and tasteless gold painted vases filled with cheap flowers, aren't too bad.

Sneaking off to get secretly married is an extra level of crazy, even for me. We told no one where we were going. We just waved goodbye and set off on a journey. If my life was a movie, I'd be Dorothy from The Wizard of Oz. Only, in my case, I didn't follow a yellow brick road... I followed a tattooed drummer to a courthouse, signed a bunch of papers and now here I am, waiting on an overweight Elvis to seal the deal.

See, I told you... I've lost all logic and reason. Call the nearest institute, they need to admit me. Pronto!

Standing in the waiting area, I scan the wall of framed photographs. Each picture shows a different couple with enormous smiles spread across their faces. Without looking back, I sense Ciaran coming up behind me. The goosebumps along my spine alert me of his presence. Carefully, he wraps his arms around my waist, then spins me around to face him. The tell-tale scent of alcohol lingers between us. Yes, we've both had too much to drink, but this... us, is inevitable.

Meant to be.

Written in the stars and all that other universe shit.

It's always been Lily and Ciaran against the world. A piece of paper will not make a difference.

"Are you sure about this, Lily Bug?" Ciaran cradles my face tenderly between the palms of his hands.

Standing on my tippy toes, I gently kiss him on the lips then pull back so I can see his gorgeous face. "Nope, but I'm not backing out now. A dare is a dare, Ciaran. You and I both know I will never back out of a dare."

The little angel sitting on my right shoulder screams at me.

You're lying. You're not doing this because of a dare, you are doing this so you won't lose him. If you marry him, then he is yours.

That's when the little devil on my left shoulder chimes in.

Yeah, hers until divorce-do-them-part.

Oh, look, we're having a party. See, this right here is why I shouldn't drink. I'm silently talking to two versions of myself.

Ciaran's deep Irish drawl snaps me back to reality. "You know if I marry you, Lily, I mean it. It's forever. I don't want you to wake up tomorrow and change your mind, you gotta be all in."

His forehead rests against mine, nothing but love shining from his eyes. Damn him and his ability to make me feel all the things I don't wanna feel.

Forcing myself to blink back the emotion his words bring, I tell him my truth. "I won't change my mind, but you have to be patient with me, I still have a lot of baggage to unpack."

He leans forward, and his soft lips gently press against mine.

Quick and fleeting.

"What some people call baggage, others call a gift with purchase."

This beautiful boy has so much love to give — love I'm still not sure I deserve. All my life he has wandered beside me, determined to prove to me I'm not as broken as I claimed to be. I fought him at every corner, only giving him tiny glimpses of my soul. I'd be a fool to release him, letting him go would be a regret I couldn't bear to live with. You can claim I'm selfish, stupid, impulsive... and yes, I am all those things. But I'm also so much more.

I want to love; I want to give my heart to him. God, I wish I could escape the crippling fear that I'm damaged beyond the point of repair, but it's not so simple. He asked me to take a leap of faith, to jump without fear or hesitation. So, here I am, barely able to contain my trembling nerves, diving headfirst, praying that I don't land somewhere I won't come back from.

If my childhood taught me anything, it's that faith is like a mirror, once broken it can never be whole again. No matter how hard you try to glue back the pieces, the cracks will always be visible. But with Ciaran, I want to try. He makes me feel and want more. He knows I am broken, but he makes the broken parts of me beautiful.

"Ciaran Maguire and Lily O'Shea." The receptionist calls out, snapping me back to reality. "You're up." She hands Ciaran a piece of paper then directs us down a large hallway that's decorated with red, crushed velvet curtains "The little white chapel is the second door on the right. Just look for the pink arch doorway and you won't miss it."

I'm sure I won't. It's not like anything in this building is subtle.

Taking Ciaran's hand in mine, I intertwine our fingers and start walking.

"Wait." Ciaran halts me. "You need something old, new, borrowed and blue." His eyes dart around the room, searching for... I dunno what.

"Well, my earrings are old." I point to the small black studs Ciaran bought me for my sixteenth birthday. "This ring," I hold up my left hand, showing off my new diamond-encrusted, black tourmaline ring he just gifted me from the pawnshop on the corner, "is new." Looking around the small waiting area of the Elvis Chapel, my eyes land on a vase overflowing with flowers. Skipping to the arrangement and taking extra care so I don't fall flat on my face right before I get married, I pluck out a handful of pink peonies. "I can borrow these flowers."

"What about something blue?" His eyes narrow in

defeat. He wants this to be perfect, well, as perfect as an impromptu Vegas wedding can be. A Cheshire smile glides across my face. With everything that has gone on tonight, Ciaran must have forgotten about his blue look. It takes everything I have to keep a straight face as I pull him over to the floor-length mirror beside the main door. "I have you, Papa Smurf."

Laughter bursts out of his mouth. "For fuck's sake! How did I forget I was blue? You know I'm gonna get you back for that little stunt."

Shooting him a wink, I walk towards the makeshift chapel. Looking back at him over my shoulder, I call out the words that landed us here. "I dare you!"

❧

TOGETHER, WE STAND HAND IN HAND, UNDERNEATH A cheap, plastic, flowered archway as some dude — who may, I add, is the worst-looking Elvis I've ever seen — recites the sacred vows Ciaran and I are committing too.

"Do you, Ciaran Maguire, take Lilyanna O'Shea, as your lawfully wedded wife?"

With a look in his eyes that sparkles like stars on a cloudless night, he lifts my hand to his lips, and kisses my knuckles. "You can bet your blue suede shoes I do."

Stuffing down my laughter, I focus on the words the officiant says.

"Do you, Lilyanna O'Shea, take Ciaran Maguire as your lawfully wedded husband?"

Clearing my throat, I deepen my voice and sing out my answer. "It's now or never."

That's all it takes, like two giddy kids, we erupt. Almost missing when Elvis pronounces us husband and wife.

Sweeping stray hairs off my face, Ciaran turns serious as he whispers in my ear, seeking permission he knows he needs. "Can I kiss my bride?"

The smile on my face gives him all he needs. His lips collide with mine, the taste of need, want, and desire lingers on our tongues.

After what feels like a lifetime, he pulls back. "Let's get out of here, Mrs Maguire."

"After you, Mr Maguire."

Who cares that we got married in a little white chapel with horrible flowery pink wallpaper, drunk off our asses with witnesses we've never met? I know I don't. At this moment, I'm the happiest I've ever been.

🍀

Using his forearms, Ciaran shifts my body a little higher. "Could you please stop wiggling? You'll end up on your ass."

"I can't. Your hip bones are digging into my inner thighs." *Who knew an Adonis belt could be so inconvenient? Not me.*

"Yeah, well, maybe if you wore appropriate footwear, you'd be able to walk on your own."

"Yeah, well..." *Nothing, I've got nothing.* It's times like this I'd love to stick my tongue out and blow a raspberry in his ear. *My inner child is a petulant, petty asshole, sue me.*

"Just hang on, we are nearly there."

Clutching Ciaran's shoulders a little tighter, I hold on as he marches us towards his suite. I like this version of us, the one where the past is exactly where it should stay — locked away and not stealing my present.

Coming to a stop outside his suite door, Ciaran whooshes me up onto his back while reaching into his ass pocket for the room key. Thankfully, he doesn't drop me. The green light flashes and he pushes down on the handle. "Okay, Mrs Maguire, over the threshold we go."

Ciaran carries me into the suite and my eyes scan every square inch, it looks similar to the one I'm sharing with Rosie and Cillian — A large open plan living slash dining area with painted white walls that stand out against the rich, tasteful dark mahogany furnishings.

My eyes flicker through the archway into a stainless-steel kitchen, one that would rival the best of restaurants. If cooking was my thing, which it is not, this kitchen would be heaven.

Before I can mentally photograph anything else, Ciaran stomps down a long, narrow hallway. We pass three closed doors, then come to a stop outside his room. Stalking towards the bed with a swagger only Ciaran could pull off, he turns around so his back is to the California King. Suddenly, I'm airborne, my body dropping onto the mattress with a soft thud.

The room spins slightly, but after three Mississippi's I'm finally able to sit up and take in the sight of my husband.

The air is thick with an awkward silence that's so loud, it's deafening. The impending question of *what now?* stands like a barrier between us. Do we have sex? Do I want to have sex? Isn't that what people do on their wedding night?

Sensing my internal meltdown, Ciaran hunkers down at the side of the bed and takes my hand in his. Eyes level with mine, he stares straight into the windows of my soul. "What's running through that wild mind of yours?"

I've never felt this kind of intimacy, it's as if there is an invisible string connecting his heart to mine and it terrifies me. To allow him to see me so bare, every emotion on display, all my vulnerabilities showcased only for him. With just one long soul-searching look, something irrevocably life-changing passes between us, dragging up emotions that I never felt before. It stirs up years of suppressed anxiety. He opened the door, just a crack, and now the sun is peeking through. I've two choices, walk towards it and bask in the warmth of his light or bolt in the other direction and hide behind the shadows I've created.

"Please, Lily... please, don't run." His words come just when I need them most. "But if you feel you need to, let it be into my arms."

Standing to his full height, he pulls me to my feet then grabs my hips with his strong, protective hold. Sliding his left hand up my side, he touches me with a tenderness that electrifies my skin.

"What are you doing?" The weight of love emulating from his eyes causes my voice to crack.

Deflecting my question, Ciaran runs his fingers along my jawline. "Do you know what I just realised?"

"What's that?"

"I haven't had my first dance with my wife."

Before I can reply, he spins me away from his body with ease, pulling me back in with one swift, effortless motion. Suddenly, I crash with a soft thud against his hard chest. Catching my hand with his, he wraps the other around my back and together we sway to the soft melody he hums. Instantly, I recognise the low whistle of Patience by Guns N' Roses and a shy smile forms on my lips. Ciaran spins me out once more and just as I fall back into him, he catches my gaze and softly sings the lyrics to me. Right there, I not only give him my heart but everything that comes with it. As the song drifts to a close, I do something I never thought I'd have the strength to do, I offer him all of me.

"Make me yours."

CHAPTER ELEVEN

SANCTUARY BY WELSHLY ARMS

CIARAN

"Make me yours." With those three words, she becomes a thief in the night, stealing all the air from my lungs.

I drag in a much-needed breath and assure her that wasn't my intention. "Tonight isn't about that, Lily."

Sure, I'd love nothing more than to slide between her thighs and bring her higher than she has ever been. I crave it — her, crying out my name in a breathless whisper as her back arches with the pleasure my touch provides. But she's not ready yet, and I'm more than willing to wait. I know from experience that backing Lily into a corner gets you nowhere. She's a scared animal who needs to trust before she'll leave her cage.

"Tonight was about showing you I'm already yours. Everything I own, I want to give to you. Everything I am, my life, my love, my last name, it's all yours. I'm handing it to you on a solid gold platter. What I'm trying to say is, I'll wait, LB." Taking her hand, I place it against my chest, right over my heart. "This is yours, and when you're ready, and only then, I'll make you mine."

Her whiskey eyes hold the fire I fell in love with. Tilting her head slightly, she holds my gaze in the same way I hold her, gently, as if she is the most precious thing that ever existed.

"Ciaran Maguire, as sweet as those pretty words are, they are unnecessary. I want this." Using my shoulders as leverage, she lifts herself higher, balancing on her tippy toes. Her lips brush against mine, teasing me with an airy breath. Then with a confident, unwavering tone, she demands, "Make me yours. I dare you."

Every conscious thought I have goes out the fucking window. All I can see is Lily, in front of me, telling me she's ready. Like a selfish sonovabitch, I take exactly what she's offering because fuck knows, when she'll give herself so freely to me again. Abruptly, I spin her around so her back is to my chest.

Wrapping her long, fiery locks around my fist, I gently

tug as I move the wavy strands over her left shoulder, exposing the right side of her neck.

Hovering just above her porcelain skin — dotted with the faintest dusting of freckles — I whisper out my next words, making her body shiver in my arms. "It's taking everything in me not to rip that skin-tight suit off with my teeth, but I know that's not what you need."

Dropping my hand to the zipper that runs along her spine, I ever so fucking slowly glide it down, stopping just above her ass. An audible gulp escapes her burgundy stained lips.

"Tell me, Lil. What is it you need?"

"Just..." she hesitates, sucking in a deep breath through her nose before releasing it slowly. "Just keep talking, I'm okay as long as I know it's you."

Moving my hands to her hips, I slowly run them up and over her ribcage, until I reach the edge of the fabric caging in her small, perky, chest.

In between dotting her neck with kisses and gentle nibbles, I assure her exactly whose hands are roaming over her body.

Tugging at the barley-there, deep v neckline of her jumpsuit, I slip my hands underneath the material and work it down until it pools at her feet. "Step out of those shoes, Bug."

Doing exactly as I ask, Lily steps forward and turns to

face me. Standing in front of me in nothing but a tiny thong — the same shade as her skin tone — I almost come undone at the sight of her. Especially when I see timidness reflecting from her eyes. I kick the material to the side and cautiously step towards her. "You still with me, Lily Bug?" My eyes roam over every inch of her face, searching for any sign that what I'm doing is not okay.

Cupping her face in my palms, I ask her to reassure me. I've never done this before, not like this. This is the scariest, most sacred moment of my life. One wrong move and she'll close up and bolt. Every step we take, we need to take together. My usual MO of rough and ready won't work with someone as delicate as my wife. She needs to be safe.

Secure.

Fucking savoured.

"Words... as much as you need mine, I need yours more. Talk to me."

"I'm here. I'm with you." Her fingers tease the hem of my black Rolling Stones t-shirt, then in one swift motion, she's lifting it, exposing my torso. Helping her, I reach back and whip it over my head.

She huffs out a short, fleeting chuckle. "I thought they only used that move in the books I read."

Setting my hands on her hips, I bend slightly at the knees and lift her from the floor. Just as I hoped, her legs instinctually wrap around my waist as she steadies herself with her hands on my shoulders. Striding towards the bed, I lower us both down. Immediately, she freezes up beneath me.

Shaking her head from side to side, I can feel her slipping into the dark. Like lightning, I flip us. Giving her full control. "Stay with me, LB."

Running my hands up and down her arms, I wait patiently for her to open those unique eyes.

"Count with me, Lil. Deep breath."

She does just as I ask, I thank fucking God she can still hear me.

"Out loud, Bug. One."

"One."

"Two," I encourage her.

"Two."

Fuck, my heart is thumping in my chest. *Stay with me, Lily Bug. Stay with me.*

"Three."

She blinks. "Three."

Nearly there. "Four."

Her eyes open wide, homing in on my face. "Four."

Lifting my hand, I run my fingers along her jawline. "There she is."

Her hand closes over mine, holding it in place. Her chest rises and falls with every breath she takes and it fucking kills me she has to fight that crippling fear, even with me.

"I'm sorry."

Shifting upward, I guide us into a sitting position. She's resting on my lap with her legs wrapped around my waist. "Hey," I grab her attention. "Don't ever, ever apologise to me. This," I motion between us. "This is your safe place. You're safe with me, Lily. I'd never do anything to hurt you or make you uncomfortable. You need a second to catch your breath, I'll give you four. If you need to pump the breaks, consider me stopped. You're in control, baby, always. I'll never push. Set the pace, and like always, I'll follow your lead."

Her fingers trace the embossed letters inked across my collarbones.

"I want this, Ciaran. I promise you, I do. Please don't stop."

"Are you sure? I don't want to do anything you're uncomfortable with."

"Safe with you?" The words come out soft but full of question. This is the most vulnerable I've ever seen her. Not only naked in my arms, but her soul laid bare too.

Kissing the tip of her nose, I pull back and stare right into her eyes, giving her everything I am with just this look. "My arms are your sanctuary and your shelter, when I have you wrapped within them, you're the safest you'll ever be."

🍀

LILY

Fuck. My heart is thumping like a bass drum in my chest as the semblance of tears burn the back of my eyes. I'd be lying if I said I never dreamt of having a moment like this. Jesus knows, I've read about it enough. All those romance novels, none of them come close.

This moment, it's mine, it's Ciaran's, it's ours, and there isn't a chance in hell I'm letting it slip through my fingers. My da took too much of me as it is, he's not stealing my wedding night. He doesn't deserve it.

Placing both hands against Ciaran's rock-hard chest, I push him back onto the mattress. Leaning forward, I hover above him and conjure the girl everyone knows me to be — The fearless, badass who takes no prisoners.

My hands sink into his hair, holding either side of his face like he's my lifeline. Dropping my mouth down, I take his lips in a kiss, hoping it portrays everything I want to say.

I love you, Baby Hanson.

That thought alone terrifies me, but I don't fall victim to its crushing grip. Instead, I lose myself in every stroke, brush, and nibble. He's intoxicating, and if I let myself, it would be easy to free fall into oblivion. Ciaran is the only person I've met who sees my weaknesses.

Over the years, I've learned, weak people get burnt, and I've been burnt enough to last me a lifetime. But somehow, he always pulls this side of me out from where I hide it — buried under sarcasm and wit.

I never thought at twenty years of age, I'd still hold my virginity, but when you spend your childhood guarding it against your own father, it becomes almost impossible to give it away. My therapist assured me when the time came, I'd know... and I do. Something passed between us tonight, and as if the gloomy clouds of my past parted, I could finally see what was right in front of me all along. I'm tired of running away from him.

Sliding from his hold, I slip from the bed and stand at the edge. Ciaran lifts himself onto his elbows, giving me a glorious view of his biceps and the muscles that dance along the tops of his shoulders. His eyes follow my every move-ment as I reach out and undo the silver buckle of his black belt. His hand moves to cover mine, making my eyes flick to his.

"Are you sure?"

Am I scared? Yes.

Am I sure? Abso-fucking-lutely.

"I'm one-hundred percent positive."

Sitting forward, he stops me from undressing him. Instead, he hooks his fingers into the side of my thong, and with a slow tortuous motion, he slides it down my thighs, until finally, I step out of it.

Never once does he take his eyes off mine — beautiful

pools of deep sea-green a girl could easily get lost in. "Are you still with me?"

I climb back up onto his lap, and rest my centre against his bulging shaft that's barely contained by the dark black denim of his jeans. "Every second of the way."

Circling his arms around my waist, he pulls me closer, slipping my pierced nipple into his mouth. Before I can stop it, a moan of pleasure ripples from my chest, escaping my lips without protest.

Peering at me under his hooded brow, Ciaran flicks the barbell with the tip of his tongue. My back arches, forcing my nipple further into his teasing mouth.

Jesus, that feels so, so good.

Switching sides, he gives my left nipple the same attention, and with no hesitation, my hips dance to the beat pulsating between my thighs. His wanting hands roam over my hips, ribcage, and spine while he nips, sucks, and licks every single inch of my chest.

"So, good." The words leave me before I can process them. My body and brain are frequenting different wavelengths.

"Lily?" His voice is deeper than I'm used to. "Need to taste you, LB. Tell me I can taste you?"

Fear barrels through me like there's a loaded gun pointed at my temple.

Nope, I won't let my fear ruin this.

Ciaran's earlier words fill my mind. *Count with me, Lily. One, two, three, four.*

Slowly, his faith in me pushes through the fear.

Faith over fear.

Faith over fear.

"Yes."

One word, but it's all it takes for him to flip me onto my back and spread me open.

I watch him intently as he cautiously lowers himself between my thighs. Taking extra care not to cage my body beneath him. *How did I get so lucky? Why did he choose me to give his love to?*

"Eyes on me, Lily Bug. Keep those gorgeous eyes on me."

Insecurity swarms me, but I force it back and watch with awe as Ciaran drags the tip of his tongue through my slit. All my inhibitions float away as Ciaran devours me with an intensity I can never explain. The raw emotion passing between us is almost too much to bear. I'm lost in all things Ciaran Maguire, floating away to the land of blissful orgasms and sedated limbs.

❧

HOURS PASS AND MY HUSBAND HAS TORTURED ME SEVEN ways to Sunday.

Sure, we met a few speed bumps along the way, but Ciaran being Ciaran walked me over every single one.

"Last chance LB. Are you sure?"

"For the last time, YES!"

Nudging forward, Ciaran's shielded, pierced Magic Cross tip enters me with a slow, cautious thrust. I wince slightly, biting down on his shoulder as the sharp pain gyrates through me. Having him towering over me is slightly unnerving, but I trust him to keep me safe. He whispers words, keeping me very much in the present moment with him, not allowing me to retreat to the dark. Stilling for a moment, Ciaran pulls his shoulders back and adores me with a look. "Tell me when I can move? You're in charge, always."

Nodding through his words, I drag in a large, much-needed breath, unintentionally tightening my inner walls.

"Jesus H Christ." His eyes narrow. "Are you trying to kill me?" The cheeky smile on his face highlights his dimple and I realise he is trying his damndest to keep this moment as light-hearted as he can.

Laughter bubbles in my throat at the discomfort that works across his furrowed brow, only reassuring me of my decision. This moment always belonged to Ciaran, there's no one else I would feel this comfortable with. My husband, my sanctuary, my best friend. Time to put him out of his misery. "You can move now."

"Thank fuck!"

I never meant to fall for him. I swore I wouldn't. But somewhere between midnight and three am, he showed me rules are there to break, and even broken souls can feel whole again.

CHAPTER TWELVE

TATTOOED HEART BY ARIANA GRANDE

LILY

I WAKE TO AN EMPTY BED, AND ALTHOUGH THE SPACE beside me is cool to touch, Ciaran's signature citrus scent is still embedded in the hotel's linens.

With a sleepy stretch, I reach up over my head, my body protesting as my muscles — ones I wasn't even aware I have — ache. Using my arms, I push myself into a sitting position and scoot back against the headboard.

My eyes wander around the room as I search for my phone. I spy it plugged in, charging on the bedside locker, and a wide smile spreads across my face.

How cute is that? He charged my phone.

Before I pick it up, I spot a piece of paper tucked beneath it with the words **READ ME** scrawled in all caps.

Sliding it out, I unfold it.

And if possible, my smile gets even bigger.

Good morning, Wifey for life.
On the off chance, you wake up before I'm back, stay put.
I'm making your beautiful, sassy ass breakfast in bed.
DO NOT MOVE AN INCH.
Love to love you.
Yours always, your extremely sexy and very well endowed,
Husband xx.

After placing Ciaran's note back on the nightstand for safekeeping, I grab my phone and scroll through my missed messages, all of which are from my best friend.

Rosie: Hey, where are you? I just checked your room, you're not there.

Rosie: Lily? I'm getting worried. Please text me back.

Rosie: Are you dead?

Rolling my eyes at her protectiveness, I text her back before she comes looking for me.

Lily: Jesus, you're worse than my mother. I'm alive and FULLY satisfied. *Corn on the cob emoji* *Eggplant emoji* *French breadstick emoji*

Just then, the bedroom door swings open. Standing, taking up most — if not all — of the doorway is my mouth-watering husband. He is wearing nothing but low slung, black track bottoms, leaving his glorious torso and tattooed arms on full display.

Ciaran strides across the room, holding a tray of food fit for a queen. "Morning, Bug." He tips his head towards the tray. "I hope you're hungry."

"Starving."

Woah, slow down, Slutty Sally. Just because you opened your legs wider than a bus lane last night, doesn't mean we're ready for a repeat.

He places the silver tray on my lap, then leans in and brushes a chaste kiss on my forehead before climbing back in beside me. I take a moment to scan the spread in front of me. Two servings of perfectly scrambled eggs heaped onto one plate, four slices of toast, two glasses of freshly squeezed orange juice, two ibuprofen, two forks and a little vase holding one of the pink peonies I 'borrowed' from the Little White Chapel.

"Did you make this?"

His cheeks turn a cute shade of pink as he nods his head.

Aw, is my lovable asshole embarrassed?

Leaning over, I carefully place a small, fleeting kiss on his lips. "Well, thank you, it looks amazing."

"It was no stress, LB. Now first, take those tablets, I don't want you to be sore."

I pick up the two painkillers, pop them into my mouth and wash them down with my juice. Feeling a little sassy, I wiggle my brows and open my mouth wide. "All gone."

"What? Do you want a lollipop for being an obedient patient?"

"Shut up and eat the food, Mr Maguire."

"Whatever you say, Mrs Maguire."

Passing him a fork, we both dig in, but soon, we're interrupted by the constant buzzing of my phone.

Flipping it over, I see I've three messages and two missed calls from Rosie.

Rosie: What? Who?

Rosie: Ciaran? Please tell me it was Ciaran.

Rosie: Oh, God... It was Saint, wasn't it?

Before I can reply, the phone rings again. Lifting it to my ear, I answer with a long, drawn-out, "Heeeeelllllloooo."

Rosie's voice screeches down the line in a whispered shout. "WHAT THE FUCK, LILY! You can't text me something like that, then toss your phone across the Atlantic. You need to reply."

Chuckling at her flair for the dramatics, I apologise, "I'm sorry, I got," my eyes flick towards Ciaran, who is lying back against the headboard with his signature cheeky, devil-may-care, smile. "Sidetracked. Anyway, why are you whisper-shouting at me?"

"I'm hiding in the bathroom. I didn't think you'd appreciate me discussing your sex life in front of your brother."

"Touché."

Whatever Rosie says after that gets lost in translation. All I can hear is the loud thumping in my chest as I watch the tip of Ciaran's tongue peek out from behind his perfectly straight — so white they're blinding — teeth. The dimple in his left cheek deepens, and that's it, I'm a goner. Ever so slowly, he bites down, seductively catching his plump bottom lip. Without taking my eyes off his, I hold the phone to my ear. "Rosie, I'll call you back. My husband is looking at me as if he wants to eat me for breakfast. Love you."

Vaguely, I hear her shout, "Husband? What the hell, Lily?" before I press the end call button and toss my phone across the bed. It bounces once before toppling off the edge with a loud thump. *Oops!*

Patting his thighs, Ciaran motions for me to come to him. Completely forgetting about the tray full of food on my lap, I knock it over and cringe as all its content crashes to the floor. *Oops! I did it again.*

Sniggering at my clumsiness, Ciaran grips the hem of his black rolling stones t-shirt I'm wearing and pulls me towards him.

I go willingly, swinging my legs over his and settling into a straddling position on his lap. His tattooed forearms circle my waist, engulfing me in a safe bubble of him. My eyes dart to the mess on the floor, my inner clean freak itches to clean it up.

"Hey," Ciaran demands my attention. "Leave it, I'll tidy it up in a minute."

Slowly, he leans forward, kissing the tip of my nose

while his hands travel over the bare skin of my thighs. "So, Wifey... What do you want to do today? We have the entire day to ourselves."

My eyes involuntarily wander to the tattoo that runs across his collarbones.

The words he used to keep me calm last night.

I remember the day he got that tattoo. It was the same day I got the one on my left rib cage — An open birdcage with a bird breaking free.

After they sentenced my dad to three years in Mountjoy Prison, I wanted to get something to symbolise my freedom. That night wasn't the first time he was inappropriate. It wasn't even the second.

For years, I stayed silent, acting out at everyone and everything, except the man who I called my dad. Sure, he never physically violated me. Well, not in the way you're thinking. It was more what he made me do to him.

Touch it, Lilyanna. Take it in your hand and show daddy how much you love him.

Bile rushes up my oesophagus, my skin crawling with hate.

Dirty.

Filthy.

Hate!

When they took my father away, that heavyweight

lifted. A sense of relief washed over me, and for the first time in my life, I was finally free. Later that week, I persuaded Ciaran to come with me to the local tattoo parlour, knowing full well he would. He knew I would need him there for support. He held my hand the entire time, then got one of his own. I recall asking him why he chose the words he did. The memory rushes in before I can stop it.

"Why those words?" I ask, running my fingers along Ciaran's collarbone. Where the words 'take a deep breath and count to four' are embossed in black ink onto his skin.

"I remember when I was a kid, I would rush into my ma when something was wrong. I would always be in such a panic, trying to tell her as quickly as possible. I would just blurt it all out, like one big, long word. She would take my hand and say, Look at me. My eyes would meet hers. Take a deep breath and count to four. Count with me, Ciaran. Out loud, baby boy. One, two, three, four. When she passed away, anytime I spiralled into that panicked state. I'd stop, take a deep breath and count. One, two, three, four. That one sentence is all I remember about her. And even now, when I sit behind my drum kit, it's her words I recite. Somewhere along the line, it stuck. Four breaths, four beats and go," he replied.

The twins lost their mother at a young age; she died of cancer when they were around six or seven. They moved to our town shortly after that. Their dad wanted to be close to his family, something about more support with raising two young, twin boys. They started school with Rosie and I that December, and then the anti-love story of Lily Bug and Baby Hanson began.

Suddenly, Ciaran's warm hand grazes my flushed cheek, pushing my wild hair off my face. "You still with me, LB?"

Giving him a shy smile, an idea pops into my head. "Wanna do something crazy?"

"If it's with you, always."

"Let's get fresh tattoos."

"I'm in, but first, let's get you showered. Besides, I need to scrub the rest of this blue off before I go anywhere."

❧

CIARAN

If someone stood in front of me forty-eight hours ago and told me I'd be sitting in a tattoo parlour — with my wife — getting a ladybug tattooed onto the underside of my ring finger, I'd have laughed in their face. Sure, I'm known for my random ink, and it's no secret that most of my tattoos link to my fiery redhead.

Now, here I fucking am, getting another one, even

though I'm still trying to decide whether last night was the dumbest thing I've ever done or the best.

Waking up with Lily, resting soundly on my chest, was nothing short of heavenly bliss. But I have this unnerving ache in my stomach that any minute now, she'll feed into fear and run. The uncertainty of what the hell happens next is smothering me to fucking death. I must have lay in bed for hours this morning, just wondering, what if she wakes up, and she wants to bolt out the door?

I have to show her, show her that no matter what happened last night, I'm in this thing with her for the long haul. Sure, she gets on my nerves, and there are times I want to strangle her and her stubborn ass; but aren't all relationships like that. I understand we both have flaws but blend our flaws and what you get is our special brand of imperfectly perfect.

"How're you doing over there, Baby Hanson?" Lily calls from the open cubicle beside mine.

"Nearly done. What about you?" I hiss as the tattoo needle grates against the bone. One thing about finger tattoos is the lack of flesh makes them painful as fuck. At least it's only a small design, otherwise, I'd be crying to my ma in heaven.

"Just finished." Lily chimes. "Wanna see it before Alexa covers it up?"

After spending the afternoon wandering the strip, taking

in all the sights while we were looking for a tattoo shop with a female artist, we finally found one.

Lily only allows women to ink her, but if that's what it takes to make her comfortable, so be it. "Yeah, sure thing Lily Bug."

Sliding into my cubicle, she stands on my right side. Without moving the hand Dirk — my tattoo artist — is working on, I look her way.

Fuck, will there ever be a time where she doesn't steal my breath?

Standing there in a tiny pair of black denim cut off shorts, her yellow Doc Martens, and a black sleeveless 4Clover band tee that she has tied up into a crop top, she looks divine. And she's all mine.

Lifting her left hand, she shows me her ring finger.

Running along the inside — hidden yet visible — are the words I spoke last night, inked in small cursive script.

Take a leap of faith.

It's then I know for sure she's all in, and fuck, I'm all for it.

"Love to love you, Lily Bug. So much."

✤

"I'm not getting in that fucking boat."

Laughing at her refusal, I hold my hand out to help her

step in. "It's a gondola, not a boat. Now take my hand and get in."

"If I wanted to see Venice, I'd go there. I wouldn't take a boat ride through a Vegas shopping mall."

"Do you make it your life's mission to be difficult? Get in the Jaysusin' gondola, I'm trying to be romantic here, and you're ruining it."

With an eye roll, Lily steps in and takes a seat beside me. Wrapping my arm around her shoulder, I pull her in close to my chest. "Call this an impromptu honeymoon, then when I'm finished with this tour, I'll bring you to Italy for the authentic experience. How does that sound?"

"Like I'd rather be reading."

It's then she spots the picnic basket and champagne I organised. Her eyes widen with surprise as she asks, "You planned this? When?"

"When you were in the shower this morning, I wanted to show you that there is more to life than what's on the pages of those books you read, Lil. Maybe if you just opened those spectacular amber eyes, you'd see you can have your happy ending too. Pun very much intended."

"Shut up," she says, poking me in the chest. "You're ruining this romantic moment."

"So, you like this boat ride?"

Lifting her face from where it's resting in the crook of my arm, she brings her mouth a hair's breadth from mine.

I'm seconds away from claiming her when she leans closer and whispers, "It's not a boat, it's a gondola."

Clucking at her blatant defiance, I kiss her lips, soft and fleeting. "Whatever you say, Wifey. Whatever you say."

"Get used to it, Baby Hanson. Happy wife, happy life."

CHAPTER THIRTEEN

DOWN IN FLAMES BY AJ MICHELL

LILY

TODAY WITH CIARAN HAS BEEN NOTHING SHORT OF amazing, even though I know sooner or later, we have to face reality.

For now, I'm enjoying the ease of being a girl who is falling out of hate with a boy. One romantic moment at a time.

We spent the day doing all the touristy shit Vegas offers. When the bright night lights glow, we head back to the hotel to meet the others for dinner. I'm more than certain Rosie will have a few colourful words for me, especially with how I left our phone call this morning.

Ah well, she has to deal with it; because regardless of whether she's happy, nothing will change the fact that I'm still married.

As we stand outside the large double doors that lead into a private VIP dining area of the hotel's Italian restaurant, Ciaran grips my hand. Giving it a reassuring squeeze, he lifts it to his full lips and kisses my knuckles. "Are you ready for this, Bug? We can always hide out in my room."

Sucking in a deep breath, my gaze flicks to him. He's wearing dark denim jeans tucked into his army-style boots, a plain white t-shirt, moulded to his defined chest, and his black leather jacket. Fuck me, he's like my personal James Dean. His eyes roam over my face, easing all the unwanted tension building underneath my tough girl exterior.

How did it take me this long to realise he is my counter-balance?

My safe place.

"Let's get this over with."

"After you, Wifey."

Shaking my head at that new silly nickname, I ask. "Are you ever gonna stop calling me that?"

Ciaran pulls me close and presses his lips on my fore-head. "Probably not."

We enter the room, and every face turns in our direction.

Great, just fucking great. An audience is exactly what we need.

Looks like the universe is all for shitting on my parade because everyone is here, including the four members of Sinners.

"Where the hell have you two been?" Conor questions. "We've been calling you all day."

Ciaran leads me across the low-lit room with his palm resting on my lower back. "If you must know, we were on a date."

After what feels like forever, we finally reach the large rectangular, 12-seater table where Ciaran pulls out a chair for me to sit on. Once I'm seated, my eyes lock with Rosie's. She's sitting directly opposite me, in between my brother and Cian, and judging by the scowl on her otherwise perfect face, she's not happy.

Raising her brow in question, she waits impatiently for an explanation as I pick at the white linen tablecloth and try my best to ignore her. Not that it does much good.

Her piercing blue eyes dart to my ring finger.

Searching for my ring, I presume.

Although I have one, she won't find it, it's safely tucked in Ciaran's pocket.

After we got the tattoos, we had to keep our fingers bare, to allow them to heal correctly.

Bronagh and her growing belly lean towards me, she

places her hand over mine. "I'm so happy you two finally admitted your feelings for one another. The crazy pranks — although they were hilarious — were getting a little out of hand."

Giving her a slight smile, I turn back to my best friend. The hurt in her eyes kills me. I get it, I do. If she ran off and got married to Cillian without telling me, it would piss me off too.

I hate this. Rosie is my ride or die. The only other person, besides Ciaran, who knows the real me.

She's upset with me, and it doesn't sit right, but if I could redo last night all over, I wouldn't change a thing.

For once in my life, I feel hopeful. I've always envied couples who had their shit together, and somewhere, way deep down, I always wished I could have that epic love.

Letting Ciaran love me, letting me love him, that is something I never thought I'd be ready for. But now, I feel ready to try, and sometimes that is all we need to do.

Last night, as I lay in Ciaran's arms, I promised myself I would take each day as it comes. I vowed to myself I wouldn't run.

Consider me Dory, I'll just keep swimming.

"Lily, are you okay? You're unusually quiet?" Cillian asks, his voice full of brotherly concern.

Under the table, Ciaran's hand finds my thigh, and my gaze suddenly flicks to his. With just a look, he lets me know he's there. Something unexplainable passes between us, and frankly, I don't know how I feel about it.

It's an intimacy that is so strong, it doesn't need words to communicate. It lingers there, in the space between us, floating through the silence. It's then I realise just how far I've fallen. If I'm being honest with myself, I've been falling for Ciaran for years. Slowly, little by little.

Throughout our friendship, I've given him clues to find the secret door in my sky-high walls. Last night, I gave him the key.

We're lost in each other's eyes, oblivious to everything and everyone around us as we exchange... I don't know, souls?

I'm unsure of how much time passes, all I know is, it's long enough for me to count the various shades of green in his eyes. A connection so powerful, I can hear his thoughts echoing in my mind.

Should we tell them?

Fuck no!

His chest vibrates as he chuckles, noting the panic behind my wide eyes. In his effort to calm me down, he reaches up so the knuckles of his right hand can gently caress my cheek.

My eyes close and I bask in the warmth his touch brings. His signature scent fills my senses and my lashes flutter open to find his Hollywood worthy smile. The dimple in his left cheek, deeper than ever. He looks happier than I've ever seen him, and a tiny part of me fills with pride. I put that gorgeous smile on his face.

Just the sight of him has my world tilting on its axis. It's an oxygen stealing, earth-shaking, heart-warming kind of moment, and every instinct I have screams for me to run.

My chest fills with unease. I'm not used to these kinds of feelings. Especially so openly. Suddenly, the air in the room dissipates and my breathing gets heavier.

Air, I need air.

Breaking the connection, I push my chair back and stand. "I need... uh, the eh... restroom. I'll be right back."

I see it in his eyes. He knows I'm freaking out, but he's willing to give me the space I so desperately need.

Rushing to the bathroom, I almost fall through the door. The overbearing scent of perfume smacks me in the face. Candy floss and pomegranates, the signature stench of Remington St. Claire. And also a fiver dollar hooker, but sure who am I to judge someone's taste or lack thereof.

I walk over to the sink and stare at the reflection looking back at me.

My cheeks are flush with a pinkish hue, thanks to Ciaran and his scorching touch.

"Jesus, Lily, get a grip. You're losing it."

How does someone terrified of love give it away so freely? Ugh! What is it about Ciaran-freaking-Maguire that makes me weak at the knees? With one look, he makes me come undone.

In a matter of hours, he has made me feel things I've spent years avoiding. Colour me shocked... Lilyanna O'Shea is free-falling without a parachute.

The bathroom door creaks open and Rosie comes into view. Drawing in a breath, I wait for her to lash out for my non-reply earlier, then I remember, she's not me. Rosie is the softest, most loving, unselfish person I've ever met.

"Jesus, Remi sure went to town with the perfume. It smells like a fragrance store in here." Rosie waves her hand under her nose as she takes a step towards me, and I hold back the urge to laugh at her innocence. Sure, I don't know Remi very well, but with the way she crawled all over Ciaran last night, I have more than enough reason to hate her.

Petty? Sure it is, but I'm woman enough to admit it.

When she sees my wavering facade, she wraps her arms around me. "Are you okay? That got a little intense, and I was only a bystander."

Burying my head into her shoulder, I mutter my reply into her white t-shirt. "I don't know."

Her hand caresses my spine, bringing me comfort. Pulling back, her hands hold on to my shoulders as she searches my face with her blue eyes. "I never thought I'd see the day. Lilyanna O'Shea is in love."

Brushing her hand off my shoulder, I turn away from her scrutiny. "Don't be ridiculous. I am not."

Her eyes find mine in the bathroom mirror. "Oh, don't deny it. The entire room could feel the electricity sparking between you two. You fell, admit it."

Like the sassy little brat I am, I get defensive. "I didn't fall. He fucking tripped me. He trapped me with pretty words and his killer smile. Not to mention the beautiful gondola ride with a pre-planned picnic."

With her hands on her hip, she asks, "Are you done?"

I spin to face her. "Not even close. He keeps tripping me, and like the love-struck idiot I am, I fall face-first into a steaming pile of marital bliss. I'm not equipped to handle this. That —" I point to the door leading back to the dining room. "— that was too much. He is too much. It felt like he could see right through me, Ro."

I pace the small area while my mind races with my new reality. My heart belongs to the man I've spent years fighting my feelings for.

Fuck! Stupid, stupid, Lily!

"Somehow," I continue with my rant. "He can strip me bare, and not in a literal sense — although, he can do that pretty damn well, too. No, this is fucking worse, because with just one look he can see the darkest corners of my soul. And that... that terrifies me. What was that look? Is that normal?"

A huff of laughter leaves her pouty, red lips. "Yes, Lily. It's normal. That look, as you referred to it, is love in its purest form. And regardless of whether you want to acknowledge it, Ciaran Maguire has been looking at you like that for years. The only difference is, now, you've finally opened your eyes enough to see him."

She walks over to the small chaise lounge beside the sink and takes a seat before patting the space beside her.

I drop my shoulders in defeat, then lower myself down and lean my head against her shoulder. Her head rests against mine as she continues her pep talk.

"Sure, love is scary, but it's also freeing. To love someone unconditionally, flaws and all is the most rewarding feeling in the world. There is nothing on this earth that can come close to it. Ciaran is a lucky man. I know first-hand what it's like to have your love. Without knowing it, you've given me enough love to last a lifetime. Loving him, sure it will be different, but you can love, Lil. You don't have to be so scared."

Standing to her feet, she holds out her hand. "The best kind of love is earned, not gifted. Ciaran has been fighting for you since we were kids, I think it's past time you put him out of his misery. Let him love you, and most importantly, let yourself love him. You deserve happiness. Don't be a by-product of your father's hate. Let love in, I promise you, it's worth it."

Finally, I take her waiting hand, and she pulls me up.

My eyes flick to the small white bandage covering my fresh tattoo. I can't see the words, but I know they're there.

Take a leap of faith.

With a recurring smile, Rosie nods towards the door. "You ready to head back out there?"

For once, I don't feel so afraid. "Yes."

"Good. Oh, don't think you've gotten out of explaining how you got married without me. I'm giving you a pass, for now. But, sooner or later, I'm getting all the details."

Shaking my head, I swat her ass and push her out the door then walk straight over to my husband. He's looking directly at me as he mouths, "You still with me, Lily Bug?"

Smiling widely, I sit onto his lap and wrap my arms around his shoulders. I lean my forehead against his. "Let's tell them, I'm ready."

His blinding smile hits me right in the chest. "On four?"

"On four."

Together, we take a deep breath, turn to face all our friends, then count to four.

"Hey!" Ciaran grabs their attention. He looks back towards me as he addresses the room. "I'd like to introduce my wifey for life. Mrs Lilyanna Maguire."

The room erupts into chaotic shouts and gasps, but I don't hear any of it because right then Ciaran's lips meet mine and everything else fades away.

CHAPTER FOURTEEN

IF YOU'RE MEANT TO COME BACK BY JUSTIN JESSO

CIARAN

As I exit the bathroom, I wipe my damp palms on the dark denim of my jeans and head back down the L-shaped corridor, leading to the private dining area where we are all having dinner. Rounding the corner, a body crashes against my chest. Instinct kicks in and my arms wrap around a small feminine waist, saving her from landing ass first on the floor. A sweet, sugary scent fills my nose and immediately, I recognise it as Remi's perfume.

Once she is standing steady on her feet, I pull my arms back and shove my hands deep into my jean pockets.

Remi St. Claire is a walking 50s pin-up girl with her retro style and ink-covered skin. With her tiny waist accentuated by curves that could rival a country back road, even Ray Charles would see she is gorgeous. But she's not Lily.

"Oh, hey. Sorry I didn't see you there. Are you okay?"

Her hand reaches up as she tucks the feathered strands of her chocolate brown hair behind her pierced ear. "Yeah." A slow smile creeps across her pink painted lips. "I was looking for you."

Shit! I should have suspected this was coming, but I was so lost in all things Lily, it never crossed my mind.

Closing my eyes for a split second, I think of a way to explain this to her. "Look, Remi..."

Holding up her tattooed hand, she stops me midsentence. "Ciaran, you don't have to explain. It's not as if I didn't know about Lily. That first night, you told me all about her. When we agreed to do this friends-with-benefits thing, I knew your heart belonged to her. And, as much as I wish things were different, they're not. I'm a big girl, I can deal."

"Still, I should have said something last night when we were at the bar. Things between me and Lil, they're complicated. When we're together, we move to our own beat. I know you and I were just casual, but you deserved better than a public announcement. So, I'm sorry."

Something foreign glints in her eye, then suddenly, she

wraps her full-sleeve, tattooed arms around my neck and pulls me into a hug. Her breath heats my ear and the urge to pull back grows with every millisecond she lingers.

"Don't worry about it," she whispers against my neck. Pulling back, her hand touches my cheek. "All I want is for you to be happy." Before I can stop her, she raises onto her tippy toes and moulds her plump lips to mine. Shock rattles my bones, freezing my body in place.

Gripping her waist, I push against her hip bone and force her to step back. A loud thud grabs my attention, turning to see what caused it, the heart in my chest pounds against my ribcage.

Fuck!

Standing there, with an expression similar to a deer trapped in headlights, is my wife. Her black purse has fallen to her feet. There is not much that renders Lily speechless, but with her mouth agape, she's silent as she takes in every inch of Remi and me.

Raising my hands in surrender, I take a step towards her, slow and careful. Terrified that one wrong move would spook her fragile demeanour even more. "Lil, that..." I look over my shoulder at the chick that possibly ruined my life. "That was not what it looked like."

Her heavy breaths are visible by the rise and fall of her chest.

Just one more step and she'll be in my arms.

Glassy amber eyes brimmed with unshed tears lock onto mine. "Don't."

That one word cracks a hole in the centre of my chest.

Clenching her teeth with flared nostrils, she spits out her next words with venom. "Do not fucking touch me."

"Lily Bug, please."

"Don't beg, Ciaran. It's as pathetic as your side piece." Bending at her waist, she picks her clutch off the floor, then spins on her heel. "And, don't dare follow me."

"Lily, wait."

My hands grip my hair as my life walks out of the narrow hallway. "Fuck!"

A hand lands on my shoulder, and my skin burns with rage. Spinning in place, I knock Remi's hand away. "What the hell? You saw her, didn't you? You kissed me on purpose."

Remi swallows back a nervous gulp. Her eyes bulge out as I take an angry step towards her.

"Answer me!"

Lowering her head, shame washes over her delicate features.

"I'm sorry, Ciaran. I... I don't know why I did that."

"Sorry? You're sorry? My fucking wife just walked out on me because of you and your petty jealousy. My life is not a game, Remi."

"She doesn't deserve you. When will you open your

eyes and see she's playing you for a fool, and you're letting her," she roars.

"You're right!" I bring my face inches from hers and capture her pebble-grey gaze. "She deserves a lot better than me. I could give her the world, and still, she would deserve more. At least with her, what you see is what you get. She is not fake, and she would never do what you just did. Now, if you'll excuse me, my wife needs me."

"CIARAN!"

"Fuck you, Remi."

I STORM THROUGH THE DINING ROOM WITHOUT stopping, not giving a single fuck about the obvious stares coming from my friends. I'm sure there's more than one question directed at me, but I don't stop to answer.

Lily! I need to get to her now.

Remi.

FUCKING REMI.

I should've had more sense. I knew when I slept with her it was an awful idea, but did that stop me? No, and now I'm stuck in a sinking ship without a life jacket.

When I first got involved with Remi, I was so upset with Lily. She told me to let her go, live my life and fuck my way across the world. And like a stupid sonovabitch, I did just that. Except, instead of dicking a busload of faceless strangers, I fucked someone who is an essential part of my career. I should have known it would end in flames. The stupidest ideas always do.

Stepping into the elevator, I press the button for the top floor then watch as the red digital numbers flash as it climbs each floor.

Why is this thing so slow?

Finally, the door opens, and I take off running.

Out of breath, I reach her room. Gripping the architrave on either side of the frame, I rest my head against the wooden door.

"Lily?" Her name, a shouted plea from my lips. "Let me in, Lily."

"Go away, Ciaran. I'm not in the mood. The last thing I need right now is to get blinded by your pretty words." Her muffled words are barely audible, but I hear them loud and clear.

"I'm not leaving, not until you open this door and let me explain. I'll stay out here all night if I need to. Open the door, Lily."

Clutching at straws, I try the one thing I know works every time. "I dare you."

Seconds pass, and nothing.

With a clenched fist, I raise my hand to bang on the door. Just before my hand meets the wood, it flies open.

"You have five minutes and not a second longer," she throws over her shoulder as she walks back towards her room.

Five minutes, I can work with that.

A relieved breath rushes from my lungs as I follow her through the suite she's sharing with Rosie and Cillian.

Lily shuffles around the room, grabbing everything she owns before dumping it into the open suitcase that rests on the centre of her bed.

"Going somewhere?" The words tumble from my mouth before I can stop them.

Her body goes rigid as she glares at me with fiery eyes. "As a matter of fact, yes, I am. I'm going home. Away from you and your lies."

"Don't do that. Don't assume you know what you saw, because you don't. I have never lied to you, LB. Never."

Taking a step towards me, she closes the distance between us. "Really? Well, Mister Honest, answer me this... Have you slept with Remi St. Claire?

"Yes, but..."

Cutting me off mid-sentence, she asks, "When?"

"When, what?"

She's so close, directing her murderous gaze right at me. You know that saying... if looks could kill? Consider me deceased.

"When was the last time you stuck your dick in her? Jesus, Ciaran, do you need me to draw you a diagram?"

Fuck, she had to ask that, didn't she? The one question that will make this situation ten times worse. I promised her I'd never lie, and I won't.

Lowering my head, I mutter my response. "The last time was the day I found out you were coming to Vegas."

"But I only decided at the last minute. That means... FOUR DAYS AGO!!! Are you fucking serious?"

Her dainty hands shove my chest, but I barely move. Gripping her shoulders, I hold her steady but her hands clench into fists and she thumps them against my pecs.

"Stop, Lily."

"No! How could... how could you ask me to fall when you had no intention of catching me?"

"It wasn't like that, Lily. I didn't know."

She steps back and runs her fingers through her flame-red hair.

"When I left for this tour, you told me to move on. What was I supposed to do, Lil?" I close the distance she created. "You told me not to wait. For months, I did nothing. Then when I finally release myself from your hold, you show back up and wrap me around your finger all over again. What is it you want from me? How was I supposed to know you'd one day want me? I've always wanted you. Every time you say jump, all I do is ask, how high? I can't do much more to make you see that it's always been you."

Black stained tears streak her cheeks. "That's not the point. It's the fact you asked me to marry you when you're involved with someone else. You didn't tell me. I can't do this, Ciaran. This is too much. I can't compete with her. She's perfect. She's not stuck under a mountain of childhood issues."

"Jesus, Lil. I thought we had passed this. Fuck after everything, after last night, you are still letting your past dictate your future, our future. Remi means nothing to me. We were just messing around. You are my wife, the girl I've loved my entire life." Raising my hands, I cup her tear-stained cheeks. "In all my life, my heart has only belonged to two women, my ma, and now you. She left me, I can't lose you, too."

Lily pulls my hands from her face. "I'm sorry, I can't."

"What are you so afraid of? Tell me, if you could look back at your life forty years from now... what would you regret more? Living your life full of fear or breaking through it and letting love consume you so much so, you'll never have to be afraid again?"

"I don't know."

"Well, I do. I know that no matter how far, how hard, how fucking stupid, it is to fall for you, I still jump every time. Because you, and only you, are worth the risk. Don't break my heart, Lily. Just let yourself love me. I dare you."

She turns away from me, zips up her suitcase then pulls it to the floor. Without making eye contact, she walks by me, pausing when she's parallel to my body. Her hand lands on my shoulder, but I don't look at her. I can't watch her leave.

"I'm sorry, Ciaran," she chokes out. "I guess you win because that's a dare I can't take. Love to hate you, Baby Hanson."

My jaw tightens as tears sting the backs of my eyes. Turning just in time to watch as she pulls the door open, I give her the truth instead. "This is not the end of our story, LB. It's just a plot twist."

She pauses for a beat, then with a raise of her shoulders, she's gone.

✥

LILY

Heartbreak is a gut-wrenching feeling in the pit of your stomach. It is the tightening in your chest that causes every breath of air you inhale to cut your lungs, a sensation sharper than any razor blade.

It is reminding yourself you are better than the anger

burning under your skin, but also not caring if that anger boils over.

Heartbreak is something I never wanted to feel, but as I walk away from my hotel room, it's clear that's exactly what I'm experiencing.

I swallow the bile rising from my stomach. The ache in my chest is crippling. I've never felt pain like this before. Like I've got pierced in the chest with a thousand tiny cactus needles.

Why? Why did he ask me to be vulnerable if he had no intention of protecting me? Why did he make me fall when he wasn't willing to catch me? He spent years convincing me he isn't like the rest, and when I finally believe him, he proves he is so much worse.

I'm stuck somewhere between broken and pissed off. I gave Ciaran Maguire my heart, and within forty-eight hours, he tore it from my chest then stomped on it with his stupid army boots. Loving him is not an option.

There was a time, I swore to myself, I would never allow a man to have that much power over me. Today I got a glimpse of what giving away my power does, I can't live like that.

Dragging my suitcase out of the elevator and through the lobby, I send Rosie and Bronagh a joint text.

Lily: I'm sorry, I had to leave.

Please don't come after me. Enjoy the rest of the weekend. Time is precious, spend it with your boys. I'll see you on Monday. Tell the lads I'll see them when the tour ends. Love you both, Lx

With that, I turn my phone off and make my way outside to grab a cab to the airport. I need space. Space to think, to learn, to grow.

I wish I knew then what I know now. Ciaran and Conor wouldn't return to Ireland after that world tour.

Part Two

The Intermission

CHAPTER FIFTEEN

THIS IS THE PLACE BY TOM GRENNAN

ONE YEAR LATER - LOS ANGELES

CIARAN

WITH A SLIGHT SMIRK, I LEAN AGAINST THE DOOR JAMB and watch my wife prance around our kitchen with a large mixing bowl curled into the crook of her left arm.

Fuck me, she's a sight.

Nothing but an old, raggy, band tee covers her fair skin, and yet, she's as beautiful as the day I married her.

Lost in her own little world, she doesn't see me as she fiddles with the buttons on the built-in surround sound.

Suddenly, the song changes to something a little more sensual and her hips swing to the beat.

Stray strands of her vibrant hair hang from her messy bun and her fresh morning face shows off the dusting of freckles I love so much.

Unable to stay away, I push off the doorway and stride across the room within seconds. Sneaking up behind her, I wrap my arms around her growing baby bump and kiss the back of her neck.

"Good morning LB, Can't sleep?"

She sets the glass mixing bowl on the counter then covers my hands with hers. Looking over her shoulder with a glowing smile, she steals all the air from my lungs.

I've toured the world, seen cities some people only dream about, but nothing compares to the vision before me.

"What have I told you about creeping up on me, Baby Hanson? One of these days, I'll shank you, and it will be your own damn fault."

My hands move to her hips, and I spin her to face me. "You'd never hurt me. We made a deal remember?"

Her amber eyes crinkle in amusement. "Oh, was that the deal where you promised me morning orgasms or the one where you promised not to break my heart, but did anyway?"

Suddenly the room turns black and Lily slips away. I reach for her, but I can't seem to get any grip. My voice, calling her name, fades into the nothingness, just as she does. She's gone, and I let her go.

I wake with a startle, sweat dripping off the strands of hair stuck to my forehead. Raising my hands, I scrub them over my face, desperate to erase the images burning in my mind.

Every night, for the past week, it's been the same fucking dream, again and again. If you could even call it that. It's borderline nightmare territory.

Swinging my legs over the side of my California king, I drag myself up and head to the bathroom.

It's been nearly a year since Lily walked out of that hotel room. It's been a year since our fleeting marriage went down in flames. I could lie and say I haven't been avoiding her, but the fact of the matter is, that's exactly what I've been doing. I never went home after the Sinner's tour, instead, I've been hiding out in the Los Angeles apartment as far away from my little redhead as I can get. Sure, we've been home once or twice, for Christmas, birthdays, the week we were recording the newest album, and right after everything that happened with Bronagh, but never for long. And although Lily isn't the only reason I've stayed away, she's an enormous factor.

The man staring back at me in the bathroom mirror makes me realise just how much the past few months have worn me down. Black circles rim my eyes displaying my lack of sleep, and my once bronzed skin is ghostly. Turning on the tap, I cup my hands, fill them with water and splash my face. My hands grip the edge of the sink as I peer at my reflection.

You look like shit.

A loud crash, followed by a long drawn out, "Fuckkk!" pulsates through the air.

Rushing from the bathroom, I sprint down the hallway towards Conor's room.

Without stopping, I push through the door to find my brother clutching his chin-length, blonde hair in his fists.

Glass litters the floor, tiny shards glisten under the glow of the Californian moon seeping through the open balcony doors. Picking up the broken picture frame, I stare down at Conor's wide smile as he kneels in front of Bronagh, holding my mother's engagement ring. Jesus, it only seems like yesterday, but in reality, it's a lifetime ago.

Setting what's left of the framed picture on the chest of drawers beside me, I step over the remaining shattered fragments.

Conor is sitting on the floor with his back to the base of the bed. His knees are buried against his chest, and his arms are slung around his shins. Sinking beside him, I wrap my arms around his shoulder until he falls against me. "It's all right, I got you."

His shoulders shake as silent sobs rip through his chest.

I hate this.

In the last eight months, I have watched as my brother slips further and further into this unrecognisable person. When Bronagh left, she took a part of him with her, and I'm terrified he'll never get it back.

Looking at him falling apart, I wonder if staying away from everything we've ever known is doing him any favours. I've tried everything to help him, but he's only getting worse.

My shoulders hitch as I draw in a deep breath, "Con?" I lean my head against his. "Maybe it's time we head back home? Staying here, it's not helping either of us."

Rearing back, he glares at me with red-rimmed eyes. "Move on? Are you shitting me, Ciaran? That's a little rich coming from you." Palms flat against the wooden floor, he pushes himself up into a standing position.

Dragging myself off the floor, I stand too.

"Fuck's sake, Conor. I'm just concerned." Looking around the trashed room, I drive my point home. "Open your eyes, you're a mess. At least in Ireland, we have friends. Fuck, they're family."

Scrubbing his hands down his face, he steps forward into my space. "I didn't realise you were a priest, Ciaran. Keep your preaching to yourself."

"I'm not preaching."

"You are! Maybe you should take your nose out of my business and focus on your own. Where exactly is your wife, brother? Oh, that's right, she left you too, and by the looks of Saint's Instagram feed, he's been having a grand time replacing you."

I'm not gonna lie, his words hit me hard.

"That's different and you know it," I protest.

"Is it though? Because from where I'm standing, we are two eejits, both wishing we could turn back the hands of time." He spreads his arms wide. "Newsflash, we-fucking-can't."

Turning away from him, I head for the door. I've had enough of his shit for one night.

"What's wrong, Ciaran? Can't handle the truth?" He roars, stopping me in my tracks. My hand hovers over the doorknob, but I make no move to leave. "Don't think I didn't see the divorce papers on your desk. Maybe instead of trying to fix everyone with your overbearing hero complex, re-evaluate yourself. Next time you come in here and tell me to let Bronagh go, make sure you're taking your own damn advice. Let her go, Ciaran. Sign the damn papers. She's better off without you, anyway. They all are. Maguire men, we're cursed. Destined to fall in love young, but never strong enough to keep or save our woman. Da tried with Ma, you tried with Lil, and fuck knows, I tried with Bronagh. But guess what, Lil Bro? We all failed."

With a flick of my wrist, I pry the door open. "Fuck you, Conor."

✤

With my left hand raised above my head, I lean against the glass window wall of my office and watch as the sun replaces the moon on Venice beach. It's times like this, I can feel every mile between us. I know the relationship between us was less than short, but before we ever became a thing, we were friends. She's the person who makes me laugh, the one I want to share my day with, the phone call I want to make when I need to talk, and without her, I'm trapped inside my head.

Conor's words play on repeat. *Let her go.*

I wish it were that simple, but it's not. Lily's ingrained in every aspect of my life. Both personal and professional, sooner or later, I need to deal with her.

Sinking into my office chair, I pull open the desk drawer and remove the A4 size manilla envelope.

Sliding the documents out, I focus on the bold heading:
PETITION FOR DISSOLUTION OF MARRIAGE - SIMPLIFIED DIVORCE.

What a load of shit!

I read over it a few times and... I don't know what I'm trying to achieve, it's not like the dried ink will somehow magically disappear.

Throwing the pages onto the desk, I reach for the Waterford Crystal decanter and a glass. With a pop, the bottle opens, and the rich aroma of Irish whiskey fills my lungs. Whiskey isn't my go-to drink, but right now I need something strong to take the sting away.

Let her go. Let her go. Let her go.

Maybe Conor is right? Pulling my phone from my tracksuit pocket, I click the small multi-coloured camera logo then search Saint's handle, @heavens_orginalsinner. *What a dick!*

Scrolling through his feed, I see picture after picture of him and the band travelling across Europe. After the tour, they took some time off to see the sights. When you're working full time, you only see the inside of a hotel or stadium. I'm about seven pictures down when a pop of red catches my eye. The picture is of him, standing on The Hill of Tara. Half of his smarmy face is cut out as he stands with his hand open. In the distance is Lily, arms stretched wide with a beaming smile on her face. The way he took the photo, it makes Lily look like she's standing in his palm.

I flick down to the caption and my stomach flips.

What better way to explore this gorgeous country than with my favourite Irish lass! #PrettyLady #Igotthewholeworldinmyhand #Ireland #SinnerstravelEurope

Fuck it, I'm texting her.

Ciaran: Jax St. Claire? Is he the reason for my special mail delivery?

Delete.

Ciaran: I miss you. I miss your sassy attitude, your built-in comebacks, and your overbearing need to always be right. I miss your smiles. Your cackle, and that sexy resting bitch face I want to kiss so badly. I miss it all.

Delete.

Ciaran: I swore, I wouldn't do this. I wouldn't be the guy who pines after a girl. Yet here I am, thousands of miles away, and still missing you. You know, I'm sitting here in the dark, watching the sunrise over the ocean, and the only thing I can think of is I want to watch it with you.

Delete.

Ciaran: Fuck Lily? Divorce? Is that what you want?

Delete.

Ciaran: Hey, LB. I got the papers. If divorce is what you want, I'll sign the papers. All I ever want is for you to be happy. Promise me something though, if you ever need me... call me, okay. It doesn't matter if I'm down the road, or an ocean away. You need me, and I'll come running. Every time. I'll always love to love you. Xx.

Sent.

I need to stop trying to turn a period into a comma. I fought and lost. Lily O'Shea is not mine — not anymore. Grabbing a pen, I scribble my name where I'm supposed to. Downing the rest of my drink, I fling the crystal glass across the room and watch in slow motion as it explodes against the wall. Anger replaces my sorrow, filling every molecule of my body. I'm so fucking angry. Why does life bend us past the point of breaking, then fuck us up the ass? First my ma, then Da and Con, now me. Life keeps shitting on us. Maybe Conor was right, we're cursed.

I drop back into the chair and run my hands through my hair.

"Looks like you took a page from my book." Conor saunters into the room, eyeing the broken glass on the floor. "Feels good to break shit, doesn't it?"

Taking a seat on the opposite side of the black leather desk, he spies the freshly signed papers in front of me. "So, you signed them."

Acknowledging him with just a nod of my head, he picks up the papers and scans them. "Is this what you want?"

Peering over my brow, I level him with a glare that screams, *what the fuck do you think?*

"Look Ciaran, I'm sorry. I projected my shit onto you, and that's not fair. If you want to let her go, do it. But, if there is even a tiny part of you that believes this," he waves the documents at me, "is the wrong choice. Then don't. Some of us, we have no choice, but you do."

Passing the documents to me, I take them without protest.

"What will it be, brother? In fifty years... who will be the woman standing by your side?"

It's a split-second decision... but one, I know I won't regret for the rest of my life.

I tear them up.

Fuck Lily. Fuck Saint. And fuck these divorce papers.

Lily Maguire promised me forever, and if she thinks she can back out of that dare now, she is sorely mistaken.

CHAPTER SIXTEEN

WORKIN' ON IT BY MEGHAN TRAINOR, LENNON STELLA AND SASHA SLONE

LILY

THE FAMILIAR SCENT OF LAVENDER AND BERGAMOT fills my senses as I step into Dr J's office.

Dr Janet Monks — aka Dr J — has been my therapist since I was seventeen. Her methods are more holistic than conventional, but she is the only person I ever feel truly at ease with.

"Lily, darling." She opens her arms wide and I step into her warm, welcoming embrace. Her long, natural brown hair flows in wild waves around her wrinkle-free face. The woman is well into her fifties, but she doesn't look a day over thirty-five. Barefoot, wearing a vibrant silk kimono over a plain yellow tank top and black yoga pants, she is effortlessly beautiful.

"How are you?" Her soft gentle tone instantly calms me. Pulling back, she gently grips my shoulders as she takes me in from head to toe. "Oh, sweetheart, what's wrong?"

I can never tell how she does that, with one look she can gauge my mood. It's as if she has a sixth sense.

"Ciaran got the divorce papers."

Her soulful brown eyes turn sorrowful. "Okay, well, that was a big step for you. Kick those boots off and take a seat, it sounds like we have a lot to unpack today."

Once my Docs are off, I take a seat in the large armchair and allow my body to sink into it. I tuck my feet under my bum and make myself at home.

Dr J holds out a soft, white, fur-like blanket for me to take and I wrap it around my shoulders like a shield. This is what I love about these sessions, they are personal. Dr J knows exactly what I need when I need it, and right now, I need comfort.

She takes a seat in the chair across from me then picks up her brown leather-bound notebook. Flicking it open, she plucks her pencil from between the pages. "So, you said Ciaran received the papers? How did he react?"

I think back to the text message he sent last week. I've read it at least a thousand times, memorising every word.

Ciaran: Hey, LB. I got the papers. If divorce is what you want, I'll sign them. All I ever want is for you to be happy. Promise me something though, if you ever need me… call me, okay. It doesn't matter if I'm down the road, or an ocean away. If you need me, I'll come running. Every time. I'll always love to love you. Xx.

"Erm, surprisingly well, I think. He said he just wants me to be happy."

"Are you happy?"

Such a loaded question.

Avoiding eye contact, I stare at the hand-painted, silk, wall tapestry hanging behind her. It's a woman meditating while seven vivid colours swirl through her body — each colour representing a chakra. It's a beautiful piece. Dr J painted it herself at one of her healing yourself from the inside out workshops.

My eyes flick back to hers, but she doesn't push, she never does. Inhaling, I fill my lungs with some much-needed air.

"No. I'm not happy about ending my marriage — if you

can even call it that. It was about time though. It's been a year, and we've hardly spoken. Only when it was unavoidable. He needs to move on, and as long as that piece of paper ties us together, he won't."

Her pencil moves across the page at lightning speed, the lead scratching against the paper with every word she writes.

"So," she draws out. "What you're saying is that you sent him those papers to set him free, is that correct?"

Ugh! Why is she so infuriating?

"In a way, yes." My shoulders sag, and a sigh escapes my lips. "But also, because I need to learn how not to depend on him. He's always been my life jacket. The one person who stops me from sinking. I think it's time I learn to swim. He can't hold me up forever. I won't let him."

Her eyes crinkle into a frown as she focuses on my face. "That sounds familiar to what you said when you let him go, before he left for that first tour. What makes you think this time will be different? Have you asked yourself why you're so determined to walk this road on your own?"

Contemplating her question, I search for the right words. "I guess it's because when I'm with him, the anxiety eases. It's like all the hurt and fear dissipates. His energy is all-consuming, and suddenly, I forget how broken I am. He makes the emptiness disappear and that's dangerous because I'm terrified the minute he walks away, I'll plummet further into the abyss. And sure, he masks the internal scars, but he doesn't heal them. That is something I need to do myself. I can't keep using him as a security blanket because I know, deep down, one day, my demons will rear their ugly heads and we won't survive it. I don't want to lead him on anymore, he deserves better. As for it being different, it has to be. I need to lose him so I can love me first."

She nods, scribbles something onto the page but doesn't delve any further.

"And what about everything that happened in Las Vegas? She pushes. "Have you both spoken about that?"

"Not really, no." I'm sure my face is saying what my words aren't. *I don't want to talk about him with fucking Remi.*

"Um-hmm. You're not ready to unload that so, let's try something else. How's Saint? The last time you were here, you two where getting close."

"You make it sound like we're intimate, which couldn't be further from the truth. Our relationship is strictly platonic, but to answer your question, Saint is good. We talk at least twice a week. I'm thinking of visiting him in Los Angeles. Michael wants me to convince the band to switch to Sham-Rock Records. If I can get them to sign, it could be huge for my career."

A smile graces her face, lighting up the already bright room. "Finally!" She shouts. "That's the first genuine smile

I've seen on your face in months. Work brings you joy. Let's grab onto that feeling and build the momentum." She holds out both arms and rotates them in a clockwise circular motion like she's stirring this giant cauldron of joy. "Tell me, Lily, what is it about work that excites you?"

Taking a second, I think about it. One-word sticks in the forefront of my mind. *Power.*

"It makes me feel powerful. I could stand in a room full of men and I know that I am the one in charge. I give the orders. I call the shots. It's the one place I can truly strive. Nobody dares mess with me, I am the queen when it comes to spotting raw talent. In the past twelve months, I've signed a mixture of eight new artists and bands, and six of those have reached Ireland and the U.K.'s top 10. I'm good at my job, I manage ten acts, 4Clover included. I can run that label better than any other asshole that works there, and I do it all on an apprentice wage."

Leaning forward in her seat, Dr J rests her elbows on her thighs. "Have you tried asking for a raise? Maybe a commission-based salary?"

My eyes involuntarily roll back into my sockets. "Yes, I have asked more than once, but Michael insists I need to complete my online course before he can," lifting my arms, I mimic inverted commas, "officially promote me."

"Lily, we've talked about using a sarcastic tone to brush

over underlying issues. I want you to close your eyes and use your visualisation tool to connect to your inner child."

Doing as she asks, I shut my eyes, and picture my younger self. It doesn't take long for the image of me in a red and black ladybug t-shirt and dungarees to appear.

Dr J's voice is strong and calming as she guides me through the visualisation.

"Now, once you've found her, take her hand in yours and lead her over to the small bench under the large oak tree. Once you're both seated, I want you to ask her how she's been."

I'm fully aware that to outsiders looking in, I'd look certifiably insane, but this method has proven rather successful in the years I've been attending Dr J's sessions. Inner child therapy is highly effective in dealing with childhood trauma, connecting with yourself on an entirely different level allows us to dig deeper into how and why we behave the way we do.

"Now I want you to ask her, why? Why are you so agitated by Michael?"

My answer flows out before I can even register it. "Because, if I were a man, they would pay me more for everything I do."

"And this upsets you?" She prompts.

"Yes! In every aspect of my life, men have always tried to control women to some degree. My dad, he beat my mother into submission. When I got older and bolder, he tried to do the same with me. Michael, he knows the work I do is invaluable, and yet he treats me like an over-glorified intern. Then there is Ciaran, who wants to save me. He is hellbent on being a fucking hero, but I don't want a hero. Why does he assume I am this damsel in distress? Why can't he see I'm strong enough to save myself? Why can't I be the hero of my story? Women can be heroes too, you know."

I open my eyes to find her staring at me with a beaming smile.

"Why are you looking at me like that?"

"Because, my dear, you just had a breakthrough."

My brows scrunch together to form a deep v. "I did?"

Her soft chuckle reverberates around the room. "Yes. Every problem in your life connects to a time where you felt powerless. So, your gut instinct is to never feel that way again. You pride yourself on being the strongest person in the room. Your dad made you feel weak. Michael makes you feel less than your worth, and Ciaran, although it's not the same, he still makes you feel vulnerable, so you push him away because you're not willing to let your guard down. You've not learned how to be strong and vulnerable, simultaneously. And, until you do, you will always push back, because power is your motivator. Once you learn how to stand in your own power in every aspect of your life, then and only then, you will stand in your vulnerabilities too."

❧

AFTER LEAVING DR J'S OFFICE, I FEEL ON TOP OF THE world. Sitting into my brand new, orange mini-cooper, I take my phone from my bag and switch it back on. An onslaught of messages come through, one after the other. They're mostly work-related, and one from Rosie wanting to do drinks later. Just when I'm about to pop it back in my back it beeps again. My heart jumps right out of my chest as Ciaran's name blinks across the home screen. I haven't heard a dicky bird from him since he agreed to the divorce. Drawing in a deep breath, I click the message and suddenly, the last hour of therapy seems wasted. All the work undone by one text message from across the ocean.

Ciaran: I know I said I'd sign the papers, but I've changed my mind. You promised me a lifetime and I intend to cash in on that. Prepare yourself, LB. I'm coming back to you.

Well, shit!

CHAPTER SEVENTEEN

SUPERHERO BY CHER LLOYD

LILY

THE TAXI PULLS UP OUTSIDE THE GOLDEN BARREL, AND instantly, I regret agreeing to go out tonight. "Karaoke? Is this supposed to make me feel better?"

After Ciaran's text, all I want to do is curl up in bed with a pint of ice-cream and a good book. Drunk people whaling into a microphone is the last thing I'm in the mood for.

Rosie stops in her tracks and spins to face me. "Yes, karaoke is good for the soul." Taking hold of my hand, she pulls me along until we reach the large, dark wooden doors that lead to the lounge. "Besides, you used to love coming here every Sunday. Come on, it will be fun. Just like old times."

I haven't stepped foot inside this bar since Bronagh stopped working here. Before Vegas, before life turned into a steaming pile of shite.

With a sigh of protest, I follow Rosie into the dimly lit space. It's still early, so there are plenty of tables to choose from.

Leading the way, Rosie heads for the large round table to the left of the makeshift stage.

"Is there a reason we need such an enormous table? It's only the two of us."

"Oh, well…" She looks everywhere but at my face. "Cillian and Cian are coming too. They'll be here shortly."

I eye her closely. "Why do you look shifty as fuck?"

"No, I don't." Changing the subject, she asks me what I want from the bar, then stalks off before I can interrogate her further.

I take a seat and peer around. The place hasn't changed in all the years since I've been here. Ebony oak tables with matching stools are spread across the open plan area, and with the horrid shade of salmon-pink gracing the walls, it's as if it got trapped in 1992.

"Well, if it isn't Lilyanna O'Shea." A deep yet cheery voice booms from behind me. Glancing over my shoulder, my eyes land on Ronan Brady. Ronan is only a few years older than me, but he's been running Karaoke here for as long as I can remember. Pulling out a stool, he drops into the seat beside me. "How have you been? I haven't seen you in forever."

"I've been good, busy working, you know how it is. How's Mark? Are you guys still together?"

"Of course," he flicks his non-existing locks over his shoulder. "That man wouldn't know how to function without me. We've been living together for five months now, and still, he can't manage the washing machine. Every Friday, he brings his unmentionables to his mother's. He thinks I haven't noticed, but Doreen Daly is the only woman I know who irons socks. I thought I was extra, but that woman takes laundry to a whole new level. Anyway," he places his hand over mine, "enough about me. I saw a picture of you with Jax St. Claire in Starz Weekly. His name may be Saint, but that man drips sin."

With a dramatic face fan, his eyes roll back and his mouth opens to form an O.

Slapping his shoulder, I fight back a laugh. "Please stop! You look like you're being tortured."

He stands up while wiggling his perfectly plucked eyebrows. "In a good way, though. Okay, enough chit-chat. I need to get this show on the road. Don't leave before I call you up. Nobody rocks Karaoke Night like the Powerpuff Girls.

That silly name was what Ronan always called Me, Rosie, and Bronagh, but tonight it hits me like a tonne of bricks. *Bronagh should be here, but she's not.* Shoving down my emotions before they bubble over, I give Ronan a small, sad smile. "I'm sure Rosie will drag me up onto the stage at some point."

If he spots my sudden change in mood, he doesn't show it. With a cheeky wink, he saunters away.

🍀

"MY EARS ARE BLEEDING." GRABBING ROSIE BY HER shoulders, I shake her. "Make it stop. Please, make it stop."

"They're not that bad."

"Are you deaf? How can you say that? They're murdering that poor song. Nobody should sing Mariah Carey at karaoke. Nobody. Besides, It's June, not December. Why are they singing Christmas songs?"

Rosie looks over at the group of ladies, who are on stage. Five of them are wearing matching pink t-shirts with the words Sarah's Hen Party written in white glitter. The girl in the centre is the only one with a white t-shirt, Bride stretched across her enormous chest in pink glitter.

"They're having fun, leave them alone." Lifting the straw to her red lips, she sips at the strawberry daiquiri. "Do you regret it?" She looks back at the group of girls.

"Regret what?"

Her blue eyes soften. "Getting married?"

I let her question sink in. Do I regret marrying Ciaran? I'm not sure. There are too many variables. One thing I regret is the timing. We weren't ready for that kind of commitment. Honestly, we still aren't. But that doesn't mean I regret him. In another life, at a different time, things could have turned out different. If I've learnt anything in the last year, it's that chasing what if's, when's, and maybe's is not healthy. I need to focus on the here and now or else I'll blink and still be stuck living in a hell I created. Self-healing is important, it's not something you can pack away and forget about. It needs to be a priority. If you threw a stone into the sea, would it ripple from the outside in? No, it wouldn't. It starts from the inside and travels out. So why would loving someone be different? I have to start with myself first.

Then there is the Remi issue. Logically, I know I have no right to berate him for sleeping with someone when we weren't together, but his blatant omission of the fact still stings. He should have told me, it's not as if she was some random person he would never see again. Remi is a permanent fixture in his life. She will always be around, lurking in the shadows, rearing her beautiful head and making me feel less than. Silly? Sure, but it's the truth.

Regardless of what I show the outside world, underneath the give-no-fucks attitude, my self-confidence is still fragile. Remi St. Claire is the total package. She's a badass Rockstar with buckets of sex appeal, her confidence radiates off her in waves, she is fearless. Both inside and out. I can't compete with that.

One day Ciaran will see that she is everything I am not. And when that day comes, he will regret chasing me to the end of the earth because what he'll find there is nothing but a barren wasteland, scorched by the demons of my childhood past.

"No," I finally speak. "I don't. Do I wish things could be different? Sure. But they aren't Rosie. This is me, it's who I am. I can't love someone like Ciaran Maguire. He wears his heart on his sleeve. He demands affection, craves it even. He is full of pretty words and romantic gestures. He yearns for someone he can love and protect. On the outside, he's sarcastic and snarky, and always up to mischief. But underneath his tattooed exterior is a little boy who lost his mammy too young. And now, he aches to replace her. I can't be her Rosie. I can't be the girl who fully loses herself to a man. I've seen first-hand what that does to someone. Look at my mother. Fuck, for years, she was so lost on my dad she avoided reality. It took her a lifetime to escape the world he built around her, then when she was finally free, she had nothing. Nothing, Rosie. No education, no career, no financial freedom. For fuck's sake, if she wanted to buy a pair of knickers, she needed to ask him for the cash to do so. Then, when she finally escaped, all she had was a broken heart and the mental scars he gave her. I'm not saying I never want to fall in love because I do, I really do. But first, I need to become strong enough to carry myself, I need to know that if, and when, it all goes down in flames, I can rise from the ashes."

Her head bows, her eyes suddenly invested in the old cigarette burns that mark the hardwood floor. Her muffled mumble barely reaches my ears, but I still hear it. "I'm sorry. I shouldn't have told him to come."

Confusion works its way across my brow line. *What the hell is she talking about?*

"Rosie? What are you talking about?"

Without answering, her attention flicks to the entrance behind me. Peering over my shoulder, I follow her line of sight, and suddenly, everything around me fades away, my breath hitches in my chest, and my lungs fight to fill with the air I desperately need. I've been anticipating this moment for longer than I care to admit, and now that it's here... what do I do?

Ciaran Maguire strides towards me with determination roaring from his eyes. With each step he takes, every decibel of noise, fades away, and it unnerves me. Scanning his frame, I drink him, savouring every drop. His dyed black hair hangs over his eyes in slightly wet strands, as if he just stepped out of a shower. His lean torso, covered by a long-sleeved, white t-shirt, defines every single ridge of this wash-board stomach. With his sleeves rolled up to his elbows, I have a delicious view of the protruding veins running underneath the tattooed skin of his forearms. His strong thighs are covered by the dark denim jeans he has tucked into his signature combat style boots and fuck me... he is a walking lady boner.

I can't breathe, just the sight of him has stolen every molecule of air in my lungs. Cursing him and his ability to affect me without consent, I push from my chair and stand to greet him. Quickly, I pack my vulnerabilities away and put my mask in place.

"What are you doing here? Aren't you supposed to be in L.A?"

A sly smirk teases the corner of his mouth and instantly, I know I'm fucked. He is on a mission, and unfortunately, that mission is me. His eyes bore into mine, showcasing all the emotions I've spent the better half of a year running from.

"Don't ask silly questions, Lilyanna. You're smarter than that."

When I don't respond to his blatant disregard of my question, he tries again. Only this time, he steps into my space and lifts my chin with his left hand, making our staring contest that much more intimate. "Do you want to know why I'm here?"

Swallowing back the anxiety rolling up my chest, I square my shoulders. "I asked, didn't I?"

"Ah, there she is." His grin widens.

"There who is?"

"My wife."

"Soon to be, ex-wife."

"Don't think so, LB. I told you I was coming for you, and unlike a certain someone I know, I don't say things I don't mean. Buckle up, Wifey. I'm bringing out the big guns."

CHAPTER EIGHTEEN

WE ARE NEVER EVER GETTING BACK TOGETHER BY TAYLOR SWIFT

LILY

Fuck him and his pretty face. Who does he think he is? Walking in here with his bad-boy swag and kissable lips as if he didn't disappear for a year.

Ugh, I'm seething.

He better stay on the far side of this table, because I swear to God, if he comes near me, I will chop his dick off and shove it down his throat.

Look at him, sitting there, perched on his stool as if nothing ever happened, dripping his normal sexy confidence that somehow, lowers all my defences. *The audacity of this prick!*

Then he has the cheek to say, *"I told you I was coming for you."*

Who does that? My husband, that's who. His presence alone has me on edge, and I don't like it. Not one bit.

My new coffin-shaped acrylic nails dig into the palms of my hands as the sweet, delicious sound of his laughter echoes across the table. Chewing on the inside of my bottom lip, I fight back the urge to strangle him. His sinful scent wafts in my face, filling my nostrils, and soothing my soul. *Why couldn't he smell like mouldy cheese? You know, to match his stinking personality.* Ignoring him was much easier when he was on the far side of the Atlantic, but now, now that he's here, at home and in my face, it will be much harder.

His eyes burn a hole in the side of my face as I blatantly look everywhere but at him and all his cheeky charm.

"Are you okay over there, LB? There must be something interesting at the bottom of your cocktail glass, cause it sure has all your attention."

I lift my glass, and place the sugar-coated rim against my burgundy painted lips. With an exaggerated eye roll, I turn my attention to Rosie and Cillian, who are so lost in each other, they're no help in my mission to avoid Ciaran. And the jackass knows it, too. So instead of sweet relief from his asinine button pushing, I have to endure it.

Whatever floats your boat Maguire, I can play this game all night.

"You can't ignore me forever."

Watch me!

"You need to talk to me at some point," he prods, pressing every button he can think of, hoping to get a reaction. *Not happening, Maguire.*

Switching up his tactic, he leans in closer and runs his finger along the inside of my glass. Scooping up the sugar along the edge, he pops it in his mouth, and ever so slowly, licks the evidence of his finger. When my cheeks flush at his action, his lips curl into his signature smirk. *Bastard!*

"Bittersweet, just like my Wifey. So, how is Saint? You both seem very cosy on IG."

Feeling spiteful, I spit out a response. "I don't know, maybe you can call your fuck buddy and ask her. After all, he's her brother."

"Low blow, Wifey."

"The only thing that's low are your standards."

"You weren't saying that when you married me."

"Yeah, well, we all make mistakes, that's why you're my soon-to-be-ex. Maybe I should start calling you my Y instead. Because, why the hell I married you in the first place remains a mystery."

"Stop deluding yourself, Wifey. You love me, admit it."

"Stop calling me that, I'm not your wife. My phone battery lasts longer than our marriage did."

Before Ciaran can respond, Cian cuts in. "Jesus, do you two ever stop? You're like two bold children. Go fuck in the bathroom already, cause this constant back and forth is getting on my last nerve."

At the same time, I mutter, "I'd rather not," under my breath, Ciaran jumps from the stool and holds his hand out for me to take.

"What do you say, LB? Want to take a ride on Mr Boneman for old time's sake?"

Shaking my head at him, I bite out my reply. "Are you trying to annoy me?"

He lifts his left brow, almost daring me with a look. "Is it working?"

"Fuck you."

"I'd love you to." Sinking to his hunkers in front of me, he holds his tall frame in a squat and leans in. His breath brushes against the exposed skin of my neck, forcing those traitorous goosebumps to stand at attention. His voice drops to a whisper, making my cheeks flush crimson. "It's been far too long since your pussy strangled my cock."

I can't deny the jolt of want that erupts in my core, but will I fuck let him know how much his words affect me.

"Back up, Chuck. You're in my personal space."

"Not yours, Lily, ours. We're a married couple. You'd do well to remember that, and while you're at it, inform Saint too. I don't share, Lily." Pushing his hands off his thighs, he stands to his full height. "You are mine," he winks. "Until death does us part."

Shoving his hands into his pocket, he turns and heads for the bar.

"He's got one thing right: death will do you both part. It's only a matter of who kills who, first," Cillian chimes in, just as I pick my mouth up off the floor.

🍀

CIARAN

She's different. I can't quite put my finger on what has changed, but something has. There is a new spark in her eyes that wasn't there before. A blazing feistiness, raging with strength and determination. Excitement boils under my skin, the desire to push every single one of her buttons becomes too much to bear.

Daggers shoot from her glare, burning into my skin as I walk back from the bar with our drinks.

Fuck me, I missed this — the underlining lust she disguises as hate.

Lily O'Shea is a beautiful chaotic hurricane brewing

beyond the horizon. With every glance she steals, she gains momentum; heading my way, determined to whisk me off my feet, leaving my world in an irreparable mess of unfinished business. She has another thing coming if she thinks I'm bowing out without a fight.

Taking a seat on the stool beside her, I place her strawberry daiquiri on the table while she continues to ignore my existence by pretending to be in deep conversation with Rosie.

I scoot closer and her body tenses. *Like it or not, LB, I still affect you.* Drawing in a deep breath, I allow her cherry blossom scent to fill my lungs. "How long are you going to keep this up?"

"For as long as it takes you to get the hint." Her tone drips venom, a complete contradiction to the goosebumps that run along her bare arms.

"I'm not the one lying to myself. That's all you, Wifey."

Peering over her shoulder, her amber eyes find mine, and for a moment, time stops. It's there, in the pursing of her lips and the crinkle of her eyes, I know I'm getting to her. Plastering on a cheeky smile, I dare her with my eyes. *Keep fighting me, Bug. I like it.*

Ronan's voice bleeds through the speakers diverting our attention to the stage. "Folks, up next is my feisty friend, it's been a while since she graced us with her presence, so please, give a warm welcome to Miss Lilyanna O'Shea."

Pushing off her stool, Lily shoots me a wink. "This one is for you, Hubby," she mocks in a sarcastic tone, fuelled by the fire burning in her eyes. Before I can respond, she strides towards the karaoke machine with that bad-ass confidence I love so much, and the punters cheer her on.

Her long, unruly hair hangs over her bare shoulders, tumbling down her back in untamable waves. Wearing nothing but a skin-tight, black strapless dress that stops mid-thigh, and a pair of thigh high, burgundy stiletto boots, she looks good enough to fucking eat. A low groan bubbles in my throat. *Christ, she's breath-taking.*

Cian's hand lands on my shoulder. "Close your mouth, mate. You're catching flies."

"Can't help it, man. My wife is pure fire."

"That's the problem, Ciaran."

Tuning him out, I focus on the stage. Laughter barrels from Ronan's mouth when Lily whispers in his ear, then suddenly, the recognisable sound of *Taylor Swift's, We Are Never Ever Getting Back Together,* pumps through the surround sound.

Her lips curl into a smug smile as her gaze locks on me. Raising the microphone to her painted lips, she belts out the first verse with ease. I laugh at her over-dramatic actions, lift my pint to my lips and continue watching her performance over the rim of my glass. *Come at me, Lily. Show me what you've got.*

Defiance lights her gorgeous face. Her expression tells me everything I need to know. *Game on, Baby Hanson. Game on!*

The second verse kicks in and she steps off the stage — the mic clutched in her left hand. In four strides she's standing behind me, running her long, painted black nails across the width of my shoulders, singing about picking fights and how she's always right. Before I know it, she's holding out her hand for Cian, gesturing with a nod for him to help her step up onto the small stool. Suddenly, he stands from his seat and grips either side of her waist. Bending at his knees, he effortlessly lifts her and places her dainty frame onto the table, just in time for the chorus.

Thrusting her free hand into the air, she shouts, "We," then holds the mic out so the crowd can join in and sing along to the iconic lyrics. The pub erupts in an off-key rendition of the T. Swift classic, and Lily, she's in her fucking element.

Her hips sway to the pounding beat, a smug smile a mile wide housed on her pouty lips.

Dropping low, she puts her face in line with mine, and with an airy, condescending tone, she speaks out the bridge. Tilting her head to the side, her smirk crinkles the corner of her eyes, and fuck, I want to kiss it right off her face. Her lips gravitate towards mine, then suddenly, she brings the mic between us, then preaches, "Like. Ever."

When the song finally ends, she jumps from the table, landing right in my lap and the place erupts with hoots and hollers.

On instinct, her hands wrap around my neck. "Was that clear enough for you, Baby Hanson?"

Tightening my hold, I pull her closer. "If you think we're through, you're more delusional than I thought. Everyone in this fucking bar can see we only exist for each other. You can tell yourself a million times that we're just friends, but, at the end of the day, month, year, hell even this decade... I'll still be the guy. It will always be me, LB. Always." She pulls back, ready to run, but I hold on tighter. "You wanna be friends? Fine. But one day, I'll prove to you, you are worthy of an epic love story. Those heroes you read about they won't hold a candle to the hero in your story... because your hero is me."

Finally, she frees herself and stands to leave, but just before she walks away, she looks over her shoulder. "I don't need a hero, Ciaran. I can save myself."

This time, I let her walk away.

"Good luck, man." Cian offers. "You're gonna need it."

Without taking my eyes off Lily's retreating frame, I reply, "I don't need luck, I have faith."

CHAPTER NINETEEN

GIVE IT TO YOU BY JULIA MICHAELS

LILY

If Mondays were shoes, they'd be Crocs. Nobody in their right mind loves those dignity stealing monstrosities.

Today has been a cluster fuck of epic proportions.

I have the worst hangover known to woman, and Lord knows the four hours of broken sleep I had last night is doing nothing for my less than sour mood. I'm one email away from sticking an out-of-order sign on my forehead and calling it a day. To make matters worse, my coffee cup is empty, and I'm up to my tits in paperwork for the up-coming 4Clover tour that kicks off this November.

This is all his fault, showing up the day before our one-year-anniversary, he's trying to rattle my cage. Unfortunately for me, it's working.

Ugh, Ciaran Maguire, the bane of my existence. He's like a haemorrhoid, just when you think you've got rid of it, that fucker pops back up and insists on being a pain in the ass. To hell with him and his persistence.

Last night he continued to push every single one of my buttons until I got so drunk, Rosie had to bring me home and put me to bed. For hours, I lay awake thinking about the depth of his sea-green eyes, and tethering along a line of what if's, and what never should have been.

Resting my forehead against my desk, I release a weighty sigh. "Fuck this day."

A deep chuckle interrupts my mid-morning breakdown, the sound so potent it steals my ability to move. I don't need to look up to know who it is, it's a sound I'm all too familiar with.

Lifting my head a fraction of an inch, I drop it back down again, knocking it lightly against the glass work desk. Repeatedly.

"Careful there, LB. You might knock some sense into that stubborn head of yours."

Frustration assaults my already rigid shoulders, and tension decides he will join in and beat me in the head with his can't-catch-a-break stick.

Slowly, I raise my head, ignoring the luminous green

post-it that's taking up residence on my forehead, and glare at the man who insists on ruining my already bad day.

"Well, if it isn't the haemorrhoid."

"What?"

"Oh, that's what I'm calling you now. Well, in my head at least."

Ciaran's wide shoulders lean against the doorjamb with his arms folded across his chest. How do men pull off that casual lean? The — oh, don't mind me, I'll just stand here looking as if I belong on the cover of GQ — look.

He's utterly edible in his tight, long-sleeved black tee and black ripped jeans. He flashes me his dimpled smile, which only makes my irritation flare.

"Did anyone ever tell you you're a bit of a weirdo?" He states as he saunters into my office as if he owns the place. Lifting his hand to his forehead, he sasses, "You've got a little something stuck to your face."

Pulling the post-it off my face, I crumple it up and throw it across the room, into the overflowing waste bin. "Did anyone ever tell you you're like a foul smell? Lingering where it's unwanted."

He lowers himself into the chair and kicks his feet up onto my desk, then he lifts the neckline of his t-shirt to his nose and sniffs. That move alone sets my memory off, and suddenly I'm transported to a time where his warm citrus scent, mixed with the perfect amount of spice, brought me comfort. *Lily! Sort your shit out, your self-control is slipping, and fast.*

Turning my attention back to Ciaran, my annoyance rises tenfold. I pick up my stapler, and chuck it at him. "Get your feet off my desk."

Unfortunately, the shithead has the reflexes of a cat and dodges right before my weapon of choice hits its target.

"Jesus, you could have killed me. What did I ever do to deserve such animosity?"

"Your presence alone is enough to ignite my inner psycho. Now, what do you want? I have work to do."

"Can't a man visit his wife at work on their first-year wedding anniversary?"

I try to hide my shock but judging by the smug look on his handsome face, I'm not doing a very good job. "Eh, how... you remembered?"

Do you ever look at someone and think: *God must have been in a good mood when he made you?* Because that's what happens when I look at my husband.

He's the perfect blend of a young Johnny Depp with a pinch of Skeet Ulrich, circa 1996 — bad-boy beautiful.

His face softens, but his green eyes turn serious. "I'll never forget the day I made you mine." His words carry so much conviction, they steal mine. So, instead, I nod my head and start fiddling with some paperwork on my desk.

Breaking through the awkward silence, he pushes himself out of his chair. "I got you a present."

I watch him as he strolls towards the door, then suddenly he disappears behind the wall before re-entering with the most beautiful bouquet of Forever Susan lilies and a matte black gift bag.

He passes me the black and silver vase first, and I lift it to my nose and bask in the sweet smell. Forever Susan's are my favourite of the Lilium family, their vibrant red, yellow, and deep purple petals are stunning.

I stand, and with the vase clutched tight in my grip, I walk over to the window and place them on the sill. Running my fingers over the delicate petals, I thank him. "They're gorgeous."

Suddenly, he's right behind me. His six-foot frame against my back. "They remind me of you, bold and beautiful."

I fight against the tears that are pricking the backs of my eyes. "Ciaran..."

His hands reach out, gently caressing the skin from my shoulder to elbow. "About Vegas, and everything with Remi... It didn't mean anything, Lil. I swear, once I heard you were coming, that was it. She was a distraction. Something to take my mind off how I felt about you... How I still feel."

"I know... I got your emails. I just couldn't. It was never

about Remi... It was the omission. You broke my trust. You asked me to leap, but you weren't honest with me, and I landed in a pile of shit I wasn't equipped to deal with."

"I'm sorry. I know how much honesty means to you. And if I could go back and redo that trip, I would have told you. I was just so caught up in making you mine, it didn't register until it was too late."

Screw him and all his pretty words.

I turn in place and look up into his eyes. "You know, you're making it hard for me to hate you."

A lazy yet beautiful smile lights up his face, but instead of replying he turns and heads back to the chair without a word. Following his lead, I head for mine.

Once I'm seated, he lifts the gift bag off the floor and holds it out for me to take.

"The flowers weren't the actual gift. I read somewhere that you should give paper for your first anniversary."

Silently, I take the bag and open it. Inside is the most beautiful, black marble music box. It's lightly dusted with tiny flecks of silver, making it look like a night sky. After gently placing it on my desk, I lift the lid and a familiar melody fills the room.

"Is that," I can't finish my sentence, the emotion brewing beneath my skin is too much.

"Patience by Guns 'N' Roses." Ciaran finishes for me.

"It was our first dance as a married couple, it will always remind me of you."

I'm lost for words. His thoughtfulness has stolen my ability to speak. Closing my eyes, I force back my unshed tears. When I open them again, I notice the rolled-up piece of paper resting inside the box. Taking it out, I ask, "What's this?"

"Open it and see."

I undo the thin black ribbon then peel the scroll open. Suddenly, the tears I fought so hard to keep locked away, finally fall.

Star Certificate

The star with the co-ordinance RE: 13:03:33.35 DEC: 49:31:38.1. was successfully entered into the star registry under the new name of:

LILY BUG

To my Wifey for life,
This is to remind you that when you feel trapped in the darkness, you still shine.
I will always love to love you.
Baby Hanson.

Lifting my hand, I use my fingertips to wipe the moisture off my cheeks. "Ciaran... this... it's, thank you."

He pushes from his chair, circles the desk, and drops to his hunkers in front of me. He takes my hands in his and looks up at me with a puppy dog expression. "Have dinner with me, tonight?"

"I... I can't."

His hopeful face drops, and he begins to stand, but I stop him by placing my hand on his chest.

"I want to, I really want to. I just can't, not tonight. I'm flying out to Los Angeles this evening."

His chin lowers to his chest, and he looks... defeated. "Are you going to see him?"

His words are so low, they're barely audible.

"Yes, but..."

He holds up his hand, cutting off my words. "Don't. Do not say you're just friends."

I've seen Ciaran and all his many sides — the fun carefree prankster, the loyal friend, the protector, the hopeless romantic — but never, ever have I seen this side. He looks as though he's seconds away from saying fuck this shit. It's there, brewing in his irises, burning with bright green jealousy. I don't deserve a guy like him; I know that. He loves with every bone in his body, and even though it might not look like it, I do care about him, more than he knows.

"We *are* just friends. Nothing more."

Standing to his feet, he shoves his hands through his hair. "The same way we're just friends, right?"

"No, it's not like..."

He paces up and down the length of my office. "I see the way he looks at you, Lily. It's the same way I look at you and that, that can never be a just friend's relationship. You're kidding yourself if you think otherwise. I am telling you right now, if you gave him the opportunity, he'd stick his dick in you faster than you could say condom."

I stand in front of him, forcing him to look at me. "Ciaran, what he thinks is irrelevant, I've told him, friendship is all I can offer. I'm not looking for a relationship, and if I was, it wouldn't be with Jax St. Claire."

Cupping my cheeks in his palms, he begs me to prove him wrong. "Don't go then. Stay here with me. Fight for us, for once in your life, fight for me."

This right here, it's a pivotal moment. One wrong move and we will tumble down faster than a tower of Jenga. I wish I could give him what he needs, be the girl who gives it all up for love, but I can't. My career and my need for independence are crucial to my healing process. I have to learn how to stand on my own two feet.

Flying to Los Angeles has nothing to do with my friendship with Saint, it's strictly business-related. If I can get Sinners to sign on the dotted line, I am one step closer to where I want to be.

"I can't. This trip will further my career. Michael said if I get Sinners to move to Sham-Rock Recordz I can manage them. This is everything I've been working towards. I have to go. I can't let this opportunity pass. I need to grab it by the balls."

Tilting his head to the side, he forces me to drop my hands. "See that's the problem. You won't ever put me first. I get that you're working through shit, Lily. But there needs to be a time where you decide what the fuck it is you want. I've been more than patient with you. I've done everything your way. You needed time. I gave it to you. You needed space. I fucking moved to the far side of the world. For once, I wish you would give me what I need. Which is for my wife to choose me!"

He steps closer, closing the space between us. "When you sent me those divorce papers, I was ready to throw in the towel, but I couldn't, not without making sure what we had wasn't salvageable. So, I got on a plane and rearranged my life... for you. When I got here, I knew I made the right choice because I see it in your eyes, you love me, Lily. Stop lying to yourself and let this happen. There will be other opportunities, other bands you can sign. But this," he gestures between us. "This is once in a lifetime. So, what will it be, Lily? Flight or fight?"

Looking at him now, I know that his arms are strong enough to hold me through the fear, and his fingers, nimble enough to piece every broken part of me back together. Ciaran Maguire could be the one to heal me, but that would mean I would give up on healing myself. All the work, all the progress I've made, it would go to shit. I need to do this... for me. Loving him is easy, it always has been. Loving myself, that's where it gets hard. If I walk away from this deal now, I will lose the part of myself I've been working so hard for. It took everything I had to find me. I can't lose myself to love someone else. I just can't.

The lump in my throat grows with my rapid heartbeat, swallowing it down, I stare at the boy who held me in the dark, the man who made me believe I was worth saving, and I do the hardest thing I've ever had to do. I break his heart.

"I'm sorry, Ciaran. I'm so, so sorry, but I can't. You're right, I love you. I can't deny that, not anymore. I love you so much, it scares the crap out of me. I want to fight for us, but I also need to fight for myself. For the little girl inside of me who needs to be strong and stand on her own two feet. I need to become the woman I needed growing up. I can't give up my independence for a man. It's too important."

"Why did you marry me? Why promise me forever if you weren't going to try?"

"It's not like that. I didn't jump into this on a whim. I wanted this. I still want this. But you have to understand, if I walk away from this record deal, I will lose the girl I've fought so hard to become. I need this, I need to breathe air that isn't supplied by your love. You give me wings, Ciaran, but if I don't do this, I'll never learn how to fly."

His teeth sink into his lower lip, and he swallows back the tears forming in his eyes. His eyes close briefly, and I know that this is it, the end before we even have begun.

Without another word, he turns and walks away, leaving me to wonder if I just made the biggest mistake of my life.

CHAPTER TWENTY

UNLOVING YOU BY ALEX AIONO

CIARAN

I'm done. No matter how hard I want to fight, I can't anymore. I'm bowing out and waving my proverbial white flag.

There was a time I thought I'd chase Lilyanna O'Shea to the ends of the earth and back again, but now, I don't know what to do or where to go.

I never felt this kind of deflation before. How is it, I can give her everything, and still, she can't see me?

I'm done begging her to stay, hopelessly pleading with her to choose me for once.

It's exhausting, for years we have been repeating the same pattern, over and over, rinse and repeat. It's my fault, I made her my priority; when to her, I was the second choice.

I will always be put after her need for growth, and although that is not necessarily a bad thing, it still fucking stings because I can't compete with her unabated need to save herself.

I wish she would just fucking see that I want to help her, I want to walk beside her on her road to freedom. I want to be the man she leans on when the load gets too much for her to bear.

There is a part of me that wants to hate her for always pulling away, but I can't. Her resilience, determination, and strength are all reasons as to why I love her so fucking much.

She is the strongest person I've ever met and the fact that she's unaware of how strong she is, makes her unbreakable. Most people run from their demons, but not my Lily Bug. No, she looks her shadows in the eye and says, come at me fuckers, let's see what you got. She is not afraid to fight for the light she seeks, and for that, I admire her even more.

Unfortunately for me, I fell for a girl who doesn't need a counterpart to feel strong, she has got this all on her own. I wish I had a choice, but I don't. Loving Lilyanna O'Shea isn't something I have a say in, it just... is. It didn't happen overnight, instead, it snuck up on me, slowly pulling me under and capturing my heart piece by piece. Until one day, I realised there was no escaping. Love is not a Netflix subscription, you can't just cancel it because you don't want to pay the price, no that fucker is a life sentence, and me, I am a prisoner to it.

No matter what I do, how much distance I put between us, she's tattooed onto my skin, both literally and figuratively. Call me an idiot, because I'm a fool for loving someone who is so emotionally unavailable, but the fact of the matter is, it will always be her. I am hers. I was put on this earth to love her and all her fragmented pieces. That might sound fucking ridiculous, but it's the truth, I feel it in my soul. It's in the way I calm her restless storm when the darkness threatens to pull her under. I know her, and not just the silly surface stuff, but on a deeper level. We are connected by something powerful.

Without her, I have nothing to fight for.

Walking away from her is the hardest thing I've ever done, but it was necessary. She needs that push, the now or never ultimatum, otherwise, she will continue to fight me at every turn. I need her to push against the fear of falling, to want to fight for something bigger than herself.

Then there's Saint, I don't know what is going on between them, but the jealousy that rushed through me was untamable. I hate that he gets pieces of her when she hides them away from me. I despise that she can lean on him and not feel like she is losing a part of herself. What I don't understand is, how? What has he got that I don't? Why is it that she can run to him when it's me who is waiting to catch her? All these fucking thoughts that I can't process because she won't stay in place long enough for me to ask.

Putting my Jeep in park, I stare out at the empty grave-yard in front of me. Coming here wasn't part of the plan, but after I left Lily's office my body went into autopilot mode. It's been too long since I stepped foot inside the black iron gates of St. Margaret's Cemetery, but the tug in my chest is all too familiar. Drawing in a deep breath, I grip the handle and pop the door open. My feet carry me, step by step, past all the faceless names on the headstones, until finally, I'm where I need to be.

"Hi, Ma." Sitting on the grass surrounding her graveside, I wrap my hands around my knees. "Sorry, it's been so long. Life, well it's been busy. Conor and I, we moved to Los Angeles for a bit." My fingers itch with uneasiness, restlessly seeking for something to do.

I always found this kind of thing weird, talking to a stone in hopes that she can hear me, wherever she may be. I'm not saying I don't believe in heaven. It's just, I don't know what that looks like and it's hard for me to envision it in my mind.

When we were younger, Dad would bring us here, every

Wednesday without fail. Wednesday was my ma's favourite day. She'd always say: midweek means the worst has past, and now, we have something to look forward to. It's always good to look forward, Ciaran, that way when it does come, we appreciate it more.

I guess somewhere in the old man's mind, he tried to keep her alive in whatever way he could. Even now, he comes every week, no exception. My eyes fall to a bunch of daisies resting in an outdoor vase in front of her headstone, the petals slightly damaged from a week's worth of weathering. A small chuckle leaves me, she hated those flowers, but Dad being Dad, always got them for her. I don't know whether he liked pushing her buttons, or if he just enjoyed the sassy eye-roll that she gave him when he brought her another fresh bunch. Daisy Eva Maguire kept my old man on his toes, he spent half of their marriage apologising for annoying the shit out of her, and she spent the other half loving him all the more for it.

They had the kind of relationship everyone around them envied. They were best friends until the bitter end. Dad, he never fully got over the loss of my ma. When I asked him why, he told me he could have moved on, but what he had with my ma, only ever comes around once in a lifetime. She was his everything, the only person who accepted him and all his flaws, without complaint. "You're a lot like her, you know," he once said. "You see the best in everyone, and you gravitate towards the most broken of souls. She was always trying to save everyone around her, so much so, when the time came, she had no energy left to save herself."

I never really understood what he meant by that, to me, my da has always been strong and resilient, but apparently, that wasn't always the case. Before my ma, he had a storage unit full of issues to unpack and she stayed by his side, helping him sift through every box. I suppose that's where I got my hero complex from, and maybe why I'm so drawn to Lily. History sure has a habit of repeating itself, right down to the sassy girl with a flower name.

Shifting forward, I pull the few stray weeds creeping up underneath the pebbles. "I'd say da already told you this, but I got married last year. One-year-ago today. You're probably wondering why I'm sitting here, and not spending my anniversary with my wife... well, things between us, they're complicated." *If you could even call it that.*

"Over the years, I may have mentioned her a time or twenty. Her name is Lily. You'd love her, she is feisty and independent, just like you once were. The thing is Ma, I have been fighting for her, for us, for years and I've been getting nowhere. Every time I break through one of her barriers, another one pops up in its place. How do I know when to say, enough is enough?" Staying silent, I wait for a reply I know won't come, but still, the need for my ma's sage advice burns stronger than ever.

"Please, Ma, tell me how to un-love her? Cause this stalemate, it's a slow dance to hell. I don't think I can do it anymore, but there is a part of me that knows, I'll never fully let her go either." *Take a deep breath, Ciaran. Count with me... one, two, three, four.*

I inhale, holding the air in my lungs then release it with a heavy sigh. I repeat over and over until finally, my erratic heart slows to a steady beat. Resting my forehead on my knees, I seek the answers to my impossible question. "What do I do, Ma? I'm at a loss here, standing at a crossroad, and not knowing where it is, I have to turn. If by any chance you can hear me, please, tell me what I am supposed to do."

Seconds pass and nothing, not that I was expecting her voice to suddenly whisper the words I need to hear. Things like that, they don't happen in real life. My ma is gone, she is not here to help me choose which path to take, or even beat my ass for taking a wrong turn. It's time to face the fact, I need to be the one to make the choice, either continue to fight or let her go. Either way, I've got to pick one, cause this limbo we're in, it's not healthy for either of us.

Standing, I brush the grass off my back pockets and bring my fingers to my lips to kiss them, then place them on the top of my mother's headstone. "Good chat, Ma. Love you."

As I walk towards the gate, a flash of white catches my eye. Right there, lying beneath the large, outdoor, grandfather clock is a daisy. I shake my head in disbelief, closing my eyes only to reopen them and find it's still there.

Time, Ciaran. Give her time.

CHAPTER TWENTY-ONE

SHOULDN'T OF SAID IT BY JULIA MICHAELS

LILY

THIS CONSTANT BATTLE BETWEEN MY HEAD AND MY heart is back breaking, no matter what I choose, I lose something or someone.

Ciaran caught me off guard.

I wasn't expecting him to show up at my office, and I certainly wasn't ready for him to throw down an ultimatum, but instead of running into his open arms, I fled.

I've done a lot of soul-searching in the last year. Weekly therapy sessions, along with daily meditations, have helped me deal with a lot of my issues. I'm stronger now; I'm not the same girl I was in Vegas. Sure, I still have cracks, and more triggers than I care to admit to, but slow progress is still progress.

I know what you're thinking, in my fight for self-love, I've become selfish. But, is putting myself first really that bad? Does choosing myself make me a bitch? It really shouldn't. Every woman on this planet should put herself first because she's all she has. Nobody should ever love you more than you love yourself. I'm not talking about appearance — although that's important too — but on a deeper, soul level.

When Ciaran walked out of my office, my heart plummeted to the deep end, and suddenly I was drowning in a sea of regret. For the first time in a long time, I wasn't sure if I was making the right choice. I could see it on his face, the look of defeat, he's had enough.

I suppose I had it coming. Ciaran has been waiting for me for too long, sooner or later, he was bound to reach his breaking point. I hurt him, and believe it or not, that's the last thing I ever wanted to do.

The world seems to be turning, but it's never in our favour. Our timing has never been right—the constant push and pulls' detrimental to both of us. In my search for myself, I've lost the one person who makes all this fighting worthwhile.

There isn't a doubt in my heart that Ciaran is the endgame, but right now, my mind is still at half-time. Sure,

I've been working on myself for a long time, but it's a process.

Mental and emotional scars don't heal overnight; they fade with time and patience.

I can't pretend those years of suppression and abuse don't exist, because they do. It's up to me to unpack, to sort through the shit and decide what to let go of, so I can finally move on.

I'm so close to the finish line, and if I drop the ball now, I'll be right back at the beginning. I'm sure I sound like a broken record, but it's the truth. I'm constantly battling between what I want and what I need.

Ciaran Maguire has the power to make me feel worthy, to crave the happy ending he promises, but I don't want to depend on him to feel love. I don't want to become this needy, insecure person who is entirely out of touch with herself. But maybe, just maybe, there is another way—a way where we can hold on to ourselves while holding onto each other.

I stuff all the paperwork I need into my briefcase, gently place the music box into the gift bag, grab my handbag, and finally rush from my office with full arms, and a mind full of what next's?

Once I get to my car, I pull out my iPhone and dial Saint's personal number. The overseas dial tone rings and rings, and then his broad, melodic, SoCal accent floods through my Bluetooth.

"Hey, Pretty Lady. It's 4 AM, is everything okay?"

Wincing at my ignorance, I apologise. "Shit, I'm sorry. I forgot to check the time difference."

There is a lot that people don't know about Saint. He comes across as this cocky, arrogant Rockstar, but deep down he lives in a world of hurt. Music is his lifeline; the only thing keeping him from submerging into a very dark place. He reminds me of my brother, Cillian — except his vice isn't alcohol. It's sex, drugs, and rock n' roll.

The music industry is a very dark place, and it's easy to fall down the rabbit hole and never re-emerge. Saint, he walks along the edge, one step from falling. He found me when he needed a friend, someone he could be himself with, someone who wouldn't judge him and his habits. He's a straight shooter with no filter, and those are qualities that I admire. We've become close over the years, and after Rosie and Ciaran, Saint's my best friend. That's why this career move is crucial to both of us.

His current manager doesn't give two fucks about the band and their mental health. He's all about the money. With me, I put my clients first. If they need downtime, they get it. If they have personal issues, we find solutions because, at the end of the day, their health is all that matters. Being the professional I am, I put my difference with Remi aside and offered Sinners a contract they couldn't refuse.

"Why did you pick up? Can't sleep?"

His touch of laughter is forced and almost sarcastic. "You know me; sleep is not my friend. Anyway, as much as I love hearing from you, is there a reason for this impromptu phone call? I've got a hot blonde laying in my bed, and I need a snack. And by snack, I mean her pu—"

Rolling my eyes at his crassness, I cut him off before he can finish, "You're a pig."

"But you love me anyway. So, what's up? I wasn't expecting to hear from you until tomorrow. Are we still on for dinner?"

"Bout that, I'm not..." The words lodge in my throat, but with a deep breath, I'm able to continue. "I'm not coming to L.A. Something came up."

"Hang on, let me get my smokes."

I hear shuffling and what sounds like a door opening, before a click and a deep inhale. "Has this got somethin' to do with Ciaran? A little tattooed birdie told me he was back in Ireland, and by little, I mean Cian."

Before I know it, I spill today's event's down the line, telling him all about Ciaran and his attempt at salvaging what's left of our marriage, and how I threw it back in his face.

"Shit, Pretty Lady. That's hella heavy. What are you going to do?"

"Honestly, I don't know. All I know is if I get on that plane. I'll lose him — for good this time."

"I get it, do whatever it is you have to do. Look, I'll speak to the rest of the guys; I know they're all for jumping ship. It's just a matter of signing the papers, and that can wait for a few weeks. Our contract is up at the end of August, so as long as it's before then, we should be golden."

"Sorry for all this messing around, I would never usually mix my personal life with business, but this, it's too important. I'll call Olivia now and have her send the contracts directly to you. I'll be free to fly out at the end of the month, and we can go through any issues you have then. Is that okay?"

"Of course, babe. Now, fuck off and get your man. I'll expect an invitation to your second wedding at the end of the week."

"Har-Har, very funny. I'll call you later, once I get a handle on all this other stuff."

"No stress. Later, Pretty Lady."

🍀

I'VE CALLED CIARAN AT LEAST TEN TIMES, AND nothing, just a full voicemail. So, here I am, standing at his front door, hoping his dad knows where I can find him. I knock, then hold my breath. Finally, the door swings open, giving a full view of an older version of Ciaran.

"Well, if it isn't my favourite daughter-in-law," Dave Maguire greets me with a smile similar to his sons. "Come on in."

Stepping over the threshold, I look over my shoulder and watch as he closes the door behind me.

"How many times have we been over this, Dave? I'm your only daughter-in-law."

"Even if you weren't, you'd still be my favourite." With a wink, he strides past me towards the kitchen. Following his lead, my eyes briefly scan the numerous photographs hanging on the hallway wall, each picture telling a different story.

"Tea?"

Taking a seat at the small round table, I pick at my acrylic nails. "Emm, yeah. Sure. Two sugars and just a splash of milk, please."

Placing the hot mug of sweet tea in front of me, he takes a seat on the far side and raises his brow. "So, I take it you're looking for my son?"

"Am I that obvious?"

Deep gruff laughter escapes him. "Hate to break it to you, kid, but yeah, you are. It's been a while since you've been in this house, and with the way Ciaran has been stomping around, I figured you two disagreed on something. Not that that's a new development."

Avoiding his sharp glare, I lift my cup to my lips and swallow a mouthful of tea.

"So, what did he do now?" His emerald eyes watch me as I mull over his question.

"It's not a matter of what he did. It's more what he didn't do that's the problem." Making eye contact, I spill out all my frustration. "You know, it's been a year since I left Vegas. A whole year, and just when I start to gather my shit and put everything behind me, he shows up like no time has passed, demanding we give whatever the hell this thing between us is, another shot."

"Lily, I don't think he meant to stay away as long as he did, but Conor, he was in a dark place. He needed Ciaran to keep him afloat. Ciaran being the type of person he is, he put his life on hold to help his brother. Then you served him those papers, and he panicked. He doesn't want to lose you, darling, so he came out all guns blazing. When he was away, he called me every day, without fail. Mostly to see how I was doing and if I needed anything. But not once did he hang up without asking about you. He may have kept his distance, but he never forgot Lily, not for a second."

My eyes close, holding back the tears welling in my eyes. "I don't... I don't want to lose him either. I just don't know how to balance it all."

The corners of his lips lift into a sad smile. "Can I give you some fatherly advice?"

"Sure."

"My wife, she once told me communication was the key to all lasting relationships. At the time, I thought it was all a crock of shit, her way of getting me to open up about my messy past. But, after a couple of late-night talks, I let her in. That woman, she knew me inside out — every demon, every insecurity, every doubt. Everybody has flaws, Lily, but when we choose to share our weaknesses with the person we love, it makes us stronger. If you're in love with my son, open up and let him in. If you need more time, let him know. I promise he'll understand. All he wants is to be a part of your life, but until you two talk, you won't know what that looks like. Relationships, they come in all shapes and sizes, sit down, talk, and figure out what's best for both of you."

"How do I do that when he doesn't return my calls? I've spent the entire day looking for him, and he's ignoring me."

It's hard to decipher the look on his face, eye wide, brows raised, and lips drawn in tight. "What's the one thing you've been asking him for?"

The answer seems obvious now. "Time."

"Yes, kid. Give him some time. I know my son. Where Conor is withdrawn and broody, Ciaran is heart first, head later. Give him some space, not too much, but just enough to let him breathe. He'll come to you when he's ready."

CHAPTER TWENTY-TWO

MY OWN HERO BY ANDY GRAMMER

LILY

I HAVE EVERYTHING I NEED, AND BY EVERYTHING, I mean a jar of Nutella with 33% extra free, a giant bowl of popcorn, and my fluffy unicorn onesie.

Oh, and let's not forget, my Vampire Diaries box-set — season one through three because let's face it, the only team I'm on is Stefan's.

Call me Nicole Scherzinger, cause baby, I don't need a man.

Okay, so I'm feeling sorry for myself, but who are you to judge me? It's my day off, and if I want to spend it curled up watching TV with my best friend, that's what I'll do.

It's been five days since Ciaran left my office, five days of complete and utter radio silence. He's serving me a dose of my own medicine, and I don't like it, not one bit.

Am I ridiculous? Absolutely!

Is my pity-party warranted? To fucking right it is.

Stuffing a large handful of popcorn into my mouth, I mock him to make myself feel better. "Hey everyone, my name is Ciaran Maguire, my hobbies include being difficult and ignoring Lily's texts for no reason."

"You doin' okay, Lily?"

My eyes avert to my best friend, who's sitting on the worn leather armchair beside the fireplace. Side-eyeing her from my sprawled-out position on the couch, I chuck a popcorn kernel at her. "If you want to judge me and my moping session, you can remove yourself. This —" I motion around my living room. "— is a no-judgment zone. Well, unless you direct it at a certain drummer, then and only then, I'll allow it."

Rosie sits up, and rests her elbows on her knees, giving me a sad smile. "I take it Ciaran hasn't text you back yet?"

"Nope, and I don't need you to feel sorry for me, either. I'm doing a stellar job of that myself."

"Did you tell him you didn't go to LA?"

"Nope."

"What did you say then?"

Picking up my phone, I chuck it towards her armchair.

Luckily for me, she catches it — the last thing I need is a broken screen to go along with my broken heart.

Did I mention how petty I am right now? No? Okay, I'm incredibly petty.

The audacity of Ciaran and his Houdini act has me reeling.

I place the popcorn on the table, grab my Nutella and listen as Rosie reads my texts aloud.

"Okay so, let's start with Monday evening."

Lily: Call me. It's important.

Lily: Ciaran, please call me. I need to talk to you.

Rosie looks up at me with her bright blue eyes. "Okay, so they aren't too bad. I was expecting worse."

"See, I told you. I even said, please."

I dig my spoon into the jar of Nutella and encourage her. "Keep going."

"Okay, so let's see. Tuesday at 21:43."

Lily: The purpose of a text message is to get a speedy response. If I

wanted to wait days, I would have sent my messenger pigeon.

Rosie snorts. "Well, at least you were direct. Moving on, Wednesday at 18:06."

Lily: Don't mind me; I'm just exercising my fingers.

Covering her mouth with her hand, Rosie holds back her laughter. "I... ha, I can sense your frustration, it's growing with every word."

"Laugh it off, asshole."

"Ten points for creativity, though. If you sent me that, I'd have to text back."

"I know, right? He's infuriating, not even an emoji."

Shovelling another spoonful of chocolaty goodness into my mouth, I watch as she scrolls down while wiping tears from her eyes. Her shoulders silently chuckle as she fights back her impending laughter "Thurs, ha, Thursday at 15:47."

Lily: Did you know that there are roughly 171,476 words in the English

language? Maybe try using any of those to TEXT ME F&%k!N BACK!

Raising her hand, she holds the phone up so I can see it as she points to the screen with her index finger. "I love that you bleeped the fucking, very classy. Also, did you google that fact?"

"Of course, I did. You can't win an argument with false information. Always fact check, Rosie. Google is our friend."

"You're something else, do you know that?"

With a lift of my shoulders, I retract my neck and sink it into my chest, giving her an adorable view of my triple chin, then I add a creepy smile for effect.

"Why are you so weird?"

Sticking my tongue out, I grab my popcorn and wait for her to continue. "Hurry up! We're at the part where Stefan calls Elena from the car park, and guess what Rosie, SHE PICKS UP! I need those feelings, Rosie. I need to see her answer the damn phone."

"Jeez, keep your knickers on; today at 04:53." Her gaze flicks to mine. "Wait, why are you texting him at that hour?"

"Really?" I ask. "He hasn't texted me back for days, and you're worried I woke him up."

"Valid."

Lily: Hey? What's up?

Lily: Oh, nothing, you know, just chillin' wbu?

Lily: Oh, same, how crazy is that.

Lily: Any plans for the weekend?

Lily: Nah! Not really, kinda tied up with something.

Lily: Oh yeah, what?

Lily: WAITING FOR MY HUSBAND TO TEXT ME THE FUCK BACK!

Lily: Do you remember that time I forgot to text you back for like a year? Well, if you text me back, I won't forget again.

Lily: Text me back, I dare you.

"That one is my personal favourite," I state. "It was the most thrilling conversation I've ever had with myself."

The phone buzzes in her hand and time all but stops. "Is it him?"

Rosie freezes, her eyes darting between me and the phone. "I don't know."

"Well, can you check? The suspense is killing me."

I wait with bated breath as she ever so fucking slowly glances at my home screen.

"Well?"

"It's your Ma. She wants to know if you turned off the immersion?"

"Of course, I did." *Did I?*

"You don't look too sure."

"Yeah, maybe I should double-check."

🍀

"You two disgust me. Can you please take all your PDA somewhere else? My retinas are burning. I can't take it anymore."

I'm teasing. I adore that my brother finally pulled his head out of his ass long enough to get the girl. Anyone with functioning eyeballs can see their love for one another. Rosie is the Yang to Cillian's Yin, the light to his dark, they complete each other in every way, and it's revoltingly cute.

Cillian's eyes catch mine over Rosie's shoulder, and he winks. This morning, while Rosie and I were hosting my pity-party, he was out, putting together the finishing touches for his surprise proposal. It's been a long time coming, and I don't doubt by the end of the weekend, Rosie will be well on her way to becoming my sister-in-law.

Kissing the tip of Rosie's head, Cillian turns his attention back to me. "Any word on Ciaran?"

"Nope. Have any of the lads heard from him?"

"Nah, Conor said he was heading west for a few days, but he hasn't spoken to him since he left on Monday. Cian is like an anti-Christ. He's missed two recording sessions."

It's not like Ciaran to go MIA, sure he's the prankster of the foursome, but he's dependable. He hates letting anyone down, it's not in him.

"I'm sure he'll show up, eventually."

My mind wanders back to Monday, and the look on Ciaran's face as he left my office was so broken. I know I'm responsible for him taking time away, but fuck, if he just answered his phone when I called, we could have avoided this hurt.

Regret washes over me like raging waves attacking a shoreline. If I could go back, back to the moment Ciaran begged me to stay, I'd tell him I chose him.

I'd ask him if he'd be willing to stand by my side while I figure out how to wage through all my internal struggles.

Deep down, I know I'm not ready to fully commit to an adult relationship, but maybe if we communicate, talk it out, we can pave a way that leads to that.

Over the last few days, I've admitted to myself that it's Ciaran. There are no other options; there never was. Selfishly, I made him feel like a back-up plan when, in reality, he's the only plan. I was so consumed with finding myself that I forgot why I was doing it — to be happy and free, to love without fear, and mostly to love myself enough to give love to another.

Shaking those thoughts away, my eyes wander to Cillian and Rosie cuddled together in the armchair. I want what they have, a love so consuming it marks your soul. When they're together, the rest of the world fades away, and it's a beautiful sight.

Placing the empty popcorn bowl on the table, I stand to leave.

Rosie looks up from her nestled spot against Cillian. "Where are you going? We still have three more episodes left."

The house phone cuts me off before I can make up a reasonable excuse to leave them to it.

"Who the hell is that?" Cillian questions. "That phone hasn't rung in years, the only reason we still have it is for the WiFi."

I shrug my shoulders and head to the small table in the corner of the living room to pick up the landline. "Hello?"

"Hey, Firecracker. It's so good to hear your voice." My da's voice echoes through the phone, and suddenly everything around me blurs. My emotions shut down, and I become cold, fearful, anxious. The need to back away, or even better, flee, is almost too much to bear. Suddenly I fail to be the warrior I was born to be, the strong woman who can handle anything. Instead, I show the frightened child inside me, damaged and afraid, still hiding in the dark under her bed, awaiting the next beating, the next advance, the next horrifying moment. Thoughts accelerate inside my head, I want them to slow down so I can breathe, but they won't. My breath comes out in gasps as images flash like a video montage through my mind. *Make it stop. Stop, daddy. Stop!*

All the memories, giving tiny snippets of a past I had buried before blending into another. I can't quite grasp one particular moment, the anxiety rips through my veins, leaving me burning from the inside out. *Make it stop!*

My heart hammers inside my chest like a jackhammer, chipping away at everything I've worked so hard on. The room spins, and I squat on the floor, trying to make everything around me slow down. The demons grip my throat, cutting off what's left of my air supply. I'm vaguely aware of

Rosie's arms wrapping me up and keeping me safe. *He can't get me. He can't get me.*

Her gentle voice whispers words, but I can't hear them, all I hear is the sound of my fear, thumping in my eardrums and pulling me under, undoing everything I've become.

Placing my hands over my ears, I try to silence my thoughts. "Stop! I'm safe. I'm secure. I am safe. I am secure."

Cillian appears before me, kneeling on the worn, carpeted floor. His lips are moving, but I can't hear him over the white noise. His hands move back and forth, just like the tide. Ebb and flow. In and out. In and out.

"Ciaran." One word falls from my lips like a plea, but it's the only one I need.

Ciaran, I need you.

CHAPTER TWENTY-THREE

BACKUP PLAN BY PLESTED

CIARAN

"WHERE THE FUCK HAVE YOU BEEN?" CIAN'S LARGER than life frame takes up most of the space in my tiny living-room.

Can't a man take a few days to gather his fucking shit without an interrogation?

My Granny Bridy lives on the west coast, just outside of Westport, so I went there to clear my head. I spent the entire week moping around like someone kicked my puppy, while she force-fed me soda bread and apple tart 'til it came out my ears. It's been years since I sat down and had a hearty

Irish dinner, but if there's one thing my Granny does right, it's ham and cabbage with creamy mash.

She was delighted to see me, but that doesn't mean she didn't threaten me with the wooden spoon for being, and I quote, a sexist pig with old fashioned values. When I told her what I said to Lily before she left for Los Angeles, the eighty-two-year-old beat me with a tea-towel. I'm not joking, she chased me down the hall like I was a bold child.

"Hello to you, too." Dropping my duffel bag in the entryway, I stride into the open plan living room and vault over the couch, landing next to my brother Conor. Wrapping my tattooed arm around his broad shoulders, I pull him closer to my chest. "Hey, Bro, are you doing okay?"

He runs his hand through his shoulder-length hair, before nodding his reply with a quick dip of his chin.

Conor has always been a man of few words, but after everything that happened last year, he's become worse. Most days, I have to drag the conversation out of him. I could go into detail, but that's his story to tell.

When we were kids, Conor and I were identical, but over the years we've changed slightly. Although you'd know we were related, people can tell the difference. We've developed our own, individual style — Conor has that hipster-hobo look, where I am a clean-cut babyface, with punk rock vibes. The most significant difference is our hair, mine is slightly long and dyed ink-black, where he sports our natural shade of ashy blonde and falls around his face in wild waves. Our eyes are identical in hue, but Conor's, they lack life, muted by the hand God dealt him.

Reaching toward my black army-style boots, I grip the heels and pull them off. "I needed a few days to myself, is that too much to ask?"

Cian's steel grey eyes narrow. "No, it's not, but next time, take your fucking phone with you. In between babysitting his ass —" he points at Conor "— and my sister constantly asking if I've heard from you, I feel like your secretary. There's also the matter of the recording sessions you missed. We've got a tour in November, and we've no new tracks. How we'll ever be ready is beyond me, nobody gives a shit. Cillian is busy planning his proposal, and you're disappearing."

"Look, I'm here now." Jumping from my seat, I grab my bag and pull out my black leather notebook. Throwing it into Cian's lap, I gesture for him to open it. "I even got some lyrics down. Cillian will have to tune them a little, but they're relatively good."

He opens the black leather laces that keep my notebook together and flips it to the last few pages covered in ink.

I don't have a problem with her wicked games,
her ever-changing rulebook or the way she plays.
I don't have an issue with her tryna find,

herself among the ashes of her childhood mind.

All I have,
and all I see,
is a lifetime of moments,
where she lovin' me.
All I want,
and all I need,
is to be the man on which she leans.

Oh, she wants to free herself.
Oh, she needs no one else.
Oh, I'm tryna make her see,
she may not need a hero, but she's getting me.

I don't have a problem with the power-crazed,
sassy execution of her crazy ways.
I don't have an issue with her tryna free,
her overthinking mind from all the misery.

Oh, she wants to free herself.
Oh, she needs no one else.
Oh, I'm tryna make her see,
she may not need a hero, but she's getting me.

All I have,

and all I see,
is a lifetime of moments,
where she lovin' me.
All I want,
and all I need,
is to be the man on which she leans.

Oh, she's a queen on her throne,
Oh, she wants to rule alone.
Oh, but what she doesn't see,
she's a prisoner of her kingdom,
And I'll set her free.
Oh, I'm tryna make her see,
she may not need a hero, but she's getting me.

"It's good. How do you hear it?"

"Electric guitar counting in the intro with a steady 4/4 bar strum. Then kick in with a heavy drum beat and a wicked bass line for 12 measures. Add in the vocals and keep it edgy."

Cian looks down at the lyrics as he envisions a melody. His head bobs to a non-existent tune, as each note forms in his mind.

When he flicks his steel greys back to mine, a wide Chester smile highlights his face. "Magic, Ciaran. Fucking magic."

❧

Gunshots blast through the surround sound as the Xbox controller vibrates against my palm. "What a wanker! I shot you first."

Conor's deep chuckle shakes the two-seater as he basks in Cian's victory. "Call of Duty is not your thing, Ciaran. Don't sweat it, there's always Mario Kart."

"You're right, Con. Princess Peach is more his speed."

Lifting one of the throw-pillows, I chuck it at Cian's head. "Just 'cause you're a jammy bastard, doesn't mean the rest of us are. Anyway, you spent the entire game camping in the corner, so shut it."

Cian's phone vibrates against the glass coffee table and Cillian's face lights up the screen. Leaning forward, he swipes the screen and puts the call on speaker.

"What's up?"

"Cian, please, tell me you've heard from Ciaran?"

The panic in his voice has me sitting up and reaching for the phone. "Hey, I'm here, what's wrong?"

"Thank fuck. You need to get here now. Lily, fuck. I don't know what's wrong, Ciaran. I think she's having a panic attack. She needs you." The rest of his words blur, all I hear is, Lily, panic attack, she needs you. Keeping the phone on speaker, I toss it onto the chair beside me as I pull on my boots. He continues to tell me what happened, but nothing registers.

"Tell her to count. Tell her I'm on the way, and to count for me, okay?"

"What the fuck does that mean?"

"Just do it, Cillian," I bark. *Keys, where the fuck are my keys?* "She'll know what it means. Tell her to count out loud."

Cillian's voice seems further away like he's pulled the phone from his face.

"Snow? Tell her to count. Ciaran wants her to count."

"Out loud, she needs to do it out loud."

Frantic, I pat down my pockets, and lift all the couch cushions, searching for my jeep keys.

Suddenly, Conor tosses me his bike keys. "Here! Take the bike, you'll be quicker."

"Thanks."

"I'm on the way. Tell her I'm coming." The words fly from my mouth as I rush out the door.

❧

COMING TO A STOP OUTSIDE LILY'S HOUSE, I KICK DOWN the side stand, pull off Conor's helmet and race up the narrow drive with my heart pounding in my chest. After ringing the doorbell, I shove my hands into my jean pockets and bounce on the balls of my feet, impatiently waiting for the door to open.

The door swings, and Cillian stands there, ready to attack whoever is on the other side. "Jesus, Cillian. Put the hurl down. Who do you think you are, Cú Chulainn?"

Looking over his shoulder, my eyes land on my heart. Any other time, I'd laugh at her and her ridiculous unicorn onesie, but now, she looks so fucking fragile, and it kills me. At that moment, I don't just see her, I feel her. Every ounce of her pain, sorrow, and despair floods through my veins. My strong, fierce, wife has shattered, maybe beyond repair. Her tear-filled eyes find me through the darkness, and she comes running into my open arms. Lifting her off her feet, I let her wrap every inch of her trembling frame around me.

"You came?" Two words, but they pierce my lungs.

How can she still doubt me? Haven't I proven, over and over that I'm going nowhere?

"I told you, Lily Bug, no matter what, you need me... I'll be here, anytime, day or night."

Her arms tighten around the back of my neck as she holds onto me like a lifeline.

Nestling my head into her neck, I promise her, I'll keep her safe. I won't let anyone hurt her, not even the demons in her mind. "Stay with me, LB. I'm here. I got you."

Walking over to the armchair with Lily still in my arms,

I lower us both onto the soft, brown leather and pull her into my chest. Her wild hair tickles my face, but I don't care.

"Do you remember what I told you the night we got married?" I ask, needing her to remember. "I told you, my arms are your sanctuary and your shelter, and that when I have you wrapped within them, you're the safest you'll ever be. Do you remember that, LB?"

"I remember." Her words are so soft, so low, if I weren't paying attention, I would have missed them.

Hours pass and Lily hasn't moved an inch. She's clutching my t-shirt as her silent sobs soak the cotton material. Now and again, I whisper in her ear, letting her know I have her. Meanwhile, Cillian is trashing the house, and drowning his feelings at the bottom of any bottle he can get his hands on. He's a mess.

Lifting the near-empty bottle of vodka to his lips, he swigs it back then drops it to the table and grabs his keys. "Fuck this shit."

Panic lines Rosie's face as she pleads with him not to go. "You can't drive like that, you're pissed."

"Whether you think this is a good idea or not, I'm going to find him. He needs to know he can't hurt my family, not anymore. I'm not the same kid he used to slap around. I'm a grown man who won't hesitate when it comes to putting his pathetic ass down."

I've known Cillian a long time, and I've never seen him

this worked up, but Rosie is right, he's fucking hammered. There's no way in hell he can drive and even less chance of me letting him.

Rising from the chair with Lily's tangled limbs still wrapped around me, I lower her back onto the chair and brush the damp strands of hair off her face. "I need to stop your brother from making the biggest mistake of his life. I'll be as quick as I can. Then, I'll be right back, okay?"

She nods in acknowledgement.

"I promise you are safe."

Gently, I place my lips against her forehead, then turn towards one of my best friends. "If you're determined to do this, I'm coming with you. And before you get any ideas, I'm driving. Rosie is right, you can't get behind the wheel like that. I'm not prepared to lose someone else because some drunk dickhead got behind the wheel."

I knew my words would hit him hard, and I'm not surprised when he hands the keys over.

"Fine, just don't try and stop me. This —" his eyes flick to his sister "— it needs to end tonight."

Leaving him to say goodbye to Rosie, I hunker down in front of Lily and take her hands in mine. "I love you, Lily. Even in the dark."

CHAPTER TWENTY-FOUR

PAPER HEART BY EMILY JAMES

LILY

Do you ever just lay in bed and feel nothing?

No want, no desire to lift your head and greet the morning — not even with a middle finger — because you can't feel anything but the overbearing numbness of... nothing.

The last thirty-six hours have been a complete cluster fuck. The dominos were laid out, and one after the other, they tumbled — taking out everyone that stood in their wake.

While my world imploded, suffocating me beneath the ash and rubble of my life, my brother, Cillian, was busy burning his to ground. There was no stopping the aftermath of my da's release. One phone call gave way to the demise of Cillian's relationship, and almost his career, too.

Then there's me; I'm sinking so far down the rabbit hole, there's no way out. My thoughts are so fucking loud, they're deafening. Everything I've ever believed in has disintegrated along with the strength I thought I had.

I lift the neck of the black and yellow Nirvana hoodie I'm wearing to my nose, and Ciaran's signature scent fills my lungs, wrapping me up in a proverbial security blanket.

It's been three days, and Ciaran and I still need to address the giant elephant in the room. I know I am not mentally able to have that conversation, but it needs to happen, and soon.

Ciaran has barely left my side, other than to shower or eat, always lingering, making sure I'm okay. My answer remains the same — I'm fine.

Fine! Ha, what a load of shite.

If hurt, bruised, and irreparably shattered is the definition of fine, then yeah, I'm fucking dandy. When will we admit *I'm fine* is biggest lie we tell ourselves? Truthfully, I'm exhausted, so fucking bone-tired trying to emulate this strong, unbreakable person and it has me drained. Every ounce of my energy is depleted, my progress catapulted to somewhere out of my reach.

My life feels like a game of snakes and ladders. One

minute, I'm nearing the finish line, ready to tell my demons to suck it, then one wrong roll of the dice and I slide back to the start. Only this time, the desire to get up, brush off the dust, and roll again is non-existent.

People don't understand how stressful it is to explain what's going on inside your mind when you don't understand it yourself.

The bed beneath me shifts as Ciaran rolls over in his sleep. For two days straight, I don't think he so much as blinked, he's worn out, but he refuses to leave me.

I roll over onto my side to face him, and tuck both hands under my cheek. The duvet is wrapped around his waist, leaving his bare chest on full display. Every rise and fall of his ribcage, steadies my erratic heartbeat.

How do you do it? How does your presence alone bring me so much comfort?

Tattoos — everything from quotes, lyrics, lilies, and skulls — are sporadically placed on his arms, and on anyone else, they'd look ridiculous, but on him, they seem to fit. My eyes scan the sculpted lines and edges of his face, noting every minuscule detail. Even with his pouty mouth slightly agape and the tip of his tongue resting on his bottom lip, he's undeniably handsome. My fingers itch to touch him, to trace the countless beauty spots that decorate his otherwise flawless skin — especially the three on his left cheek. I don't do that though because he needs to sleep.

Carefully, I push the covers off myself, slide from the bed, and tiptoe to the door. I take one last look over my shoulder, at my husband, my heart, my hero, before leaving him to get some much-needed rest.

✤

THE BUBBLING FROM THE KETTLE BRINGS ME COMFORT as I sit in the darkness. With my elbows on the counter, I rest my head in my palms and inhale a deep breath.

Get it together, Lily.

Suddenly, the overhead light flickers on, illuminating the old-fashioned wooden kitchen and forcing my gaze to dart towards the doorway. There's a sad smile on my mother's face as she walks towards me tightening the belt of her blush coloured dressing gown. Reaching up, she pulls two mugs from the overhead press and places them beside the boiling kettle. "Can't sleep?"

I shake my head and swallow the lump in my throat.

Arms held open she takes a step towards me. "Come here."

I sink into her embrace, and she wraps me up in a motherly hug. Comfort consumes me, and without warning my tears start to fall.

"It's okay, sweetheart. Let it out."

"I thought," I hiccup. "I thought I'd dealt with this. I was so sure I was stronger. Then…" I sob harder, snotting all over her silk robe.

Blinking back the tears, I will them not to fall. "I am supposed to be strong. I'm supposed to have no fears. So why, why do my tears keep falling? If I am so fucking strong, why am I breaking down?"

Gripping my shoulders, she pulls back and searches my face. "Listen to me, darling. It is okay not to be okay. You don't need to be a pillar of strength all the time, you are human. Your emotions are real, chaotic, and deserve to be acknowledged. I know you are dealing with a lifetime of issues, and I'm so sorry I didn't shelter you from that. Believe me, it's my biggest regret. But, please, Lilyanna, don't desensitise to the world. Don't harden your heart to protect yourself. You have so much love to give, and once you learn how to love yourself, it will ripple out to everyone around you."

Pulling me closer, she rests her head on my shoulder. "What your father did, to you, to me, to Cillian, it's unworthy of your soul. Do not let him win, Lily. Claim your life back. Fight for your freedom. Show him you are the hellfire we all know you are. You are not a victim, darling. You are a warrior."

Her words register, but in reality, it's easier said than done. I've spent time and energy attending my therapy sessions, only to be set back by one fucking phone call. Is it worth it? How do I know if I'll ever get to the place I'm trying so desperately to reach? Simple answer, I don't. All I know is, I can't become the person I want to be by remaining who I am.

"Thanks, Ma. I love you. You know that right?"

"Of course I do. You may not always say it, but contrary to what you think, your emotions are always written on your face — the good, bad, and the sarcastic."

Sensing my need to wrap up the heavy conversation, she pulls back and offers me her brightest smile. "Pancakes?"

"With Nutella?"

A small smile tugs the corner of her mouth. "Is there any other way to have pancakes?"

🍀

WITH A FULL PLATE OF NUTELLA PANCAKES IN HAND, I make my way up the stairs to my bedroom and push the door open with my foot. Ciaran is still sound asleep, only now, he's turned onto his stomach with his hands tucked under the pillow. Captivated by his glorious back, I etch closer. I don't know what it is about this man's back, but fuck me, it's drool worthy. All those years he's spent drumming has done wonders for his trapezius and rhomboid muscles, and let me tell you, it's a sight.

I place the stack of pancakes on the nightstand, sit on the edge of the bed and brush the wild, jet-black waves off his face. His long lashes flutter open and those green orbs latch onto my face. "Hey."

"Hey, yourself."

He rolls over, bringing his tattooed hands to his face, he scrubs the sleep from his eyes. "Sorry, I was knackered, I must have fallen asleep."

"Don't apologise, you've been here day and night. You can't run on fumes."

Using his forearms, he pulls himself into an upright position and leans his head back against the headboard. His curious stare turns in my direction, "How'd you sleep?"

"Not very well, but I'm good." Gesturing to the food, I say, "I brought you some pancakes."

Awkward, that's the only way to describe whatever the hell is floating between us. I get it, I brought most of this on myself. Ciaran doesn't know where the line is because we haven't drawn one. Now we are skirting in the in-between, terrified of making any wrong moves. If the last few days have taught me anything, it's that I take Ciaran for granted. I push him away constantly, yet every time I need him, he comes running. It's not fair to him, and if roles were reserved, I would have told myself to fuck off years ago. He's become a crutch, a natural drug I use to quench my anxiety, but he's also so, so, so much more. He's everything.

I pick up the plate, and pass it to him.

"Thanks, LB." A deep, throaty groan escapes his mouth,

and suddenly, I'm clenching my thighs together to dull the ache in my Toblerone tunnel.

What is wrong with me? Why the sudden urge to jump his bones?

Maybe it's the messy bedhead look he's sporting, or the tenderness exuding from his eyes, but whatever it is, I need to get it under control, and pronto.

"So..." I look anywhere but at him.

His brows crease, forming a v above his eyes. Swallowing back his mouthful of pancakes, he drops his fork back onto the plate and takes hold of my right hand.

"Hey, what's wrong?"

My shoulders rise as I draw in a deep breath. "You know I love you, right? That I'm not just using you or whatever."

Ciaran lifts the blanket then pats the space beside him. "Come here."

I crawl in beside him, tuck myself under his arm, and rest my head against his chest.

"Lily," His deep lilt grabs my attention. "I never doubted your love, not once in all the years we've been doing this dance. I see it in the way you look at me, I feel it in my bone marrow, and most importantly, I hold it in my heart, right beside my love for you."

Leaning up on my elbow, I search his face, and I don't like what I find. "But?"

"Sit up, I need you to hear every word of what I'm about to say."

I do as he asks — sit back on my ass with my legs beneath me. His strong arms grip my waist and pull me into his lap so I'm straddling him. "That's better."

Tears well in his eyes, and I know what's coming. This is the end of our story. All those books, every silly fairy tale, they all lied. Happy ever after, it doesn't exist, not for people like me.

"Lilyanna O'Shea-Maguire, there hasn't been a day in the last ten years where I didn't love you."

My eyes close, holding back my tears. His words, although they say everything I want to hear, it's his tone — weary and shaken — that shreds the damaged pieces of my already battered heart.

His thumb swipes at my wet cheek, catching the tiny droplets of water that have escaped without my permission. "But I get it now. It's taken me a few years to understand fully, but when I saw you so irreparably broken, it finally hit me. I can't save you, Lily Bug."

Reaching forward, I take his tear-stained face between my palms and watch as he bite down on his lower lip. He gathers his emotions, just enough to continue. "I want to, trust me when I say that. There is nothing in this world I want more. But I can't. For years you've tried telling me you need to do this on your own, and I haven't listened. I realise now, I need to let you go, fully this time. I don't want to, Bug. I don't fucking want to."

His forehead falls against mine as we break, fastened in each other's arms.

"I will always love you, Lilyanna Maguire. And maybe one day, our stars will align."

Our lips collide, sealing our final goodbye. On his tongue, I taste his sorrow and pain, but I can't stop. I need to sear this moment into my brain, lock it away so I can live off it forever.

"I will never stop loving you, Baby Hanson. And one day, I will prove I am ready for your epic love, all those books I read, they won't hold a candle to our happy ending, because our love is worth fighting for."

CHAPTER TWENTY-FIVE

LAY BY ME BY RUBEN

CIARAN

I PULL OUR BODIES CLOSER, AND DROWN IN HER KISS. The softness of her lips drag me into the deepest waters of regret as the turbulent waves of what should have beens, pull me under. I don't want to do this. I don't want to let her go, but I have to. I know what I'm doing, I'm breaking my heart and giving her the pieces. All so she can repair her own.

For the first time, I see her, really fucking see her. And it hurts.

I hate that she feels so fragile, so broken. I despise that

her Da — the man put on this earth to protect her — has shattered her gypsy soul.

I wish I could take away the pain she feels, banish all the hurt, kiss every one of her eternal scars. But I can't.

She's right. I can't be her hero. I can't be her crutch, not anymore. It's taken me a long time to fully understand where she's at, but seeing her crumble so easily made me realise just how brittle she is.

Together, we are wildfire and torrential rain — one cannot exist alongside the other.

I've never had a life that didn't revolve around her. She's my best friend, always has been. There are times when I think I was put on this earth for the sole purpose of loving her.

How? How am I meant to walk away from that? From everything I've ever known. I don't know how to do this. How to look at her like I'm not in love with her.

My heart is hers. To hold, to keep, to love, to break, and everything else in between.

Savouring each brush of our tongues, I commit each stroke to memory.

One. Slow and uncertain. *Two.* Soft and sweet. *Three.* Forever and always. *Four.* Starving and desperate.

I tighten my hold around her waist, hanging on with all I have. I'm not ready. I can't leave, not yet.

"Lily." Her name is a hopeless, needy plea from my lips.

She pulls back, and I rest my forehead against hers. "I don't wanna go." My voice cracks. "I want to stay right here with you. But, I can't be the man who keeps you in a cage."

Teardrops decorate her cheeks, leaning forward, I kiss them away.

She takes my face between her palms as her shoulders rise with an intake of breath. "Ciaran Maguire, you are the most unselfish man I've ever met. There has never, nor will ever be, anyone who loves me the way you do. When I get my shit together, I'm gonna come for you."

Her lips gently brush over mine, and our eyes lock. "But until then, we have this moment because when the sun comes up, we will go our own way. We need to learn who we are without each other."

My fingers tease the stray thread that has come loose from the hem of her t-shirt. Biting down on my bottom lip, I drag it through my teeth, close my eyes and inhale. Suddenly, all the air rushes from my lungs as Lily reaches down, grips the bottom of her shirt and lifts it over her head in one swift motion.

"What... what are you doing?"

Her t-shirt hits the floor. "I'm making memories. Ones we can hold onto."

My hands travel up her sides. The static between us burns with desire as I trail over her softer-than-silk skin. My tingling fingers stop at the lace band of her bralette as our eyes stay locked. I hate what I see — whiskey coloured pools glazed with a sorrowful goodbye. My stomach tightens with penitence. I wish it didn't have to be this way. Fuck, I'd give up everything I've got to help her. I'd beg, borrow, and steal if it meant she could be free from her chains.

This is what she needs.

This is what we both need.

Logically I know that, but the wounded heart in my chest doesn't agree. If I do this; if I love her the way I want to, will I be able to walk away?

Running my thumbs across the delicate fabric, her body instantly reacts to my tender touch. Her back arches, deepening the curve of her spine and bringing her chest closer.

"Are you sure this is what you want?" If I were wise, I would just follow her lead, but I need her words. The last few days stirred up a lot. I need her to be a thousand percent certain.

Steadying herself with her hands on my shoulders, her coffin-shaped nails dent my skin. "I'm sure." Her words are strong, unlike this moment. There has never been a time where I have felt so exposed, stripped fucking bare at her feet.

Slipping my fingers beneath the lace, Lily raises her arms, helping me slide the barely-there material off her pert chest. I drop it to the floor then grip her hips, drawing her body closer. Gently, I push her wild locks over her shoulder and lean in. My hot breath dances across the curve where her jaw meets her neck, forcing Lily's head to fall back and expose even more of her velvet skin. Her hands tangle in my hair, tugging at the crown as I trail hot breath kisses over her bare chest. A low throaty moan pushes past her lips, her body vibrating beneath my touch.

When I left Los Angeles, my only intent was to claim my wife back. Prove to her that we could make this thing between us work. Not once did I think I'd have to release her and cut the ties that bound us together. Emotion consumes me, ripping my chest open with sharp razor-blade edges. This is it, the last time I'll have her like this. Naked. Raw. Vulnerable.

Lifting her hips slightly, my arm circles her waist as I flip our position. Lily's back greets the mattress with a soft thud, her arms land above her head, begging to be restrained. Staring down at her, I see a lifetime of stolen chances. In another world, at another time, we could have had it all. We are an incomplete story, desperately seeking a happy end. I could live a hundred lifetimes, and still, I would wander the earth looking for her.

I trail my fingers up her arms then gently grip her wrists. "Is this okay?"

Dark desire flashes across her face. "Yes," she whispers. "I'm safe with you."

I kiss the tip of her nose. "Always."

It's my heart that's not safe with you.

Lily drags her long nails over my back, and shivers travel up my spine. Our lips move in perfect synchronicity, speaking the truths we don't say out loud.

I love you.

I need you.

Please don't leave me.

When you're ready, come back to me. I'll be waiting.

With my free hand, I trail my fingers down her spine until I reach the seam of her black lace hot pants. Goose-bumps rise on her skin as my soft feather-like touch caresses every inch. Within seconds, I have her bare, her panties discarded on the floor along with my own. Trailing my tongue down her body, I kiss every freckle before finally settling between her thighs.

I look up at her through my lashes, holding eye-contact as I devour her pussy with my mouth.

With one hand gripping my hair tight, her hips grind with each swipe. Sensing her need for more, I tease her entrance with my thumb, slowly running my callous pad over every nerve-ending. Her hips buck, and the sound that escapes her lips has me harder than a rock.

"More, Ciaran. I need more."

Hearing her command, I thrust two fingers deep, curling them against her inner walls. She tightens with every thrust, her body arching, fighting against the pull. "Let go, darling. Come for me."

"I need..." Her words get lost as I run my tongue over her most sensitive parts. Her body shakes, falling off the edge. Another swipe of my tongue and the high she's chasing finally peaks. "There. Oh God, there!"

The look on her face almost puts me over the edge. Fuck me, she is beautiful. Wild with lust. Untamed by desire.

I kiss my way up her body; paying extra attention to her bare breasts, I flick the matching rose gold barbells with my tongue. Finally, our lips connect with a ferocious need, and I wrap my arm around her waist. Moulding her to my chest, I flip us over, so Lily is straddling my waist. Her hands move to my shoulders while mine grip her hips. She rises to her knees, and positions herself above my cock.

"Please tell me you're on the pill?"

I almost come there and then when a slow, sassy smirk curls on her pouty lips.

"I'm on the pill."

"Thank-fucking-Christ." It's not like I was planning for this, I haven't had sex in a year. Not since I married Lily. Say what you like about me, but regardless of our relationship status, at the end of the day, she's still my wife. When we said our vows, I meant them. Since then, she has been the only woman. *Always.*

Time slows as she slides my dick between her slick folds.

My breath hitches as she lowers herself over me, inch by torturous fucking inch. Fully seated in her depths, I hold her in place. Closing my eyes, I give myself a second to gather my shit.

If she moves, it's game over.

Four breaths and open.

Lily's hooded gaze locks on mine, amber pools of lust scanning my features with adoration. Slowly, I drag my bottom lip between my teeth, biting down as I lift my hips. My fingers dig into her hips as I guide her up and down my length. Each movement is slow and sensual. Lifting my left hand to her cheek, I tell her all the things she needs to hear. "Lilyanna O'Shea-Maguire, you are strong. You are beautiful. You are brave. I know I said this already, but I need you to understand that I am leaving because I know you need to do this alone." In one swift movement, I flip us around so she's beneath me. Deepening our connection, I grind into her with slow, deep thrusts. "The only reason I am walking away is because I know someday, you'll come home to me. Only when you do, you will be ready for all the love I have to give you."

Tears gather in her eyes, the moment too fucking much for both of us. The pressure builds as Lily tightens around my cock. Her hands circle my neck. Dragging me closer, she brushes her lips over mine. Whatever I'm feeling, it's indescribable. We're just two souls on the verge of breaking, hanging on to our last moment with all we've got. "When I look at you, I see the rest of my life. But, for now, we have to bend so we don't break."

Kissing away the tears from her cheeks, I hold her as if she is everything precious in the world because to me she is. All too soon, we find release, collapsing into a heap of tangled limbs. Wrapping my arm around her waist, I pull her back against my chest and hold her until she falls asleep.

Once her soft sleep-filled mummers fill the room, I push the dishevelled waves from her face and whisper my good-bye. "Some insects open their wings and take off within seconds. But not the ladybug, she's a little slower. She keeps her wings hidden underneath her hard shell, safe and out of harm's way. I've been your shell for far too long, and now it's time I let you go." Leaning forward, my lips brush her fore-head. "But that's okay because I have faith that you'll come back to me when you find out who you're meant to be. Your wings are open now, Lily Bug. All you gotta do is fly."

Part Three

The Encore

CHAPTER TWENTY-SIX

NOT 20 ANYMORE BY BEBE REXHA
3 Years Later

CIARAN

ONE MORE SHOW AND THEN WE FINALLY GET SOME time off. I'm over sharing a tour bus with Cian, Cillian, and Conor. Don't get me wrong, I love those assholes but after six months of trekking across Europe in a sleeper coach, I need some personal space and my super king bed.

As I lie in my tiny bunk, I strain to hear the conversation happening upfront in the makeshift living room. You're probably wondering why I don't just lift my ass and walk the eight steps to find out? One word. Lily.

For the most part, she sticks to her bus, but before a

show, she's here, in ours — making calls, giving orders, and being her general sassy self. Don't get me wrong, I love having her around, but sometimes pretending I don't want her gets too much.

Over the past few years, we have developed a friendship, and I'm good with that as long as it guarantees I can have her in my life.

Lily's voice travels up the narrow pathway, bouncing off every wall in the enclosed space, and making my longing double. Some days are easier than others, mainly because I can see the progress she's made, and I'm certain that the distance between us is helping her grow into her skin. But then, there are days like today, where I just need a minute to myself because if I don't walk away, I'd grab her by the waist, pull her close and kiss her sassy mouth until she can't deny what we have anymore. Our relationship is a double-edged sword piercing the centre of my chest.

Suddenly, the all too familiar scent of cherry blossoms floods my lungs. She's close. Too close.

"Cillian O'Shea!" Her voice is sharper than a razor blade. "Get your ass up and shower. You smell like a fucking brewery."

As I tap my drumsticks off the ceiling, I peek through the small gap in my bunk's curtain.

There she is, standing — hand on hip — beside Cillian's cubby. She's wearing distressed cut off shorts over fishnet tights, a black and green 4Clover band tee and a pair of black Doc Martens. Her hair is pulled into a messy bun on the top of her head and her flawless face is free from any makeup. *Gorgeous, always gorgeous.*

His grumbled protest is barely audible but that doesn't deter Lily.

"I don't give two fucks. Get up. It's not my problem. My problem is getting you sober before you get on that stage tonight. Suck it up and do as you're told."

When he refuses to move, she lifts her bottle of water and dumps its contents over his head.

"Jesus, Squirt! Was that necessary?" He pounces from the bed, water dripping from his shaggy brown hair.

Laughter ripples from my mouth. You would think he'd have learned by now: What Lily says, goes.

"Yes, yes it was. We have a phone interview with eRadio in twenty minutes. I want your ass out front in ten."

Suddenly, my curtain is torn open, and my eyes scan every inch of the spitfire before me. I twist my sticks through the fingers of my left hand as I drink her in.

"Something funny, Maguire?" Her right brow rises as she awaits my answer.

"Nope."

Lifting my right arm, I tuck it beneath my head. Lily's eyes widen as the muscles in my bare arms flex with the movement. She's been doing that a lot lately, and fuck me, it's taunting. *Tell me you're ready, Bug. Put me out of my misery.*

Fuck it! Swinging my feet off the bed, I plant them on the floor then pull myself off the bunk. One step forward and there's only centimetres between us. Her eyes slowly travel up my exposed abs.

"Where do you want me?" I tease.

With a swift tilt of her chin, her gaze darts to mine, just in time for me to see her swallow the sexual tension trapped in the back of her throat. "I... sorry, what?"

My lips curl into a teasing smirk. "For the interview... where do you want me?"

She's flustered, and because I'm a sexually deprived asshole, I kinda like it.

"Ermm, erm... the living area is fine."

"No bother." Pushing past her in the small space, my shirtless chest brushes against her bare arms.

I fight the laughter that tries to escape when she closes her eyes and drags in a deep breath.

Nearly there, Lily Bug. We are so close. I can almost taste it on my tongue.

❧

LILY

Some days I love my job, and other days — like today — I've had enough. We are on the last stop of 4Clover's *Long Road Home* tour, and I'm exhausted, dehydrated, and in desperate need of a hot bath filled with my favourite essential oils.

For months, we have been doing this same thing, night after night, and still, there's always one idiot who does something to piss me off.

"HOW THE HELL DID YOU LOSE HIS GUITAR?"

Thomas, our *head* guitar tech, shifts on his feet. "I, eh... It was on the bus last night. I put it there myself. It has been misplaced. I'll find it."

I pinch the skin between my eyes. "You better. Conor will not play without his Fender. I don't care if you have to walk to Belfast and back, find it before he realises it's missing."

His low muttered reply is muted when the pre-programmed ringtone blasts from my iPhone. I shoo him away with my left hand. "You've got an hour."

I lift my right hand to my ear, and press the accept button on my Bluetooth earpiece. "Michael." I greet. "What can I do for you?"

"Lilyanna, just as pleasant as always, I hear."

Rolling my eyes, I release a frustrated breath. "I'll be

sure to tell my diary all about your displeasure with my annoyance. Now, as riveting as this conversation is... can you get to the point? I have a show to prepare for. Conor's guitar is MIA. Cillian's drunk off his ass, and the other two are fighting over a fucking Subway sandwich."

"If this is too much for you to handle, I can get someone else to take over."

Is this asshole for real? I've single-handedly dragged these gobshites through fifty American States before carting their tattooed backsides across Europe.

"Order your own sandwich, Cian!" Ciaran wails.

Ignoring Michael's blabbering, I let out a roar. "FOR THE LOVE OF GOD! Somebody, please, get Cian another sandwich before Ciaran starts crying."

I take three steps until I am standing over the two children. Holding my hand out, I then flick my fingers in a *gimme* gesture. Ciaran's shoulders drop, and without protest, he hands over the footlong. "You can have it back when you learn how to share."

"Lily?" Michael's voice is laced with irritation. "Have you heard a word I said?"

"Look Mickey, I'm kind of busy, so unless —"

Just then, I catch Thomas sneaking towards the bathroom. "Thomas!" I scold. "Unless Conor's Fender is somehow in there taking a piss, I suggest you go look somewhere else. You don't get to stop until that guitar is in my hand. Do you understand?"

"Yes, Lily."

"— as I was saying, unless someone is dying, you'll have to wait. I've got a soundcheck to oversee. Chat soon."

"Lilyanna, I..."

Pressing the end call button, I hang up before he can annoy me any further.

"Okay, boys. Let's get this show on the road."

🍀

"MARLAY PARK! How the fuck are we?" Cian hollers into the microphone as the energetic crowd at the erupts into ear-piercing screams. "Who's ready for the final song of the night?"

There isn't a feeling in the world that compares to the electricity of a live performance with forty-thousand people in an open-air space, chanting 4Clover until their lungs bleed.

In perfect sync, Cillian, Conor, and Ciaran hit the first note of their newest single, Long Way Home, sending the fans into a frenzy. Cian holds the microphone towards the crowd, and right on queue thousands of voices recite every lyric, causing goosebumps to erupt along my skin.

"Tell me, how long should I wait?/ How long will you

take?/ Cause baby, we're taking a long way home / Oh, call it luck / call it love / Maybe it's faith from the Gods above?/ But I have hope in you and me / We're just taking a long way home."

It's moments like this one that make me appreciate what I do.

Leaning against a backstage speaker, I watch as all the hard work we've put in comes to fruition when the roar of the crowd carries over the music. And even though I'm not on stage with 4Clover, I still get lost in the high of every single chord, beat, and lyric.

There is nothing quite like watching these boys make magic. Cian is in his element, working the stage as if he was born do this, and only this. Cillian has his head bowed as his fingers dance across the strings of his electric Gibson LP 56 Black Beauty. The only thing in this world — other than Rosie — that he adores. Conor has his eyes closed, and his chin tilted as he plays his bass — like always — to the sky. Finally, my eyes wander to Ciaran as he beats against the skins of his kit. Over the years he has grown from cheeky-faced boy to drop-dead, pantie melting, gorgeous man.

It's been hard keeping our relationship platonic, probably because every devilish smirk he throws my way makes me want to jump on him as if he's a fucking trampoline.

For weeks now, the tension between us has been building, slowly gaining momentum with every stolen glance. I'd be crazy to think that we weren't close to combustion. I can feel it, whether I am ready or not.

Oh, you're ready.

As if he can feel my stare, Ciaran's eyes find mine. His lips curl into a side smirk and he winks, causing butterflies to take flight in my stomach.

I see it, in his smile, and in the crinkle of his eyes, he's proud of me. I did it. I, Lilyanna O'Shea, have carted these boys across the world and skyrocketed them to fame. I arranged every interview. I organised every detail of every show, and now here we are, back in Dublin with a park full of fans who adore these boys as much as I do.

4Clover are now one of the world's top Indie Rock bands, and I am their manager. I've come a long way from the broken girl with big dreams. All my hard work and struggles have finally paid off, and finally I am where I always wanted to be. I take one last look at Ciaran, his dark hair soaked with sweat, a black drop armhole tank and black track bottoms, and I realise what I need to do.

Overwhelmed with my sudden revelation, I shoot him one last shy smile. I push from the speaker and head back to the bus, needing alone a minute to gather myself. The booming music travels through the backstage passageway as I walk past staff members who smile and congratulate me on another epic show. I did it, I became who I wanted to be. I should be on top of the world right now, but there's just one thing missing. My drummer boy.

The music reaches a crescendo and Cian sings out those last few lyrics. Lyrics I know Ciaran wrote.

"You need to walk this path alone / but I'll be waiting, Baby / as you take the long way home."

CHAPTER TWENTY-SEVEN

SOLO BY DEMI LOVATO

LILY

"Lily, darling, it's so good to see you."

I enter Dr J's office, and she wraps me up in an inviting hug. It's been eighteen months since we last had a face-to-face session, and although we FaceTime once a fortnight, I still missed the comfort that her Holistic infused space brings.

Crystals — everything from amethyst to tiger's eye — adorn the windowsills, and countless Tibetan singing bowls decorate the natural bog wood shelves. Not to mention the hand-painted pieces adding colour to the white walls, giving the place an overall, earthy-hippy-vibe.

Releasing me from her grip, she waves her hand towards the chair. "Sit, sit. We've loads to get through."

Kicking off my shoes, I sink into the softness of the fabric seat. A calming comfort washes over me when the all-too-familiar scent of lavender and bergamot wafts from her oil-burning diffuser. I don't know what it is about that scent, but it always grounds me.

"So, how are you?" She tucks her yoga-pant covered legs beneath her, and questions me as she taps her pen against her black leather-bound notepad.

A soft, unforced smile forms on my face, and it feels so fucking good. "I'm doing well. I've been doing my daily meditations, and I also found an online yoga class I could do while on the road. I'm no Deepak Chopra but it seems to be helping."

"Why do you sound so surprised? You've been putting the work in. Now," she spreads her arms wide, "it's time to reap the reward."

She's right, I've given everything I've got to get to a place where I genuinely feel happy, and although I've had to lose a lot to reach it, I'm still proud of myself.

"Yeah, I know. It's just... it can all get a little overwhelming. For once in my life, I seem to have all my shit together. Life is good, at least from a professional point of view."

An unfeigned smile highlights her wrinkle-free face. "That's fantastic."

I swear this woman has the fountain of youth in her garden because she still looks thirty-five; there isn't a wrinkle in sight.

Taking a moment, I think about all the things I've accomplished in the past few years, and a spark of warmth ignites beneath my skin. Pride flows through me, prompting me to sit taller. I've come a long way from the girl I once was, and finally, I'm at a point where I am independent.

In three years, I've travelled the world twice over, once with Sinners, and then again with 4Clover. I've seen things that most twenty-four-year-olds can only dream of. For once in my life, I'm finally able to breathe without the heavy-weight of my past crushing my airways. I bought an apartment that I share with my best friend, Rosie; and I have a team of people who look after the bands I manage, leaving me with more time to focus on my top two clients, 4Clover and Sinners. So yeah, she is right — it's fan-fucking-tastic.

Scribbling something onto her jotter pad, she asks. "And what about your personal life? What's going on there?"

Ugh, she just had to ask, didn't she? Way to make a girl doubt her progress.

"I haven't had the time to focus on the personal aspect. I've been up to my eyes with work."

Raising her brow, she gives me a pointed look, and I know what she is going to say before she even says it.

"Balance, Lily. We've talked about this. You need to find

the right mix. Don't let your work life steal all your focus. Make room for both."

"I know, and I plan on doing that now the 4Clover boys are slowing down. The guys have decided to take a few months off, which will clear me up for some much-needed R&R. Also, my best friend is getting married in a few weeks, and even though Sean is the last man on the planet I would have picked, it's Rosie's choice, and I have to accept that."

That answer alone shows how far I've come. A year ago, I would have flat out told Rosie to put that man-boy in the bin. He's a sleazy, arrogant, sonovabitch with zero respect for my friend, but she's determined to go through with it, and I need to support her choices because that's what good friends do.

"Exactly. I'm so proud of you, Lily. You've truly grown. What about you? Are you seeing anyone?"

Like hallucinations? What does she think this is, an episode of Stranger Things?

Instead of telling her no, I mess with her a little. "Well, I'm seeing Peter at least three or four times a week."

Sitting up in her chair, she leans forward, "Oh, Peter. He's new. I haven't heard you talk about him before. Tell me about him. Where did you both meet?"

It takes everything in me to keep a straight face. "Well, we met online. I was a little apprehensive at first, but one of my online book club friends recommended the site and I thought fuck it, I'd give it a go."

Ha! She looks so pleased. Wait until the penny drops, Dr J!

"Oh, this is such a big step. I never thought you'd try online dating. Tell me about him? What does he do?"

"The better question would be: What doesn't he do? We have this intense relationship. He can make me come at the flick of a button, and he drives me insane in the best way. I swear to God, I never had a moment where Peter doesn't bring happiness into my life." Chewing on the inside of my lip, I fight to contain my laughter. "I have to admit, it was the best seventy euros I've ever spent."

Confusion crosses her face, and I can't take it anymore. My laughter erupts like fireworks on the 4th of July. "Did I mention he comes with eighteen built-in speeds? Funny enough, I come with all those speeds too."

Her hand flies to her chest, covering the black tourmaline pendant hanging from her neck. "Well, I see you haven't lost your sense of humour. What on God's earth possessed you to name your sex toy Peter?"

Really, that's all you took from that.

"He's a rabbit. It seemed fitting."

Shaking her head, she places her pen into her open notebook. "All jokes aside, it is excellent that you are exploring your sexuality. The sacral chakra is a key player in your development. When it's blocked, it represses creativity and causes emotional isolation. So, knowing that you're working on opening your sensual centre is a giant step." Changing gears, she switches topics. "So, I know from our FaceTime calls that you are just back from the 4Clover world tour, how did that go?"

I know what she's doing; she is leading up to the big question. For months she has circled around it, never forcing me to hand over the information, and like a pro, I have deflected her efforts every time. But something tells me, today, I won't be so lucky.

"The tour was great, we played one-hundred and eighty-two shows over ninety-five cities, all of which were amazing, but let's just say I'm glad to be back in my bed. As much as I love my job, it's exhausting. The lads desperately need a break, as do I."

"And Ciaran?" *There it is!* "How are things between you?"

Falling back into the chair, I raise my chin to the ceiling and release a long, over-dramatic sigh.

Ciaran... hmmm, what to say about him?

The past few months have been tortuous, watching him from the side lines, knowing that I am the reason we are apart. Every longing glance, near kiss, and electricity-filled moment, has worn my black heart down.

I miss him. I understand that's a bizarre thought, especially since I just spent months in his company, but it's not the same. Mostly, we developed this strange — for want of a better word — friendship. Then if we were alone, we would avoid each other, barely speaking, and never making eye-contact. Never allowing ourselves to cross the invisible line we've drawn. He knows how important this journey is to me, but recently, I'm wondering if it's time I ask him to walk alongside me. Deep down, I'm petrified that maybe one day, he'll find someone else, someone that will appreciate how fucking great he is. We both agreed to our separation because it was for the best. I had to learn to fly with the wings he'd given me, and he had to learn to let me go.

"Erm, awkward, but that doesn't feel right because it's not. Every moment with him is natural, but then the tension looms, drawing us closer with magnetic force, and I have to fight against the pull every time. With Ciaran, there is this, I want to say feeling, but it's more than that, it's as if the universe is rooting for us to be together. When I am around him, I lose sight of everything else, and everything about him completely consumes me. It's powerful, taking over not only my mind but my soul too. When we are in the same room together, there is no time, it just stops, and that fucking terri-fies me more than anything because I can't control it. It's impatient, violent, unapologetic, but I need it, I crave it. Our connection is like a wild animal on a leash, and no matter how tight I grip the reins, it keeps fighting. It's untamable, grappling to get free. Any day now, it's going to escape, and when it does, there'll be nothing I can do to stop it." Drawing in a deep breath, I steady my erratic heart. I know that battling my feelings is unhealthy, but I need to make sure I'm ready before I can act on them.

Wide eyes home in on mine, watching me with fascination. "Do you feel ready to unleash it?"

The answer is simple, and although I've spent months avoiding it, I know I need to open my burgundy stained lips, sooner rather than later.

I know what I want, I always have, but I had to work on what I needed first, self-healing. I'm better now. Not perfect, but better. I love myself, and everything I've accomplished, all that's missing is sharing a part of myself with the person I love most in the world. "If I said maybe, would you call bullshit?"

"If I said bullshit, would you say maybe?"

This is what I love most about Dr J — she pulls no punches. She knows better than I do that once I pull the trigger, I need to act. She also knows I'm the only one standing in my way. So, the question is, what am I waiting for? Why haven't I bitten the bullet and gone for it?

Because you're scared.

As much as I hate to admit it, my inner voice is right. Ciaran put his heart on the line more times than I can count, and each time I shot him down, assassinating every ounce of faith he put in us, who's to say he won't do the same now that I'm finally ready to give in to the feelings he evokes within me. I'd be stupid to assume he still feels the same, but I'd be a complete idiot if I don't fight for us. After all, we're still technically married.

"You're right." My shoulders drop with defeat. "I'm ready, but I can't just waltz back into his life and demand he loves me, that's not fair to him. He deserves better."

Her head nods as her lips curl into a blinding smile. "So, Lily... tell me, how are you going to win him over?"

"Honestly, I have no idea."

If this were a romance novel, now would be the time where the hero comes up with this grand gesture, pulling out all the stops, and riding in on a proverbial horse, ready to win the heroine over. But this is not a book, it's real life, my life. I've been so caught up with becoming my own hero, I've lost sight of what Ciaran wants and needs. Someone to fight for him, someone to show up and fucking stay.

He wants an epic love, and that's what he'll get.

Get ready, Maguire. I'm coming for you.

CHAPTER TWENTY-EIGHT

1000 TIMES BY SARA BAREILLES

CIARAN

IT'S SAID THAT IF YOU LOVE SOMETHING, SET IT FREE, and if it comes back, it's yours. What they don't tell you are the stipulations. How long you need to wait or when to give up and just move the fuck on?

It's been three years, and still, I'm the poor mother-fucker that would wait for three more without complaint.

Setting Lily free was the hardest thing I've ever done but watching her grow into a wildflower with unbreakable petals is worth every millisecond I spend without her by my side.

I can see she is stronger now. Her strength grew with

every day we were on tour, and piece by piece, she put herself back together again.

Gone is the fragile doll she used to be, and in her place is a woman who knows what she wants and isn't afraid to take it. It's written in every movement she makes, and every smile that lights her perfect heart-shaped face. It shines from her amber eyes, burning like campfire flames on a dark summer's night.

Staying away hasn't been easy, especially since we're woven together in every area of our lives. My friends are her friends, and she is, for all intents and purposes, my boss.

We spent months living in close quarters, tiptoeing around the feelings we buried. One wrong move and the distance we created would've exploded in our faces, but I refuse to be the one to make that first move — it has to come from her. So here I am, waltzing through limbo, unsure of where the fuck I'm going but still keeping the faith that she'll come back to me one day.

There is no escaping her and the stifling tension between us. It follows us around, threatening to pull us under. We've been back home a few weeks, and still, she's everywhere I go, engraved in every part of me.

My life revolves around her, just like hers revolves around me. We need to learn to live with it while we try to live without each other.

Tonight is Rosie's engagement party, and here I am,

sitting alone, wanting to strangle myself for letting Lily go. My eyes haven't left her, following her lithe body around the dance floor, committing every movement she makes into my memory.

She looks breath taking, and all I want to do is wrap my tattooed arms around her and convince her never to leave me again. Her vibrant hair is pinned loosely at the nape, while stray, wispy strands frame her perfect porcelain face.

Silk — the colour of emerald — hugs her skin, showcasing every dip and curve perfectly. Two tiny straps crisscross over her exposed back, giving me the perfect view of the delicate script tattoo that runs along her spine. I'm too far away to read what it says, but that doesn't dull the urge I have to run my tongue over it. Fuck me, I would give my left nut to be the dress that clings to her lightly freckled skin.

Lifting the over-priced vintage whiskey to my lips, I drain it in one swallow as I watch her over the rim of the glass, slowly dancing to an Ed Sheeran song with Rosie.

Time for a top-up.

My feet lead me to the open bar, but my eyes never stray from my Lily Bug.

I drop into the free stool beside my best friend, Cillian — who may I add, looks forty times worse than I do — and order another drink. "Hey, man. How are you holding up?"

Tonight has been tough on him, and rightly so. Rosie was his childhood sweetheart, the girl he planned to marry one day. Now, here we are, at her engagement party, and unfortunately, Cillian is not her future groom.

He tears his longing gaze away from his ex, and his eyes find mine. "Honestly... not great." Dark circles rim his hazel eyes as if he hasn't slept in days, and the potent smell of alcohol seeps from his pores. "I don't know what possessed me to come here tonight. I should've never accepted that invitation." He lifts his glass to his lips, knocking back the shot before signalling for a refill.

Our attention flicks back to the girls as they stand in the middle of the dance floor, and my heart plummets. I may not be in the same boat as Cill, but I get it, the love of my life is on that dance floor without me too.

"If I were you, I'd have done the same," I offer, hoping to comfort him and his regrets. "Have you spoken to her?"

Running his fingers along the edge of the Waterford Crystal tumbler, he shakes his head. "No."

"Are you going to talk to her?"

He is silent for a beat, probably contemplating his next move. Suddenly, his eyes dart to mine, and what I see in them can only mean one thing... trouble.

"Yeah. I'm just biding my time until I can get her alone. I don't think she would appreciate an audience when she hears what I have to say." This could go one of two ways, bad or really fucking bad.

My shoulders slump when I release my weighted

breath. The logical thing to do is try to stop him, but if there's one thing I know about Cillian, it's that all logic goes out the window when he's drinking.

"Are you sure that's a good idea, man?" I push. "Isn't it time you let her go?"

Hypocrite.

He spins on his stool, and the potent scent of whiskey that wafts off him chokes me. His hazel eyes bore into my skin with a murderous glare. "Let me ask you something. If roles were reversed and this was Lily's engagement party... would you let her go?"

Tearing my eyes from his, I seek the tattooed pixie in emerald green silk. Head thrown back in laughter, she steals the air from my lungs. Dropping my gaze to my left hand, I trace the small ladybug on the underside of my ring finger. My eyes close, and my brow line furrows. "Not a fucking chance."

Raising his glass once more, he stops, letting it hover in front of his lips. "Yeah, that's what I thought." He throws the whiskey back in one fell swoop.

It's going to be a long fucking night.

🍀

"Are you planning to sit here moping all night or are you going to grab life by the balls and ask her to dance?"

Ignoring my twin brother, I continue to watch Lily from afar as she glides across the vinyl dance floor in Cian's arms.

I wish I wasn't jealous, Cian's one of my best friends, but I can't help it. The green-eyed monster is out in full force, and he has a hold of my heart in a death grip. Logically, I know I'm being irrational. Sure Cian and Lily are close, but he'd never make a move on her. She's like his annoyingly bossy kid sister, he loves her, but not in the same way I do. Does that stop the blood in my veins from boiling? No, it doesn't. The sight of his arms wrapped around her makes me want to punch him in his smug face.

"Bro, if you keep clutching that glass like that, it's going to shatter in your hand."

Twisting on the barstool, I glare at my brother who's donning a knowing smirk. "Piss off."

Running his hands through his long blonde hair, he pushes it off his forehead. The bright overhead lights cast shadows on his face, highlighting the small silver scar above his left brow. It has faded with time, but it serves as a reminder of the future he lost, even after all these years. "Don't be a pussy all your life. Man the fuck up and ask your wife to dance."

He's right, when it comes to Lilyanna, I'm a dickless coward. Somehow, she can crush my devil may care attitude into tiny grains of sand. Flipping Conor off, I respond the only way I can. "When did you become such an asshole?"

I don't wait long enough for his answer, instead, I slam my glass down against the bar.

"Atta boy," Conor chuckles as I rise from the stool, my sights, like always, set on one girl and one girl only — my wife.

Pushing through the crowded dance floor, I catch Cian's eye over Lily's shoulder. He knows I'm coming, and he's ready for it. Shifting slightly, he keeps Lily's back to me, making sure she can't see me stalking towards her. With every step I take, the pulsation of my heart quickens, it's been far too long since my beautiful wildfire has been in my arms. Like Kismet, the song changes to a slow, steady drumbeat. Closing the distance between us, I nod for Cian to spin Lily out. He pulls her closer as Sara Bareilles' voice bleeds through the overhead speakers. At the end of the second verse, the pace picks up, and he raises their intertwined hands, then twirls her out from his chest. Only instead of bringing her back, he releases his hold, and Lily loses her balance, falling right into my awaiting arms, just as the chorus kicks in.

Our eyes lock and time fucking halts, nothing exists, only her. Lily's body is dipped, draped in my arms as her hands clutch my shoulders. I don't miss the way her chest hitches as she draws in a breath.

Tightening my hold, my palm grips her hip as I slowly steady her back on her two feet. Pulling her in closer, I take hold of her left hand as her right travels over the shoulder of my crisp white shirt. My chin dips and my eyes scan every inch of her face.

"You are the most beautiful woman I've ever seen." The words leave my mouth before I can stop them, but I don't care. She is stunning, and she deserves to be reminded of that every-fucking-day.

Her cheeks flush crimson, but it's the unspoken words in her eyes that captivate me.

Lingering between us is the feeling of inevitability, an undeniable sense that we belong together in this crazy, fucked up world. Maybe, just maybe, we had to break to appreciate our love's invaluable worth.

I once thought Lily and I were a slow dance to hell, but what if I was wrong? What if we're a cosmic dance fated for a collision? Destined to fall apart, all so we could learn, grow, and appreciate that not all love stories are glitter and gold. Sometimes they're shattered souls, broken fragments of glass that need to be pieced back together.

Lily and I, we're not two hearts that just fell in love, we're two souls walking a path that leads to eternity.

Lily needed to find herself, become stronger, and I needed to move over and let her do that because if I didn't, we would never work. A man's role in a woman's life is not to control, but to support. A husband's role is slightly different, he needs to be a shoulder when she needs to cry, and her encouragement when she's afraid to spread her wings. He has to know what she needs when she needs it, and to be prepared to move whatever mountains are in her way. When I let Lily go, it was because she needed me to, and as her husband, it was my job to give her that. I won't lie, it was the hardest, most unselfish thing I've ever done, but I would do it all over again because, deep down, I know that our story is not over, not yet.

If possible, I pull her closer, and she rests her head against my chest. Shivers climb up my spine as I rest my chin on top of her head. Suddenly, her cherry blossom scent inundates my senses, filling my airways, bringing with it memories of a night I will never forget.

Pulling back slightly, Lily tilts her head and holds my gaze. It would be easy to lean in, steal a kiss from her pouty lips and bask in their heavenly bliss, but I don't. I promised myself I would let her make that move. But she is so close, her wine-infused breath brushing against my lips.

"Ciaran, I," she prompts, but before she can continue, I shut her down.

"Don't. Not here, not now." Resting my forehead against hers, I continue, "Right now, I just want to feel this moment. Pretend that I'm just a man, leading his breath-taking wife around the dancefloor. Can we just do that, please? Then after, when the music stops and the crowd leaves, we can go back, back to pretending that you don't belong in my arms."

A glistening tear slides down her cheek, and I swipe it away with my thumb, but she nods in agreement before resting her head against my chest, over the heart that only beats for her.

We spend the night like that, wrapped in each other's arms, and when the last song ends, so does our illusion.

Glancing up at me over her tear-stained lashes, Lily's eyes hold mine. Her mouth parts as if to speak, but I can't hear it right now. I need to hold onto this perfect moment.

Pressing my finger to her lips, I silence her words. Her eyes close and she nods her head. With one last kiss on her cheek, I pull away. "We're meant for forever, just not right now."

CHAPTER TWENTY-NINE

BLAME IT ON MY HEART BY KARMIN

LILY

Sunlight creeps through the cracks in my white Venetian blinds, forcing my eyes to pry open.

Coffee, I need coffee.

After dragging my protesting body from my bed, I head for the kitchen and follow the delicious scent of fried bacon that's wafting up the hallway.

The excruciating hangover and lack of sleep are doing nothing for the jackhammer assaulting my temples, but maybe after a greasy bacon sandwich, I won't feel like a member of The Walking Dead.

Being on the receiving end of Ciaran's dismissal stung,

but honestly, I deserved it. Winning him back won't be easy, but the best things in life are earned. Over the years, he's always been there for me. Always putting my selfish needs before his own. Last night I realised just how much I'd broken him. A kaleidoscope of pain, hurt and regret started back at me from his eyes, and yet, he held me in his arms with a tenderness fit for the royalist of queens.

The battle between his head and his heart was evident, reflecting in his every movement. Every time our eyes locked, the hands of time froze in place, leaving nothing but high voltage electricity sparking between us.

I should have kissed him, captured his lips with mine while showing him with each brush of our tongues, just how much he means to me. When he asked me to just be in the moment with him, I couldn't refuse him. He needed that, to just be without real-life fucking it all up. My feelings, although valid, didn't matter at that moment. His sinful scent of citrus and spice invaded my senses, wrapping me up in a blanket of security and promises, and I knew without a doubt, that in his arms is where I need to be. The ballroom could have gone up in flames, and I wouldn't have budged, It had to happen. It was a reassurance that no matter what happens, how much time passes, our connection lives on. Growing stronger, pulling us back together with magnetic force.

It's time.

I told him I'd come for him when I was better, stronger, and I'm both of those things. I've got a plan. Well, it's more of an idea, but you know, I'm working on it. Ciaran, he deserves it all, the extravagant gesture, topped with a double dose of romance. Most women want hearts and flowers but maybe it's time we ladies start providing the men in our lives with the same courtesy. Sure, not all men want to be romanced, but does that mean we shouldn't shower them with affection.

I know Ciaran, underneath that pantie-melting smirk and bad boy vibe, he's a giant softie. He loves rom-com movies, rainy day snuggles and holding hands. He's the kind of guy that would paint my toenails, pop on a facemask with me and demand we watch reruns of One Tree Hill.

It's taking me a long time to admit that even when we weren't officially dating, we still behaved like a couple, only minus the benefits.

It's him, it always has been. Nobody has, or ever will come close.

I trudge into the kitchen, plonk myself onto the barstool and rest my face in my palms.

"Uh oh," Rosie comments. "you look how I feel... Which, FYI is like shit."

Raising my head, I take my first look at her. Her jet-black hair looks like a bird's nest. Black streaks of mascara stain her rosy cheeks, and her eyes are red and swollen. "Jesus Christ! What the hell happened to you?"

Her shoulders rise as she draws in an exaggerated breath. "Your brother happened."

Rosie and Cillian have a fractured past. After everything that happened with my dad, Cillian lost his shit. He fell off the bandwagon, and he's been spiralling ever since. He lost Rosie to his demons, and she submitted to hers to save him from plummeting further. They still love each other, anyone with eyes can see that, but sometimes love is not enough.

My brows rise. "What did he do now? Did he say something?"

Pouring two cups of coffee from the pot, she slides one towards me. "Say something! Ha! He cornered me in the ladies' room. Lowered my defences and my dress."

My eyes widen as my coffee sprays from my mouth. "Excuse me. Did you just imply that my brother fucked you in the ladies' room? At your engagement party? To another man!"

She hides behind her coffee mug, but I don't miss the look of regret on her face. It's not my brother she's regretting, but the choices she made to save him. Sean being the prime example. I don't know the whole story, but from what she's told me, their upcoming nuptials are an arrangement, nothing more. Her feelings towards her soon-to-be husband are zero to nothing, I'd even go as far as saying she hates him, and that's virtually unheard of for Rosie. She's too nice to dislike anybody. I don't pry though. It's her story and she'll tell it when she's ready to.

"Stop that," she scolds.

"Stop what?"

"Looking at me with those sad eyes. I'm a big girl, I'll be fine. Cillian and I are done, okay?"

A sad smile curls on my lips. For as long as I can remember, Rosie has believed Cillian hung the moon. It makes me sad to think that a couple as strong as they were couldn't make it. "You don't sound so sure?"

"It is what it is. We made our choices, Lil. We need to live with them. Anyway, enough about me and my sad excuse of a life. How did things go with Ciaran? I saw you dancing, did you work things out?"

Lifting my cup, I allow the rich aromas to dance across my tongue as I contemplate how to answer. *Thank you, Coffee Gods!* "If anything, we made it more complicated. You should have heard him. He was so fucking sad and nearly killed me."

She places her cup on the counter and circles the small breakfast island in our kitchen. Suddenly her arms engulf me in a warm hug.

"What are we like?" She murmurs into my hair. "When did we become such hot messes?"

My shoulders shake as I hold back my chuckle. "I think it was around the time we discovered the pleasure of the D."

"Lily!" She pulls back laughter lingering in her blue eyes.

"Oh, shut up. Did you forget my old room was next to my brothers? Oh, Cillian! So, good, Cillian. Right there, Charming, right there. Did you know I had to wear earmuffs for two years?"

Her pale face flames with embarrassment. "You did not!"

Although her wide eyes amuse me, I decide to put her out of her misery. "Jesus, I'm joking. No need to phone the Virgin Mary for forgiveness."

"You're an asshole you know that."

Flashing her my pearly whites, I stick out my tongue. "Yes! I'm aware. Now, I could have sworn I smelt bacon. Where are you hiding the goods, Ro? You know I'm feral when I'm hungry."

❦

WHEN TWO LADIES ARE SELF-DEPRECATING, SOMEONE should hide the wine because the outcome is never good. Somewhere in the last twelve hours, Rosie and I have turned into Pinky and the Brain. Now, we have all intentions of taking over the world. And when I say the world, I mean:

I'm going to win Ciaran back with the grandest-fucking-grand-gesture known to mankind, and Rosie, she's going to kick Sean in the nutcrackers and tell him he can stick his pretentious wedding up his hairy egotistical ass. Then, she's going to go get her man.

The throwback tunes are on full blast, and the first wine bottle is nearly empty. I'm lying on the coffee table staring at the ceiling fan, and Rosie has pulled her easel and big-ass sketchpad into the middle of the sitting-room, but none of that matters, because we are plotting. We are women on a mission, we even have post-its. Luminous green post-its.

Pulling myself into a sitting position, I cross my legs, sit like a buddha, and lift the wine bottle to my lips. My eyes scan the giant story web Rosie has drawn on the A2 page. The words: **OPERATION CILLIAN AND CIARAN** are scrawled in the centre of a circle in black permanent marker.

"Okay," I announce. "First things first, we need to eliminate the target, and by target, I mean Sean. My first choice would be castration, but I'm open to any other suggestions."

Rosie holds her hand out, gesturing to the wine. "We are not castrating anyone. This is real life, Lily. Not an episode of Good Girls."

Handing her the bottle, I roll my eyes and sulk. "Why do you feel the need to suck the fun out of life? We both know he's a dick, and maybe if we cut his off, he'd learn to treat people a little better. Just saying."

"Okay, no more wine for you."

I stick my tongue out and reach under the table for the last bottle, waving it at her in victory. *How do you like them oranges?* "Okay, Mother Teresa, tell me, what's the plan then?"

A wide smile spreads across her face. "We need to get Sean out of Ireland for a few days so I can raid his office. I've already searched through Michael's and I can't find anything. There has to be something, fucking anything to get me out of this marriage."

She looks defeated. She told me everything that happened with Cill last night, and I get why she's hell-bent on trying to free herself from the deal she made with her dad. She doesn't love Sean, she never did. For her, it's always been Cillian.

"Okay... hit me with what you got!" Rolling my shoulders, I prepare myself for her master plan.

She eyes me up, giving me a look that makes me nervous. "I was thinking maybe you could ask..."

"Nope! I'm not asking Ciaran. No way! There's not a chance in the devil's lair am I doing that."

"But Lily!"

"Don't, but Lily me! You know as well as I do that Ciaran despises Sean. There's no way he'll go for it."

Her bottom lip juts out as her clear blue eyes widen.

"Stop! That puppy face might work on my brother, but I know better."

Placing her hand over her heart, she adds to her dramatics. "Look, Sean has wanted to be a part of the 4Clover group since we were kids. If we could just get any one of the lads to bring him somewhere on, I don't know, a bachelor party or something, he'd lose his mind. Cian will never go for it. Conor is, well Conor. Cillian is out of the question. That leaves us with Ciaran. You and I both know, if you asked, he'd do it, no questions."

She's right. Doesn't mean I want to do it, though.

"Let me get this straight. Ciaran and I are barely speaking, and yet, you want me to ask him to bring your asshole fiancé on a boys' weekend?"

"That is correct."

Narrowing my eyes, I send her daggers. "HAVE YOU LOST YOUR MIND? What part of that plan seems like a good idea to you?"

"All of it! One, it gives you an excuse to talk to him. And two, it gets Sean out of the way so we can get some dirt on him and his sleazy dad." Popping the lid on the marker, she drops it like a mic. 'WIN, WIN, BABY!"

This is a bad idea... a very bad idea. But you know what they say, the road to hell is paved with good intentions.

CHAPTER THIRTY

BANG DEM STICKS BY MEGHAN TRAINOR

LILY

THERE ARE SOME THINGS IN LIFE MY EYES WILL NEVER tire of.

For instance, a pink and purple sky on a dusky summer evening, or how bright the stars look on a dark winter night. But nothing, not a single thing compares to the vision before me. Beads of sweat cling to his bare chest, making it glisten underneath the studio lights. Damp, jet black unruly waves poke out from beneath his vibrant orange beanie as his tattooed arms expertly pound out the heavy beat. He's a picture of ecstasy with his green eyes closed and his bottom lip gripped between his perfectly straight teeth.

It's been ten days since Rosie's party, and I'd be lying if I said I didn't miss him.

The natural thing to do would be to make him aware of my presence, but he seems so lost in his head that it would be a shame to interrupt him. So, instead, I stay hidden in the darkness of the sound-check booth — erm, harmlessly observing — as he wreaks havoc on his kit.

Most guys go to the gym to relieve stress, but Ciaran, he takes it out on his drums. Honestly, it's amazing to see the heavy tension lift from his shoulder as one song bleeds into another. Finally, he halts, lifting his chin to the ceiling and releasing a long sigh-filled breath.

"You can come out now," he announces. Slowly, his chin dips as his eyes seek me out in the dark.

Pulling the door open, I lean against the frame and cross my arms over my chest. "How'd you know I was here?"

He picks up his plain white vest-tee from the floor and uses it to wipe the hard work from his brow. "Same way I always know when you're near..." Rising from his drum throne, he heads for the half-fridge and pulls out a bottle of water.

He turns to face me, leaning back against the fridge as he lifts the bottle to his lips — swigging it back three large gulps. Suddenly, he focuses all his attention back on me. "I could feel you underneath my skin." *Yeah, I know that feeling well.*

Unsure of how to respond, I step into the room further.

"So... How are you?" My eyes travel over him, taking him all in — bright orange beanie, shirtless torso, and matching orange track bottoms. *Can someone please explain how he oozes sex appeal while dressed like a fucking traffic cone? A sexy, mouth-watering, traffic cone.*

"You're gonna come in here and hit me with small talk? Really, Lil?"

Avoiding his gaze, I take a seat behind his kit, pick up the two hickory sticks and twist them between my fingers. "Look, I'm sorry, okay. I... I don't know how to do this." Motioning between us I point out the awkward tension. "It's weird, there's this invisible line. We're not friends, but we're not together either. It's just, it is so hard to be in your life and not know what side of the line we belong on. I get it. I unintentionally had you in this position for years, and I'm finally starting to feel how sucky that is."

Confusion crosses his brow as he steps closer, closing the distance between us. Dropping to his hunkers, he lifts my chin with two fingers, causing our gazes to lock. "What the fuck are you talking about?"

"The other night, at Rosie and Sean's party. I was going to tell you that I'm ready. But then, I saw the look in your eye, and I couldn't. I didn't want to ruin the moment."

Silence, so fucking loud yet not nearly loud enough. *Say something, anything.*

My heart pounds — rivalling the beat of a homecoming marching band — echoing in my eardrums. My hands clam up and my breath vibrates in the back of my throat, tickling my vocal cords. Swallowing the dryness in my mouth, I lower my eyes to the fingers beneath my chin until they land on the small intricate ladybug tattooed on the palm side of his ring finger. It has somewhat faded over the years, but it's still there.

His face is hard, teeth gritted together highlighting his chiselled cheekbones and prominent, strong, square jawline. His eyes are darker. Gone is the sea-green hue, and in its place is something more striking, like emerald fields of dewy grass on a damp Irish morning. They're ablaze with... I don't know — love.

"Ciaran?" I question. "Say something, please?"

"I am only going to ask this once —" his voice a raspy whisper. "— so, make sure your answer is one you can live with."

Heat trails across my skin, leaving a thousand nerve endings standing at attention.

"Lilyanna O'Shea Maguire, are you saying you want this? Me, you, together?"

There's no hesitation, nor an ounce of fear. "Ye... shit!"

Suddenly, I am airborne as Ciaran lifts me from the stool before I can process what's happening. His strong arms whoosh me up as his fingertips grip my ass. My arms wrap around his neck as my thighs grip his hips. My back hits the AcouFoam wall and Ciaran's mouth captures mine with raw, possessive need. There's no sign of the soft, sweet, sensitive man I married. Instead, he is a starved lion, desperate and controlling. I'm not sure if it's me or the build-up of adrenaline from hours of playing, but whatever it is, I am all for it. My hands dive under his hat, knocking it off his head as my fingers tease in his messy hair.

A low throaty groan rumbles up my chest when his hips gyrate against my centre, making my solar plexus tighten with crazy desire.

We're a wild storm of limbs and needy kisses, lost in every stoke, nip, and suck. His hands are everywhere, roaming my body like a crazed maniac.

"Shit! Three years, LB!" he whispers. "Tell me to stop!"

I don't.

I don't want him to stop. I've been craving his hands on me for far too long.

"What if I told you I don't want you to?"

His grip on my ass tightens, his fingertips digging into my skin. "Are you sure? I can't, fuck, I can't be gentle right now." His head dips into the crevice of my neck, his hot breath igniting a fire within the depths of my core. "If we do this, I won't be able to take my time. It's been too long."

Arching my back, I press my front against his chest. "Ciaran?"

"Hmmm," he mumbles against my goose bumped skin.

"You've got two seconds to fuck me or I'll show you how good I can fuck myself."

"Is it wrong that I'm not mad at either of those options?"

"Now, Ciaran."

"Whatever you say, Wifey. Whatever you say."

Within seconds his hand travels up my thigh, underneath the hem of my black leather skater skirt. His fingers tease the lacey seam of my Victoria's Secret thong before he grips the material and tugs. The tell-tale sound of material ripping fills my ears, and suddenly, my panties are wrapped in his knuckles. "Hey! Those were expensive."

His lips curl into that cheeky smile I love so much, showing off that gorgeous dimple in his left cheek. When his tongue runs across his bottom lip, I almost come undone. "I'll buy you a new pair. Fuck, I'll buy you the entire store."

Gripping his face between my palms, I pull his lips towards mine, stopping just a breath away. "I can buy myself knickers."

His deep chuckle vibrates against my lips. "Never said you couldn't. Now shut that pretty mouth and let me fuck you."

I capture his lips in a greedy kiss, and run my nails over his back as he thrust his fingers inside me, teasing me in the most delicious way. The pad of his thumb circles my clit and sparks ignite under my skin, drawing out a sensation that has been hidden for far too long.

The surrounding air crackles with this sense of urgency, but also this bizarre contradictory knowing that we have all the time in the world.

With every thrust of his hand, the swirling, fluttering, emptiness in my stomach becomes more insatiable. A voracious hunger that only Ciaran can quench.

Our kisses become fast and deep as his free hand holds my body weight against the wall. With Ciaran, nothing feels forced or awkward. He's just there. With me, around me, loving me how he sees fit.

My orgasm hits fast, like rapid waves attacking a shoreline. Starting in my toes, it travels up my spine until finally, it ripples from my lips. "Ciaran."

I'm high, floating on his drug-like intoxication. "I need you."

Shifting his hips, he pins me to the wall so he can remove his track bottoms. "Hold tight, LB."

Within seconds, his pants are around his knees and he's pushing inside me. "Christ! I missed this."

I'm not gonna paint this as some soul-claiming moment, cause it's not. It's a build-up of passion and sexual tension. Years of repressed feelings, finally exploding in one delicious orgasmic release. It's sweaty, filthy, rough, and selfish. Two bodies feeding into a long-awaited craving. It's pure, unfiltered ecstasy coursing through every vein, cell, and thought.

Every pump of his hips stirs the electric current building inside me. It grows stronger until every single cell in my body is screaming, "Yes!"

My body quivers in his arms as his pace quickens. My inner walls tighten around his thick length and game-fucking-over.

"Lily! Fuck."

We erupt, and my spent body collapses against him. "Shit!" he murmurs breathlessly into my neck. "I was not expecting that."

A nervous chuckle falls from my lips. "Me neither. I came here for an entirely different reason, but I'm not mad at the outcome."

He sets me back on my feet and pulls up his pants as I fix my skirt. Taking my hand, Ciaran leads me into the soundcheck booth, and over to the small sofa in the corner. He sits, pulling me onto his lap so I'm straddling his waist. His hand reaches up, smoothing out my hair before tucking it gently behind my ear. "So, LB. What is it you want?"

Leaning my head to the left, I narrow my amber eyes. "Why do you presume I want something?"

His thumb runs across my bottom lip. "This smirk right here."

"Okay, I need a favour. Well, Rosie needs a favour. But,

before I get into that, I need you to know that's not what —"
I wave my hand at the studio "— this is about. I am ready, for
whatever this is. If you want, we can take it slow, or whatever. I want to romance you, show you how much you mean
to me. That's presuming you still wanna?"

"You're kidding, right?" he laughs. "Lily, I've been
waiting for you since I was nineteen-years-old. If I'm being
honest, it was probably long before that. What makes you
think I've changed my mind? When I married you all those
years ago, that was it. I gave you my heart, and I've no intention of taking it back. It's yours, always has been."

My lips find his with a slow possessive kiss. Pulling
back, I focus on the lust brewing in his green eyes. "I missed
you."

His arms tighten around my waist, drawing me to his
chest. "I missed you, too."

I tuck my head beneath his chin and allow the scent of
citrus to fill my nose.

"So," he mutters into my hair. "What's this favour?"

"Well..." I tell him everything I know about Rosie and
Sean's — for want of a better word — arrangement.

His eyes widen. "So, you're telling me I've been
watching my best friend drink himself into an early grave, all
because he thought the love of his life loved someone else.
When in reality, that couldn't be further from the truth?"

"Pretty much, yeah."

"Shit! Why didn't she say something? We could have all put our heads together and figured something out."

There's no point in us asking *what if's* and *how come's*. Rosie did what she thought was best for Cillian and his career, and I'm sure if she could take it all back, she would. "It doesn't matter now. What matters is she's done. She doesn't want to go through with this wedding and she needs us to help her out."

Ciaran nips at my neck, his hands skirting over my ribcage, setting my soul on fire. "And... what is it you need me to do?"

I huff out a deep breath. "I need you to bring Sean to your Los Angeles apartment on a bachelor party weekend."

Laughter barrels from his lips. "No-fucking-way."

"Ciaran! Please. I'll give you whatever you want, just help her out."

"When?" he asks.

"Tomorrow."

He is silent for a beat, mulling it over in his too-handsome-for-his-own-good head. "Fine, but I want dinner with you when I get back. A proper date."

Well, that was easier than I thought. "Dinner? And here's me thinking I'd repay you in blowjobs. You've got yourself a deal."

Pulling back, I pretend to move from his lap. His strong,

tattooed hands grip my hips and in one swift motion, he flips me so I'm beneath him.

"Hold up, wifey. I'd like to amend my terms."

"No can do! A deal's a deal, remember?" My tongue pokes out from between my lips, and he leans forward sucking it into his mouth.

Pulling back, he laughs. "Why do you gotta be so sassy?"

"You love it."

His green eyes glisten. "To fucking right, I do."

CHAPTER THIRTY-ONE

WHAT A MAN GOTTA DO BY JONAS BROTHERS

CIARAN

CIARAN: THIS TRIP IS A CLUSTERFUCK!

CIARAN: YOU OWE ME, BIG TIME!

LILY: Why are you shouting?

CIARAN: HE HAS A KID, LIL. CIAN HAS A KID!

LILY: I know, I spoke to him this morning. Calm the hell down. I'll FaceTime you.

🍀

CIARAN: We just landed. Can't wait to see you.

LILY: I'm here. Hurry up and love me.

CIARAN: Turn around.

CIARAN: The other way.

LILY: Where are you? I can't see you.

CIARAN: I'm still on the plane, but I had a great laugh imagining you searching for me.

LILY: DO YOU WANNA WALK HOME?

CIARAN: I'm sorry. LOL! Miss you. x

CIARAN: Look up!

LILY: I AM NOT FALLING FOR THAT AGAIN.

CIARAN: Lily, look up! xx

🍀

CIARAN: How's your day, Beautiful? X

LILY: Busy. *eye-roll emoji* Lunch? I've got twenty mins. X

CIARAN: Can't, babe, sorry! We're flat out… I'll be at least another few hours.

LILY: Ugh, you suck!

CIARAN: Not as good as you do. *eggplant emoji*

🍀

CIARAN: Hey babe. x

LILY: Hey, stranger. What are you doing tonight?

CIARAN: Meeting Conor then heading to Da's for dinner. Wanna come?

LILY: Ugh, I wish I could but I'm up to my eyes in paperwork for Cian. Next time?

CIARAN: Do you want me to help? I can call Da, he won't mind.

LILY: No, don't do that. I'll be fine. I'll call you tonight.

CIARAN: <3

🍀

CIARAN: What are you doing tonight? Wanna come over?

LILY: What will we be doing?

CIARAN: Well, let's just say it involves me, you, pillows, and blankets. *purple devil emoji*

LILY: OMG! Are we building a fort? I'm so in! *tent emoji*

CIARAN: LOL! That right there is why you're my favourite person. If my lady wants a fort, she shall have a fort. But FYI, I'm totally fucking you in it!

❧

CIARAN: What aisle are they on?

LILY: Up where the toothbrushes are.

CIARAN: NEVER ASK ME TO DO THIS AGAIN! I AM SO OVERWHELMED!

LILY: I didn't ask. You insisted.

CIARAN: Why are there so many brands?

CIARAN: Oh, shit, someone just took a picture of me holding the heavy flow box.

LILY: CIARAN! BACK AWAY FROM THE TAMPONS! I'll get them myself.

CIARAN: No… I got this. HUSBANDS BUY THEIR WIVES TAMPONS!

LILY: FFS! Just hurry up. Oh, and don't forget my Nutella. *heart-eye emoji*

🍀

CIARAN: Morning baby. x

LILY: DO NOT MORNING ME! YOU ATE MY NUTELLA!

LILY: SO DEAD! I AM GONNA MURDER YOU IN YOUR SLEEP!

LILY: DIVORCE!

❦

CIARAN: Can I see you tonight?

CIARAN: I'm sorry, I'll buy you more.

CIARAN: Jesus, will you text me back? It's just Nutella.

LILY: JUST NUTELLA?

CIARAN: OH SHIT! I didn't mean that. Please let me come over. I'll make it up to you. *wink emoji.

LILY: Having a girls' night with Rosie and Cian's new girlfriend.

CIARAN: Are you still mad?

LILY: Did you still eat my Nutella?

CIARAN: Touché.

❧

FUCK IT, I'M CRASHING GIRLS' NIGHT!

I haven't seen Lily all week, and for some unknown reason, she's avoiding me. Okay, so it's not *that* unknown. I may have eaten her Nutella, and apparently, that move alone is grounds for divorce. Lesson learned: A man should never come between his woman and her chocolate.

So here I am, ready to apologise for laughing at her theatrics with the promise to buy her as many new jars as she wants.

Da said as soon as I realise my wife is always right, my marriage will be a hell of a lot easier. It's time to swallow my pride and hand over my man-card.

After letting myself into Lily and Rosie's apartment, I'm greeted with the tell-tale sound of feminine laughter.

"Oh, I completely forgot about the death of Adam. That one was a classic." Lily's voice travels down the narrow hallway.

"Care to explain?" Cian's girlfriend, Ella asks — her American accent gives away her identity.

Moving closer, I eavesdrop from behind the partition wall.

"Adam and Eve. You and I both know it was her forbidden fruit that killed that poor bastard, not an apple. Therefore... The death of Adam."

"Who's Adam?" I announce waltzing into the room like I'm meant to be there. After I plonk myself onto the ottoman, I kick off my boots and lift my sock-covered feet onto Lily's lap.

She growls but I choose to ignore it. "What are you lovely ladies talking about?"

Lily's murderous eyes narrow, sending daggers in my direction. "What are you doing here? This is a ladies-only zone. I'm pretty sure that means no dicks allowed. And last time I checked you were the biggest dick of them all." With a swipe of her hand, she knocks my feet off her lap.

Okay, so she's still mad. But the underlying spark in her eye tells me she's also happy to see me.

I missed you, too, baby.

"Last time I checked, you didn't seem to mind my big dick, Lilyanna."

Keeping my eyes focused on her, the rest of the room fades. *Come on, Bug. Show me that fight. I dare you.*

Her pouty lips curl into a sassy smile as she shoos' me with her hand. "In the words of Arianna Grande, THANK U, NEXT!"

Jutting out my bottom lip I raise my left brow and cup my dick with my right hand. A smug smile creeps across my lips when her gaze follows. "Aw, Lily Bug, why did you have to go and hurt his feelings? Everyone knows my Big Friendly

Giant is the most sought-after piece of equipment on the market."

Her tongue pokes out, running along her bottom lip. "Well, you know what they say, Ciaran. Low prices attract the most customers."

"So... Ciaran," Rosie interrupts. "If you're here, does that mean my brother is home?"

Without taking my eyes off my stubborn wife, I reply. "Yeah, I dropped him off on my way here."

"And, why are you here?" Lily sasses.

Dragging my bottom lip between my teeth, I shoot her a wink. "I came to see my favourite girl."

The tiny crinkles around her eyes deepen as she tries to hide the smile forcing its way onto her gorgeous face. Holding up her hand, she flashes me her middle finger. "Fuck you."

"Fuck me."

Rosie stands from her chair. "Okay... Well, I've had enough of whatever weird foreplay this is. Ella, are you ready to go? I think these two need a minute to either fuck or kill each other."

"Emm... okay. Bye guys."

As they head for the door, Lily shouts over her shoulder. "Rosie, bring the trash with you."

I drop to the floor, wrap my hand around Lily's ankle and yank, pulling her from the couch and onto my lap. My arms grip her waist as her hands grasp my shoulders. "Did you just call me trash?" My fingers trail up her ribcage hitting the spot where I know she is most ticklish.

"Stop! Don't you dare! Ciaran."

Finally, the living room door closes, shutting the rest of the world out, but that doesn't stop her from crying out. "TAKE ME WITH YOU BEFORE I CHOP HIS DICK OFF AND FEED IT TO MY TAMAGOTCHI CAT."

❦

"I HOPE YOU'RE READY FOR THIS" I shout from Lily's en-suite.

"Oh, I am so ready!" Lily's amused tone travels from the bedroom. "Okay, Let's see what you got, Maguire"

Taking one last look in the full-length bathroom mirror, I laugh at how utterly-fucking-ridiculous I look.

"Okay, I'm coming out. But I swear to God, LB. If you're recording this, I will flip my shit."

After pressing play on my Spotify app, music blasts from Lily's Bluetooth speaker filling the surrounding air. *Now or never.*

Sliding into Lily's room wearing nothing but a white dress shirt, white socks, and a pair of Lily's black Ray-Bans, I lift her round-barrelled hairbrush to my lips a sing-along to What A Man Gotta Do by Jonas Brothers.

I exaggerate every movement, making my hellish wife howl with laughter.

"OH MY GOD! What the hell are you wearing?"

With one well-timed jump, I pounce. My feet land on her mattress and I shift my hips from side to side, thrusting the air.

Her hands fly to her mouth as she fights to contain her giggling, but it's no use, her contagious cackle bursts free, only spurring me on further.

"Prepare yourself. I'm about to go full John Tra-fucking-volta."

"Enough, please. I'm gonna pee my pants."

I grip my cotton shirt and pull, sending all the buttons flying. Pulling it off, I lasso it above my head while grinding my hips from left to right.

"Dead," she cries. "I am fucking dead."

I fall to my knees and crawl up the bed until Lily is pinned beneath me. Her legs wrap around my waist and I grind against her. Bringing my lips to hers, I whisper against them. "I'm sorry."

"Sorry for what, exactly?" she sasses.

"I, Ciaran Maguire — world's sexiest husband — am so sorry for eating your Nutella."

"And?"

Rolling my eyes, I continue, "And, I promise never to leave the toothpaste cap off, ever again."

"Because?"

"Because... people who leave the cap off are wild animals."

A sexy smile highlights her face, making me fall for her a little more. "Okay, you are forgiven."

I kiss the tip of her nose. "Thank Christ."

Pulling her closer, I lift her from the bed, and I flip us over so she's straddling my waist. "Hey, you!"

Her nose scrunches in this cute little way. "Hey, yourself."

My hands roam under the silk material of her black nightdress, pulling it up and over her head. "I missed you this week. When are we going to move in together? I don't like sleeping alone."

Shrugging her shoulders, she teases me with a wink. "I don't know, I kinda like my space."

"But what about at night —" I trail my fingers over the tattoo along her ribcage "— when I'm not here, and you've no one to keep you company." I sit forward, kissing my way up her stomach.

"Who said I don't have company? I have Peter, he is excellent and keeps me satisfied when you're not here."

My eyes lock on hers. "WHO THE FUCK IS PETER?"

Laughing, she reaches over to her nightstand and pulls

open the top drawer. "Ciaran, I would like you to meet Peter. My glow in the dark, vibrating rabbit."

I see it, the humour dancing in her eyes and the laughter kissing her smile. "So, you think you're funny, do you?"

"I'm hilarious, and you know it."

Pulling the rabbit from her hands, a devilish smirk graces my face. "Wanna play a game, LB?"

She drags her nails down my chest. "What do you have in mind?"

I turn Peter on and trail him over her inner thigh until finally, I hit her sweet spot. "Let's see who can make you come harder. Me or this silicone substitute?"

Amusement shines from her face as she leans forward and whispers in my ear. "Oh, Peter. Right there."

Fuck this! The only name I want to hear is mine.

I pull back and fling that purple bastard across the room. "Changed my mind. NO MORE PETER!"

CHAPTER THIRTY-TWO

WARRIOR BY DEMI LOVATO

5 MONTHS LATER

LILY

I never thought I would be strong enough to stand outside these gates. Yet, here I am.

The fine hairs on my forearms stand to attention, and not in a good way. As much as I know I need to do this, it is not easy. Anxiety courses through me, starting at my toes and flooding every cell in my body. My stomach flips, sending a wave of nausea up my oesophagus. Over the past few weeks, I have played out every possible scenario in my head, planning what I would say when I finally came face-to-face with the man who shattered my childhood.

Nothing, not a single thing could have prepared me for this — the gut-churning ache that wants me to run in the other direction. Closing my eyes, I drag in a much-needed breath and tighten my hold on Ciaran's hand.

He squeezes, grounding me like he always does. My eyes fly open and take in the red brick building in front of me. *Do not run, Lily. You can do this. I believe in you.*

"If you want to turn around and never look back, you can. He doesn't deserve your forgiveness."

My gaze darts to the man beside me, the very man who gave me the courage to find my strength. "You're right. He does not deserve my forgiveness. But I deserve my freedom. I can never be fully free without facing him. I need this."

Ciaran nods. "If this is something you need, I will be with you every step of the way."

Hand in hand, we move toward the main entrance. Lifting my chin, I hold my head high.

With each step I take, I remind myself of how far I have come.

I am Lilyanna O'Shea-Maguire.

I am fierce.

I am strong.

I am not a broken child.

I am a badass woman.

Finally, we reach the doors leading to the designated waiting area, and I freeze. This is all becoming very real, very fucking quick. My eyes fall to the ground, and suddenly it feels as if it's about to swallow me whole.

Ciaran's soothing velvet voice breaks through before my thoughts carry me to a place I thought I'd left behind. "Lily... Are you still with me?"

I blink, forcing the negative taunts to retreat. They don't have any hold over me. Not anymore. "Yes. I'm still with you."

Ciaran grips the handle and pulls the door open for me, with a deep breath I push through the fear and step inside.

I don't know what exactly I was envisioning, but the pale purple walls I'm greeted with is not what I expected. The place has an overall reception vibe. Pushing forward, I slowly make my way over the small Perspex glass window — guarded by several thick white metal bars — and I am greeted by a female officer.

"Welcome to Mountjoy Prison. Please state who you are visiting today."

I run my tongue along the roof of my dry mouth, hoping to add some moisture. Silently, I count to four. "Damien O'Shea."

"Have you both brought a valid ID?"

I riffle through my bag, panicking. *Oh, shit. Where did I*

put my passport? Ciaran's tattooed hand lands on my shoulder. "Deep breath, LB. I have them."

He reaches into the back pocket of his dark denim jeans and pulls out both passports, then hands them to the officer.

After scanning both with razor-sharp focus, she then hands us a piece of paper. "Here is your visitor's docket. Please take a seat relative to the number provided on your docket. If you have any personal items, please place them in the lockers before being called for your visit."

I nod in understanding and head to our allocated seats.

Once seated, Ciaran places his hand on my thigh. "How are you doing?"

Covering his hand with mine, I look up into his concerned eyes. "I'm okay. Nervous but okay. Thanks again for coming with me. You didn't have to."

"Babe, I know I didn't. You are more than capable of doing this by yourself, but you don't have to. Not anymore."

Before I can reply, an officer calls out our appointed number and we are led to another building to be screened. After what feels like hours of x-ray machines, drug swab tests, and canine checks, we are finally cleared and brought to the visitors centre where we are met by another prison officer. "Please state who you are visiting today."

"Damien O'Shea."

My mind is reeling. *Is he worth all this stress and trouble? The answer slaps me in the face. No, he certainly is not;*

but you are. You are not here for him. You are here for you, so you can finally move forward and live your life free from your demons.

"Sign here, and then I will bring you into the visitor's area."

Doing what we're asked we then wait until the office unlocks the grey, metal door, and follow him inside.

Sitting behind the clear Perspex screen is my very own devil, and suddenly, every memory, every comment, every executing moment, barrels to the forefront of my mind as my father's ageing eyes bore into my skin. I push them back. *No. He has no power over me, not anymore.*

Damien remains silent as Ciaran and I take a seat on the opposite side, thankful there's a layer of protection between us.

Ciaran's eyes meet mine, and with just one look he promises he's there, with me, every step of the way.

"It's so good to see you, Firecracker. I —"

"Don't," I cut him off. "Do not call me that."

Shame washes over his face, almost making me feel sorry for him. Then I remember all the shit he put me and my family through, and the feeling quickly fades.

"I am not here for your excuses or your apologies. I am here to thank you."

Confusion works across his dark brow line. He looks so much like my brother, it's frightening. Dark wavy chocolate brown hair and deep soulful hazel eyes that carry more dark-ness than light.

Forcing back the bubbling lump working its way up my chest, I square my shoulders and harness my inner strength. "As I was saying, I am here to thank you. You showed me what a man is not supposed to be. You taught me that I am stronger than I ever believed I could be. You gave me hard life lessons and more issues than vogue, but because of you, I became the person I am today. I am a warrior. A woman who knows her value and her worth. I am a boss, a force to be reckoned with because I will never allow anyone to treat me the way you once did. I am a wife, one who appreciates her husband and every ounce of love he provides her. And one day, if and when," I look towards Ciaran "we have chil-dren of our own... I know how not to destroy them. You and your twisted ways have taught me how capable I am. I have become a better woman because I strive to be everything you are not."

I push from the chair and stand to my feet. "I will never forgive you or forget the horrific things you did. But guess what Da? I forgive myself. For years, I thought I did some-thing to deserve your sick hate, but I didn't. I am not to blame, I never was."

I spread my arms wide. "This is me, claiming back my life. I'm letting go of all the hurt and hate I carry towards you because frankly, you don't deserve my energy. I wish I could say the same for Cillian, but I can't, you destroyed him. You took everything good in his world and he is drowning in a sea of hate. One day, I hope he will be strong enough to remove your toxicity from his veins, but until then I will spend every day reminding him that he is not you."

Ciaran stands, flanking my left side. His hand lands on the dip of my back, silently supporting me.

Turning on my heel, I start to walk towards the door.

"Lilyanna. Wait," There is something in his tone that stops me in my tracks, but I don't face him. "You will never know how sorry I am for all the things I did to you... and to Cillian. I will never ask you to forgive me because I don't deserve it. I hold my hands up. I was a very sick man, but I want you to know I am working on it. Every day, I am working on being a better, decent human being. I'm happy you found happiness and I want nothing more in this world for you to be better than the life I gave you. Before you walk away, please consider taking this with you." He passes a worn envelope to the guard and after the guard scans its contents, he hands it to me.

I look down at the scribble adorning the front: *Cillian*.

"Please," my da pleads. "I know I don't deserve any favours, but please give that to my son. He will never come here. He's not as strong as you are, but he needs to know how truly sorry I am. You found your freedom, Lilyanna.

Please give Cillian that letter, and hopefully, it will help him find his."

There's a part of me that wants to tell him to shove his letter up his ass; but then there is another part that knows Cillian needs this, now more than ever.

I turn and glare at him. "I will give it to him. Not because you asked me too but because he needs it. But let's get one thing straight, a piece of paper with meaningless words will never make up for all the years we suffered. You lost your family a long, long time ago, and you can never repair the damage you caused. If I never see you again, I will die happy. Have a lovely life staring at your cell wall, and when death comes knocking, I hope you burn in hell."

❧

"I'm proud of you," Ciaran announces as we walk back towards his car. "That took some serious balls, and honestly, I'm in awe."

I lean closer, nestling into the crook of his arm. "I'm proud of myself. I didn't know if I could go through with it, but I did."

"I knew you could. You're the strongest person I've ever met. Now, how would you like to spend the rest of your day? Nutella pancakes and ice-cream?"

"You know me so well." I laugh at his adorable attempt

at trying to lighten the tension lingering after our visit. "But," I add. "Can I add something?"

He stops, spins to face me and cups my face in his palms. "Whatever it is you want, consider it yours."

"How about a happy ever after?"

He bites down on his bottom lip and winks, lighting a fire in the pit of my stomach. "Bug, I've been trying to give you that for years, you didn't want it so I returned it to Disney. Sorry no take backs"

Laughter barrels up my chest. "You're an asshole."

"Yes... yes, I am, but you love me anyway."

CHAPTER THIRTY-THREE

I CHOOSE YOU BY SARA BAREILLIS

CIARAN

IF I HAD MY WAY, I WOULD HAVE WOKEN UP NEXT TO the love of my life, but no, Lily insisted on heading home last night.

My wife is the most stubborn person I've ever met. I tried everything to get her to stay — even tried bribing her with sexual favours — yet, she's still keeping me at arm's length.

I get it, Lily likes her independence, but she's holding a piece of herself back for some reason. I've lost count of the times I've asked her if we could move in together, but she's determined to take this slow.

We've been married five years. How much slower can we get?

For the last few months, we've been working on strengthening our relationship, doing normal couple things — dinners, movies, shows, and lots of Netflix and chill — and although it's been great, I want more.

I want to wake up with her every morning and fall asleep with her in my arms each night.

We have a lot of time to catch up on, and we can't do that if she won't meet me in the deep end.

We are not like other couples, our relationship spans over twenty years of friendship, so sue me if I'm willing to dive right in without hesitation. So here I am, walking towards her building with an arm full of Forever Susan lilies — Lily's favourite flower — because I refuse to spend another minute of Valentine's Day alone.

I know she's not romantic, but I am. So, she better get used to me spoiling her because I plan to shower her with all that mushy shit she pretends to hate.

I take the steps that lead to her apartment two at a time until finally, her bright yellow door comes into view.

I'm just about to ring the doorbell when a luminous green post-it catches my eye.

Hello, Baby Hanson, I knew you'd show up sooner or later.
Come on in, and please, follow the green post-its. LB xX

What is she up to? Gripping the handle, I push down and let the door swing open. Post-its cover the hardwood floorboards, trailing up the hallway that leads to the living room. One by one, I pick them up and read Lily's scribbles.

Once upon a time...

There was a little boy with hair the colour of ripe winter barley.

One day, this boy — let's call him Baby Hanson — needed a hero.

Because this smelly bully — that no one likes — was trying to steal the most precious thing in his world.

The very last gift his mammy gave him before she moved to heaven to live with the angels.

Enter Lily Bug — the most fierce, badass in all the land.

She saved Baby Hanson that day, but what the boy never realised was, she needed him more than he ever needed her.

Over the years, he became Lily Bug's best friend in the entire world.

He made her laugh.

He kept her safe.

He became her sanctuary.

He kissed away her tears when she cried.

He taught her what it's like to love and to be loved... unconditionally.

Rounding the corner into the living room, I come to a stop when I see Lily standing in the centre of the room, wearing a red spandex superhero costume covered in black polka dots.

"Hi." A shy smile tugs on the left side of her mouth.

For the first time since I entered the room, I look around. The curtains are drawn and the dimly lit room glows from the light of countless tiny tea lights. There are burgundy rose petals covering the floor and mirrored coffee table, making the room a romantic hideaway.

Suddenly, I'm overwhelmed with emotion. She did all this, and she did it for me because she knew it would make me happy. I'm well aware Lily thinks Valentine's Day is a load of shite, but she still made the effort... for me.

"Hey." I shift on my feet, unsure of what she wants me to do. Finally, I set the flowers on the side table by the door and move towards her. "Cute story." I wave the handful of post-its in her direction. With a wide smile, I take another step. "I take it you're meant to be the fiercest badass in all the land?" I state, gesturing to her costume.

Her arms open wide as she spins in place, giving me a full view of her beautiful body. "Oh, this old thing?" she smirks. "I have had it for years, I just felt like wearing it."

"Really?"

"Yep. I didn't just buy it for today if that's what you're thinking."

Being with Lily isn't always the fairy tale I thought it was going to be. But it's moments like this one, where she does something so out of her comfort zone, it makes me fall in love with her even more. Over the years, I've learned we are not a romance novel full of unrealistic expectations. We are so much more. We are real and messy, but we spent every-fucking-day working on it because the love we have is worth fighting for. We are stupid fights, late-night apologies, midnight laughs, and chaotic mood swings but each day with her is the best day of my life. Our love is all about knowing every single flaw but loving each other despite them. Every single day is an adventure, and I would give the world to spend a lifetime by her side.

"Lily, I—"

"Wait." She lifts her hand, cutting off my words as she steps forward. Taking my hand, she then leads me towards the couch. "Sit for a second. I'm not finished with my story and I think you might like how this one ends."

I do as she asks and she sits down beside me, turning her body so we are face-to-face.

Her shoulders rise as she draws in a deep breath, then finally, after what feels like forever she speaks.

"This story, it wasn't like most. You see, Lily Bug, although she loved Baby Hanson with all she had, she still had a few things she needed to do on her own. She had to learn how to love herself so she could give her heart away to the drummer boy who loved her back to life. But the boy wanted to save her, just like she saved him. He couldn't understand why it was so important for Lily Bug to save herself. Until one day, he figured it out and he let her go." Her hands reach out and take hold of mine. "It took a while, some would say too long, but finally, she became her own hero... and she saved herself."

She chuckles, and with a heavy sigh a tear slides down her cheek and I reach up and wipe it away. "You're amazing, and I love you."

"I love you, too. But please, just shut up and let me get this out."

"As you wish."

"After Lily Bug finally destroyed her demons, she looked around and realised that the most important person in her life wasn't there to celebrate with her. In her pursuit to find herself, she lost the one person who meant the world to her."

I pull one hand free, push the fallen strands of hair from her face, and gently tuck them behind her ear. "LB, you never lost me, I was just standing on the side lines."

"Didn't I tell you to shut it?"

"Sorry, continue."

"Anyway… She realised she needed to fix things. She had to make Baby Hanson see just how much he meant to her. So, she came up with a plan to win him back because even though she doesn't need a hero… she needs him. He makes her darkest days brighter. He brings joy into her life and makes her feel as if she is finally home."

Sliding from the couch, she drops to one knee. "You taught me how to love myself by loving me enough for the both of us. You are the only person on this planet that could ever put up with me and my insane brand of crazy, and for that, I love you even more. You are extremely messy, and it grates on my fucking nerves. And for the love of God, please learn how to lift the toilet lid when you piss because I honestly can't stand when you dribble on the seat and just walk away."

Interrupting her, I point to the bathroom. "How many times do I have to tell you? That's. Not. Me."

Her brow line rises, and her face screams, *oh, really?*

"Fine, it was, but it was one time."

"As I was saying... Even though you drive me crazier than I already am, I still love you. I want to spend the rest of my life enjoying all the love, laughter, and security you bring to my life. You were the boy who kissed my flaws and made them seem perfect. You held my fears in your hands and gave me the strength to be brave. You patiently picked up every shard of my broken pieces and glued them together with your never-ending love. I know I've told you time after time that I don't need a hero because I don't. But how would you feel about being my sidekick?"

She reaches behind her and grabs a black velvet gift box from underneath the mirrored coffee table. Placing it on my lap, she motions for me to open it.

I lift the lid and a laugh rumbles from my chest. "Is this what I think it is?" My eyes widen as I gently remove the satin material. "You bought me a cape?" *I can't believe she bought me a fucking cape.*

"Every sidekick needs a cape, Ciaran." Her smile is so big it melts my heart. "Read the back."

It's there, sown in giant red letters, "BABY HANSON."

Jesus Christ, who's cutting onions?

Reaching up, her hand cups my chin. "I am done walking this road alone. I choose you, Ciaran. I still have a lot of growing to do, but I want to do it by your side, together as a team."

My — not teary, I fucking swear — eyes flick to hers.

"Ciaran Maguire... would you please make me the happiest woman in the world, and marry me? Again."

Love. I love this girl with every bone in my body, and every beat in my chest. Sure, we are messy, and we fight like cats and dogs, but there is nobody in this world I would rather be beside. She drives me crazy and I kinda love it. "Lily Maguire, my Wifey for life. I would marry you a million times if you'd let me. I've been in love with you for twenty years, and I plan to love you for at least sixty more." I slide from the chair, kneel beside her, and grip her face between my palms. "Now, get your spandex covered ass into the bedroom so I can superhero fuck you while wearing a cape."

EPILOGUE

BEST OF YOU BY ANDY GRAMMER AND ELLE KING

TWO YEARS LATER

CIARAN

With a slight smirk, I lean against the door jamb and watch my wife prance around our kitchen with a large mixing bowl curled into the crook of her left arm.

Fuck me, she's a sight.

Nothing but an old, raggy band tee covers her fair skin, and yet, she's as beautiful as the day I married her.

Lost in her own little world, she doesn't see me as she fiddles with the buttons on the built-in surround sound.

Suddenly, the song changes to All About You by McFly and her hips swing to the gentle guitar strum.

Stray strands of her vibrant hair hang from her messy bun and her fresh morning face shows off the dusting of freckles I love so much.

Unable to stay away, I push off the doorway and stride across the room within seconds. Sneaking up behind her, I wrap my arms around her growing baby bump and kiss the back of her neck.

"Hey baby, couldn't sleep?"

She sets the glass mixing bowl on the counter then covers my hands with hers. She looks over her shoulder with a glowing smile, and steals all the air from my lungs.

I've toured the world, seen cities some people only dream about, but nothing compares to the vision before me.

"What have I told you about creeping up on me, Baby Hanson? One of these days, I will shank you, and it will be your own damn fault."

My hands move to her hips, and I spin her to face me. "You'd never hurt me. We made a deal remember?"

Her tired eyes crinkle in amusement. "Oh, was that the deal where you promised me lots of orgasms or the one where you promised not to get me pregnant but did anyway?"

My hands trace the new curve of her stomach. "Admit it,

you're more excited about her arrival than I am. Don't think I haven't seen the tiny yellow Doc Martens in the nursery."

"How cute are they, though? They're just like mine, only miniature."

With a smile, I pull her close, her head rests against my chest and we sway to the music.

This is it, what life's all about — midnight pancakes, kitchen dances, and forehead kisses. There isn't anything in the world I'd rather be doing. These moments, the quiet ones where we are just two people who are madly in love, doing mundane shit, are my favourite. They remind me that when everything else fades, love remains. I don't regret a moment of my relationship with Lily because everything we went through led us here, into each other's arms. I'm the happiest I've ever been, and nothing, not a single thing, could ever compare to the way she makes me feel. I was lucky enough to marry my best friend, not once but twice. I won't lie and tell you that our story is all flowers and rainbows because it's not. There are days I feel like strangling her and vice versa, but at the end of the day, we always kiss each other goodnight. Love, it's not simple, if it were, there would be no heartbreak. But if you're willing to fight, to show up every day and work on it together, it never fails.

"Love to love you, LB."

"Love to hate you, Baby Hanson."

✦

"I HATE YOU. YOU... YOU DID THIS TO ME." THROUGH gritted teeth, Lily tells me how much she loves me. "I've changed my mind. Ciaran, please tell them I changed my mind. I don't want this baby anymore." Her gaze darts to our delivery nurse, Ashlee. "Can I return it?"

"No, unfortunately, you cannot. But don't worry, you're nearly there. You're nine centimetres dilated."

I pick up the damp washcloth Ashlee gave me, and use it to wipe the sweat from Lily's forehead. "Bug, I know you're in pain. But she's nearly here."

"Pain... You're having a laugh, I've felt pain before, and this is not it. This is fucking torture. I'm talking concentration camp type shit. Why do women do this more than once? Please explain it to me cause I'm at a loss here! My vagina feels like it's on fire."

"On fire? Surely, it's not that bad." I realise my mistake after the words fly from my mouth.

"NOT. THAT. BAD? This is coming from the man who spent four days in bed after he stubbed his fucking toe on the bedpost."

"I did not."

Suddenly my fingers go numb as Lily grips my hand to ride out another contraction. I hate this, seeing her in so much pain when there is not a damn thing, I can do about it. Her cheeks flush as exhaustion takes over.

"Okay, Lily," Ashlee announces. "It's time. I need you to take a deep breath in, and when you breathe out, I want you to push down. Okay?"

Lily nods in response, but I can see it, the underlying fear in her tired eyes.

I lean forward and kiss her temple. "It's okay, I'm right here. Count with me. Together."

"You're doing great, Lily." Nurse Ashlee encourages as she pats Lily's leg.

Lily's eyes flame as her stare darts to the nurse. "Take your hands off me. Nobody will ever touch me again." Her glare swings in my direction. "That goes for you too. No more touching. From now on, this —" she points to herself " — is a no-touching zone."

Leaning down, my breath whispers against her neck. "You love it when I touch you, don't lie."

"No... I mean it, Ciaran. Keep your filthy hands to yourself. You're the reason this little terrorist is destroying my uterus. No more, you can touch yourself from now on."

"Okay, Lily. On the next contraction, I want you to give it all you've got. Deep breath in... and push."

Squeezing down on my hand, Lily gives her all. She releases a roar. "OH, YOU MOTHERFUCKER!"

I know she's in pain, but I can't help it. "Yes! Yes, I am."

Suddenly a fierce cry echoes through the delivery suite.

Lily's body instantly relaxes and she drops to the mattress with relief.

"Congratulations, Mam and Dad... Baby Maguire arrived at 10:43 am on September 16th. We are going to clean her up and check her vitals, then we will get you to do some skin-to-skin. But first, Lily, I need you to give me one more push so we can deliver the placenta."

"FUCK THE PLACENTA! It can stay there for all I care. I'm done! No more pushing."

Brushing her hair from her face, I encourage her to keep going. "You got this, Bug. One more push."

Time blurs, and the next thing I know, the most beautiful thing I've ever seen is laid against Lily's chest.

If possible, my heart swells to twice its size. Pride rips through me. I made her, we made her. She's so precious. My fingers reach out and travel along her puffed cheeks. "Hello, Little Bug. I'm your daddy."

I watch in awe as my wife gazes down at our daughter with nothing but love shining from her eyes.

"Have you got a name yet?" Ashlee asks as she scribbles on her clipboard.

"Ivy," I announce. "Ivy Leigh Maguire. The Greeks symbolism for faithfulness."

Lily's eyes find mine. "I love you."

"I love you, too."

Leaning in, I press my lips against her forehead.

"Thank you, Baby Hanson."

"For what?"

"For proving that I'm worthy of an epic love."

THE END

ACKNOWLEDGMENTS

Andrew, my very own sidekick. Thank you for showing me a love where midnight pancakes and kitchen dances exist. I love you more than words can express. Not once throughout my writing journey have you doubted me. You are constantly reminding me how amazing you think I am. Your faith in me means more than you'll ever know. Thank you for being my very own Ciaran. You always find a way to make me laugh, even on my darkest days, and in return, I promise to always keep you on your toes with my outrageous one-liners, and sarcastic comebacks.

Joshua and Benjamin, always remember Mammy loves you to the moon and back. Never forget how special you both are. Make sure you live life to its fullest potential. You are magic — don't let anyone tell you any different.

To my wild at heart mother, thank you for showing me that without struggle, we can never truly be strong. For teaching me to never let anyone dim my sparkle; and that the "f word" is not a curse but a sentence enhancer. Love your favourite child.

To my siblings, Paul, Tony, Emma, David, and Aisling, I love you all. Thanks for supporting me on this crazy ride. Sorry if I became a hermit, ignoring all your calls. I promise to answer now. (Kidding, the next book won't write itself)

To Ruth, I cannot thank you enough for all the time and effort you put into making this book readable. Thank you for your patience, time, and most of all your support throughout this 4Clover journey.

To Daria and Dani, my soul sisters, and my ALPHA beta readers. I'm so glad I found you both on the little, strange, orange website called Wattpad. All the love for you two and all your crazy. Thank you for being my biggest supporters. You've done so much to promote my work and I love you so much for it. You truly are the greatest friends. Thank you for holding my hand, and for being my rock when I was on the verge of giving up, and for all the amazing song suggestions. You're both truly amazing. I cannot wait for the day I get to meet you, for real, and not over the internet.

To my beta and arc FAMILY, you the bomb.com. I couldn't do this without your constant encouragement. I love you all. You will never know how much your support means to me. Stay fabulous!

To my Wattpad family, without you, this book would've never reached its full potential. Thank you for giving me the push I needed, and for pulling me out of meltdown mode on more than one occasion; most importantly, sending me all those hot Insta pages when I was lacking inspiration. I love you all.

To my hoes, Emily, Cheryl, and Louise. Thank you for being my ride or dies. Your friendships are invaluable to me.

A big thank you to all the bloggers and readers who took the time to read this book. I appreciate it so much. Please leave a review on any (or if you're feeling generous) all of my social media platforms.

Much Love
    Shauna

Shauna lives in the small town land of Oldtown, North County Dublin; with her partner and her two little boys. She always loved to read, to escape reality between the pages of a good book. Her other hobbies include singing, art, all things spiritual, songwriting and binge-ing on Netflix series. She believes we all have a little light inside us, but it's up to us to let it shine. The 4Clover series is her first set of romance novels but she is looking forward to sharing more of her imaginary friends with you.

OTHER BOOKS IN THE 4CLOVER SERIES

Luck, 4Clover Book One (Cian) Available Now

Love, 4Clover Book Two (Cillian) Available Now

Hope, 4Clover (Conor) Coming 2021

🍀

Enjoyed FAITH? Make sure you stay in the loop with UPCOMING BOOKS by following me on Instagram!

@shaunamcdonnellauthor

Printed in Poland
by Amazon Fulfillment
Poland Sp. z o.o., Wrocław